A Gateway Romance

Temporary Bridesmaid

Other Books by Lu Ann Brobst Staheli

Small Town U.S.A.
Leona & Me, Helen Marie
A Note Worth Taking
Just Like Elizabeth Taylor

Timeless Romance Anthology
Silver Bells Collection: "A Fezziwig Christmas"

Non-Fiction
Men of Destiny: Abraham Lincoln and the Prophet Joseph Smith
Psychic Madman
When Hearts Conjoin: The True Story of Utah's Conjoined Twins
One Day at a Time: Teaching Secondary English Language Arts
Books, Books and More Books: A Parent and Teacher's Guide to Adolescent Literature

A Gateway Romance

Temporary Bridesmaid

Lu Ann Staheli

Copyright © 2015 by Lu Ann Brobst Staheli

Original e-book published 2014
All rights reserved

This is a work of fiction. The characters' names, incidents, places, and dialogue are products of the author's imagination and are not to be construed as real.

Cover design by Rachael Anderson
Cover image: Shutterstock #70973584
Interior design by Heather Justesen
Edited by Heather B. Moore, Michele Paige Homes, and Annalisa Thaler
Back Yard Press
Paperback edition, 2015
ISBN-10: 1941145485
ISBN-13: 978-1-941145-48-7

For my husband, Mike,
who came into my life when I'd given up the
dream.

1

Jenny tossed the wedding shower invitation onto the kitchen table. Evidence and proof. The last of her friends was getting married. Like a set of dominoes—five, four, three, two, and now Lisbeth—leaving Jenny the last one standing. Even shy Lisbeth was beating her to the altar. Jenny didn't want to believe that she would be the last single in her group, but it was true.

She knew about the proposal before Lisbeth. Gary had flashed the opened ring box into her face when they met in the apartment complex parking lot a few weeks ago.

"Tonight's the night," he'd said.

Jenny had tried to smile, but one more engagement about tipped her over the edge. Five friends in twelve months—all over thirty—finding their mates and not a single guy had asked her out in over two years.

She slumped into a chair and dropped her head onto her folded arms.

The clock was ticking, and not the one on the wall. She was thirty-nine years old—thirty-nine and never married. She had always hated the words *single, spinster, Old Maid*. Sure, society had made every effort to soften the harsh blow of being in your thirties—late thirties—and unmarried, but Jenny still felt the sting of the saying: *I'd rather be dead than single*. And that's just how she felt now.

1

She made herself pick up the invitation again and pull the card from the envelope. A tiny organza ribbon threaded the two holes punched in the upper left corner then tied into a bow. A hand-lettered card glued to the front of the invitation declared *You're Invited.* Someone had too much time on their hands.

A white orchid with a silver brad holding it to an inner card peeked out the top of the sleeve. She pulled it up to reveal a message:

Saturday, May 5

11:30 a.m. to 1:30 p.m.

Bridal Shower

Jenny's eyes burned, so she let the teardrops fall. *What's wrong with me, anyway?* When she was sixteen, she hoped she would join the parade of girls invited to sporting events, school dances, and the local movie theater. The rest of her friends always had a string of guys waiting to take them somewhere. But it never happened for her. Not once in high school in her small home town did she have a real date. There had been a couple of guys who stopped by occasionally, sometimes to talk, but mostly to get help with their homework.

At college, she knew things would be different. Hundreds of young men were around her, all looking for more than an education. Surely one of them would ask her out. And one did—a high school friend of her roommate's. He was nice-looking—not a church-goer, but it was a start.

2

Jenny liked him well enough. She would have gone out with him a second time, until she found out he liked guys as much as he liked girls. She thought she'd hit rock bottom.

She wiped a sniffle from her nose as she remembered the others she'd dated briefly, all unsuitable. Nick, who tried to kiss her goodnight by grabbing her into a bear hug, forcing her to bend backward, and dipping her nearly to the cement of her front porch, while his hands roamed all sorts of places she didn't want them to be. The blood rushed to her face thinking about it. But Nick wasn't even the worst.

That honor was reserved for Kennedy, who at least gave her warning of what he intended before his fingers made it past the bottom of her shirt. She'd yanked his wrist away and taken off on a run like she was being followed by the devil. She might well have been if she'd ever considered going out with him again. Or with anyone else who wasn't at least a practicing member of some religion that taught moral values.

Then she'd hung out with two guys in her student church group. Both were bland—boring, actually. It was a relief when summer vacation came and they returned home to Blanding, *a town appropriately named for those two*, she mused.

The memory made her chuckle, despite the earlier tears. She was almost feeling human again when her cell phone played *Sorry Seems to Be the Hardest Word*. It was Lisbeth, the youngest of her friends at twenty-nine, only a month away

3

from the big three-oh. She let the song play for a moment, wondering why she had chosen that particular song for Lisbeth's ring. *Did I sense she'd beat me to the altar, too?*

Jenny flipped open the phone, held it to her ear, and smiled. "Hello, Lisbeth." She hoped her friend didn't hear the twinge of sadness in her voice.

"Did you get it? Gary put them in the mail for my mom yesterday. You *are* coming, aren't you?" The words poured from her friend's mouth, a bubble of enthusiasm. "I told my mother you would. I'm so excited for the shower. Whoever would have thought that Stephie, Grace, Tamlyn, Kira and I would all get married twelve months apart?"

"Yeah," Jenny said. *Whoever would have thought?* The engagement and upcoming wedding had sure made changes in Lisbeth's once demure personality.

"Good thing I moved into that apartment complex so I could introduce you to Gary." Jenny kept her tone light. Lisbeth was being a ditz—in a fun sort of way—and didn't know how much her words stung. No way Jenny wanted to hurt her feelings at a joyful time like this, and she knew Lisbeth didn't mean to hurt hers. *All married . . . All but me!* The thought made Jenny feel nauseated.

"So," Lisbeth took a deep breath that Jenny could hear through the phone. "I'll see you at the shower on Saturday, right?"

"I wouldn't miss it for the world," Jenny said, and honestly, she meant it.

4

While Lisbeth prattled on about the canapés her aunt Mavis was bringing and the special punch her grandmother had devised for her own wedding nearly fifty years earlier, Jenny repeated over and over *I'm happy for her. I'm happy for her.*

"So will you?"

Shaken from her thoughts and unsure what Lisbeth was asking, Jenny gave her friend the answer she knew she wanted. "I'd do anything for you." It was going to be hard to attend one more bridal shower and wedding, but not nearly as hard as being the last one of her group of friends to still be single. Would they leave her out of everything, or even worse, would they try to set her up with some man?

"You're sure? Oh, Jenny, this would mean so much to me, but I know it will be hard on you." Lisbeth was rattling on again. "Maybe I can arrange a fitting for next week. What do you think of light blue dresses? I was thinking yours could have an empire waist and princess neckline."

The word *yours* suddenly registered with Jenny. *My what?* A thread of doubt wound its way through her mind. Wasn't Lisbeth talking about coming to the shower? Jenny twisted a thin strand of hair around her index finger—a nervous gesture from childhood—as she tried to sort through everything Lisbeth was saying. *What have I promised to do? Fitting, dresses . . .*

"Jenny, having you as a bridesmaid is wonderful, but your being my maid-of-honor will make my wedding perfect—just perfect."

5

Maid-of-Honor? The words hit Jenny like they had been weapons thrown against her chest. She fought to breathe. *She asked me to be her Maid-of-Honor? And I said* yes?

Lisbeth continued, seemingly unaware that Jenny was dead silent, "I know I could have asked Stephie or Kira, or even Grace or Tamlyn, but you're my *best* friend. Besides, I didn't want a huge pregnant lady like Grace standing right next to me in the reception line, and I don't even know if Stephie will make it since she and Phil are poor grad students, stuck clear out on the East coast."

Jenny blinked back tears again, trying to keep her feelings in check. The thought of the bridal shower and making an appearance at the reception was overwhelming enough to her. But with this—this invitation—she would not only be expected to attend, she'd have to be right there next to Lisbeth's side every step of the way. Maybe she was even supposed to be *in charge of something.*

"Kira's barely married herself and Tamlyn is throwing up all the time . . ."

And now, Lisbeth was making it sound like Jenny was the least of all evils when it came to picking a maid-of-honor. Maybe she was. Maybe Lisbeth felt sorry for her and wanted her to at least *seem* to be something special this time as they stood in the receiving line. But maybe Lisbeth really *did* want her as her maid-of-honor. After all, they *were* best friends.

"I said I'd do it," Jenny interrupted before Lisbeth got herself into any deeper water with her rambling thoughts and innocent statements. She *had* to be the maid-of-honor. No getting out of it now.

"Thanks, Jenny." Lisbeth slowed down enough for Jenny's brain to process the depth of what she was saying. "I never thought I'd get married, but it's happening for me . . . and it will happen for you. I know it will."

A gut punch might not have hurt as bad as having no marriage prospects did for Jenny. She knew she had to change the subject before her voice betrayed her emotion. "Thanks, Lisbeth. I hope so, too." She gulped in air, trying to steady her voice. "So, what's my first duty as the chief maid?" Changing the title somehow made it better. Jenny imagined herself wearing an Indian headdress, beaded in blue to match the dress, *and* her feelings.

"I'm not sure," Lisbeth admitted. "I've only ever been a regular bridesmaid, but my mom will know. Come to the shower a few minutes early, okay, and we'll work it all out then."

"I can do that," Jenny said. She tried to remember what the maid-of-honor had done for her other friends, but all she could come up with was how sad she felt about it being their weddings and not hers.

"Thanks again," Lisbeth said. "I really have to run. Gary will be here any minute. We have to go check on the invitations." Her squeal proved her enthusiasm, as though her words had not.

Jenny sighed but followed it with a deep breath, pulling her shoulders back and straightening her spine as she did so.

The change in position made her feel better—more confident she could not only do this, but that she could also feel good about it. "Talk to you later, then."

Jenny closed the phone once the screen went dark. She dropped her elbows onto the table and rested her chin in both open palms. "Why can't I get married like everyone else?" She hadn't meant to speak the words aloud. She'd always worried that if she said something negative about her future, God would hear her, and what she said would come true.

But the waiting was almost more than she could stand. There had to be a way to stop the hurt. At least Lisbeth was the last of her closest friends to *take the plunge*, as the saying went. One more time through this ordeal and it would all be over. Jenny thought she could manage to hold on. *I hope . . .*

Then the solution struck her. She couldn't believe how simple it was.

If I stop hoping and waiting to fall in love, then it won't hurt so much that it never happens. How would it feel to never be married? What would life be like? Aunt Dru was still single and look at all she had done. She'd run for City Council, was CEO of a big company, and traveled all over the world. Jenny considered the possibility. Maybe staying single wouldn't be all that bad. It couldn't hurt to try the idea of forever single on for size, like a new coat. "Better to get over it now and stop wishing." No more trying to convince herself that her turn would be next. It was over. *Unless . . .*

"Enough of this nonsense," Jenny said. Despite the fact that her friends were almost her age, and all of them married—or nearly so—Jenny figured marriage would never be a part of her own life.

She stood and carried the invitation to the wall calendar where she tucked it into the pocket meant for keeping receipts. She picked up a red pen and put a big circle around the date of the shower. Jenny had drawn a frowny-face in black ink in the middle of the wedding date square when Lisbeth had told her days ago. She felt bad about it and dug around in the drawer for some *White Out*. Blowing on the covered spot until it dried, Jenny sketched a pair of hearts into the box and wrote two words below it—*Lisbeth's Wedding*. She was sure no one would ever write the same on a calendar with her name.

"Like it or not, Jenny Grant, marriage is not in your future. Not now, not ever.

2

James Cox hated being a temp worker, hated not knowing where the next call was going to come from, although it didn't really matter. He didn't need the money but wanted to be working. James even hated the strong feelings that made him leave his business and career in Southern California and traipse to Utah, begging for a job, any job in the highly competitive programming market.

No, he didn't really hate those feelings, but they sure did confuse him.

He'd had similar impressions while serving his church in France. One of his companions insisted on calling those feelings *intuition*, but James didn't like the feminine feel to the word. Of course, he didn't think it was exactly *inspiration* either. That was more like prophesy. Nope, this was just an impression—a strong one, powerful enough to make him walk away from a six-figure income and a profitable business to move six hundred and eighty-eight miles, give or take, to find whatever it was God had in store for him.

This morning when the call had come for him to report to Tech Aide, he'd found himself excited for the first time since he'd arrived in Utah. "Three days? You bet." He scribbled the address and a contact phone number onto the back of an envelope and stood from bed, ready to run to the shower. But before he made it across the room, a whisper formed inside him. *Gratitude.* James came to a dead stop. "Whoa."

He returned to his bedside and dropped onto his knees. Head bowed, he said the prayer that should have sprung to his lips the moment he hung up the phone. "Thank you for the opportunity I have to work these days in my chosen field. If it be Thy will, give me the knowledge as to why I am here, and if this is the job opening I've been waiting for." He closed the prayer then paused, not really expecting an immediate answer, but giving the Lord an extra minute just in case.

***

An hour later, James was no closer to knowing if this job would pan out to be more than three days, but he sure did like it. Everyone seemed friendly—maybe a little too friendly in the case of Tiara Brinkerhoff. The pudgy woman touted herself as some sort of a matchmaker, claiming to have been responsible for twenty-eight marriages in the company the last year alone. One look at her told James he didn't plan on letting her make him number twenty-nine. *No hot babes or sexy chicks on* her *contact list.*

What was he thinking anyway, James chided himself. Nice men didn't think about ladies that way, or at least they were *told* not to by their mothers. Sure, he'd seen a couple of great-looking women as he came into the building and

11

checked in at the front desk, but all of them were forgotten by the near-attack Tiara had given him.

"Are you here to see someone? Do you work here now? What position will you have?"

Her barrage of questions didn't give him a second to answer, and James almost broke away from her until she asked the final one.

"Are you married?"

He'd heard this question so many times before, and yet at his age of thirty-five, it always stopped him in his tracks. He turned back to look at Tiara, stammering for a brief moment before the humor of the question struck him. He couldn't resist. "Why? Are *you* available?"

It was the first time in nearly ten years that James hadn't taken offense by what he knew was an innocent question. Too often before he had felt attacked by those words, feeling people were accusing him of some terrible deed because he was not married and in his thirties. Darn that Brigham Young quote anyway: *Any young man who is unmarried at the age of twenty-one is a menace to the community.*

Tiara didn't seem to be in the least affected by his question. As a matter of fact, she didn't even seem to have heard it. She grabbed his elbow, and tried to lead James through the building like they were participants in a marathon, albeit a *walking* one. He honestly thought she would bust a gut any minute with all the huffing and puffing she was doing.

She pulled to a stop at an empty cubical. "Where is she?" Tiara said to empty air. Only a few of the spaces had been occupied during their mad rush past them, and the two employees at their desks nearby were talking into their headsets as they each maneuvered a cursor around their computer screens.

"No one's here," James felt obligated to point out. He poked his head into the office space and looked around for effect. "Nope. Not a soul."

He glanced at the desk. A daylight lamp sat on the corner. The computer sat strangely blank, just as the rest of desktop was bare, devoid of the photographs, knickknacks, and memorabilia that clogged the other desks he had seen. The name plate—Jenny Grant—was the only clue to who lived here each day, and even that didn't indicate if she were a Miss or a Mrs., although Tiara's haste in getting him to her desk would indicate the former.

"Jenny should be here any minute," Tiara said as she continued to hold firmly onto his arm. "She's usually so punctual. I don't know what could have happened. I've never seen her this late before."

"Yeah, well I'd love to hang around, but I just got here and it's my first day on the job." James looked up to see the receptionist standing with her hands on her hips, staring at him. He gently lifted Tiara's fingers away from his elbow and took a step toward the front of the building. "Maybe I'll catch up with you later, Miss . . ."

13

"Tiara. Everybody just calls me Tiara." But Tiara Brinkerhoff seemed a little unsure as to what she should do. She gave another look at Jenny's unoccupied chair as though she expected her to magically appear.

James turned and strode toward the front of the office, back to the receptionist and the spot he had occupied before Tiara had whisked him away.

"I'll find you once she gets here," Tiara called. "You two have to meet. You're perfect for each other!"

Not if he could do anything about it, James hoped. The receptionist—her name plate said Gretchen—held her hand across her mouth, apparently attempting to muffle her laughter. It wasn't working.

"So, now that you've met Miss Brinkerhoff, Mr. Cox," Gretchen said, "I think we'll keep you out of the main office today and take you to the file server room." She chuckled again as she added, "Give Tiara a little cooling-off time. She needs it."

"I think you're right." *And I know I do after that introduction.* James hoped that the rest of the day would be better. Avoiding Tiara Brinkerhoff would be a must during his lunch break. Maybe tomorrow he'd find a reason to get out of the file servers and onto a programming computer where he could show whoever was in charge that he would definitely be an asset as a full-time employee of the company.

***

Jenny heard Tiara before she saw her. "Jenny! Jenny

14

Grant!" The woman waddled toward her through the narrow aisle between the computer stations. "Have you seen him yet? He's perfect for you, just perfect."

Not again, Jenny wailed to herself. In the ten years Jenny had worked for Tech Aide, Tiara had tried to pair her off with every new, single male employee that had come to work in their division. Fortunately, Jenny was able to ignore most of them based on age difference or just plain weirdness. Unfortunately, every one of them, even the few who *were* cute and even semi-close to her in age, ignored her as well.

"Oh, Jenny, I'm so glad I caught up with you," Tiara said, reaching out a hand to touch Jenny's arm, steadying herself as she puffed to catch her breath.

"Hi, Tiara." Jenny wondered what kind of parents could have done such a thing, naming their baby *Tiara*, like they expected her to be the crowning glory of their family or something. She hoped Tiara didn't have heart failure between the cubbies that separated the bank of computer stations from the private cubicles where Jenny had her office.

"Jenny, I had to come find you right away." Tiara lifted her hand from Jenny's arm to fan herself a minute. "He just started this morning. I think he might be a temp, but that's okay. He's probably a few years younger than you are . . ." Tiara ducked her head like she was embarrassed to say anything about Jenny's age, then rushed headlong into the rest of her message. "But, he's tall, dark and handsome—no

15

joke—and I know you're going to fall in love the minute you see him."

"Not if he's a temp," Jenny said as she moved toward her cubical a few feet down the aisle. She didn't want to meet any temp worker, especially one younger than she was. Usually temps were fresh out of college, and if this one wasn't, then what would she do with him anyway? He wouldn't stick around long, and why would a man near her age still be working in a day-by-day position?

It really didn't matter what he did or why he was spending the day in her office. Jenny might have felt desperate for a romance yesterday, but today was the first day of the future she had come to accept—living her life as a single. Actually, that was beginning to sound sort of nice. Without a husband tying her down, she could buy a house or travel to exotic places. So what if she was lonely? Even married people still felt alone sometimes, didn't they?

Tiara followed her into her office. "I know I've tried to set you up before and it didn't work out."

"Understatement." Jenny dropped her purse into a bottom desk drawer and pushed the power button on her computer. She noticed the blinking message light on the phone, sat down at her desk and picked up the receiver. "I hate to cut you short, but I'm already running behind this morning and . . ." She wiggled the handset toward Tiara to make her point. "My audience awaits."

"No problem, Jenny. I'll bring him right over to meet

16

you, as soon as I see him again," the older woman said, not in the least deflated by Jenny's obvious lack of interest about meeting the temp.

"You do that," Jenny said. "I'll be right here waiting." *As if . . .*

3

Marriage was not the idyllic world Stephie had thought it would be. Phil was not the man she had thought she was marrying. He had been sweet during their courtship—bringing her flowers, sending her text messages even when he couldn't break away from work to really use the phone, and the presents he gave her were extravagant, way beyond what she expected a school teacher could really afford. But all of that, and even simple kindnesses, had disappeared once the honeymoon was over.

Phil had become demanding. "Why isn't this laundry done? I need a clean shirt for work." His requests were simple at first, but by the end of their first month together, Stephie couldn't predict what would set him off. Three times now she'd seen him throw a temper tantrum worthy of her two-year-old neighbor before last Christmas when his mother set him straight.

Only days after they returned home from the honeymoon, Phil had returned to his old life, it seemed. Of course, he was gone all day at school—teaching—but he also wanted to get away from their tiny apartment in the evenings, hang out with his friends. At first he asked if she

18

would mind, then he just assumed it would be okay, so he went ahead and made his plans without consulting her.

And now that Phil was in graduate school, it was even worse. Stephie had hoped moving to the East coast and away from Phil's buddies would help. But since then, computer gaming had become his new friend. The hours he spent tied to the console seemed endless and a waste of time, when he should be studying, or spending time with her. But he didn't see it that way, and any effort she had made to talk with him about it had ended with Stephie running to their bedroom in tears, and Phil continuing to not only ignore her, but also to hog the only television they owned.

She was lonelier than she had ever been at home, even as a single. At least there she had Kira, Tamlyn, Grace, Lisbeth and Jenny. Here she had no one, not even her husband. Money was tight because Phil wasn't working, and his graduate credits were expensive. Her savings had gone for the wedding and the expenses that came from the move. Stephie didn't know how much money Phil had saved before they were married, but he told her often they couldn't afford to go out for dinner, see a movie, or pay for her to have a cell phone or use his minutes for calls to her mother, let alone her friends. The question was how could they afford the growing stack of electronic games she had watched pile up since they had arrived in Boston?

Jenny opened the oven door to check on the macaroni

and cheese casserole. The fragrance reminded her of home, her mother's kitchen, and feeling loved. Her mom had tried to be everything for her daughter, even though it had been difficult for the two of them living alone. Stephie often wondered what it would have been like to grow up with two parents who loved her, and each other. She had hoped she'd be able to have a family herself like that someday, but her relationship with Phil didn't seem to be working out that way.

The slamming apartment door told her Phil was home. She gently closed the oven and tucked a loose strand of hair behind her ear. *Showtime.* The only problem was Jenny never knew if the audience would be indifferent or agitated. She forced a smile onto her face, ready to greet her husband, still hoping that miraculously things would return to their state during the courtship.

"Hi, honey," Stephie said as she left the kitchen and entered the living room.

Their cheap apartment was better than the dorm she had lived in during her own college years, but not much. Phil was already slumped into the bean bag chair in front of the television, his racing game had booted and the bright colors of a sports car flashed across the screen. His thumbs worked the controls, and all of his concentration was on the speeding car.

Stephie decided to try again. "How were your classes, Phil?" She bent over to place a kiss on the top of his head.

Phil grunted then jerked away like he was trying to avoid a pesky fly. She felt a spark of hurt, but she didn't want to completely give up, not yet. "Dinner will be ready in five minutes." No response.

She let a sigh escape from her lips before heading back into the kitchen. At least she could set the table, just big enough for the two of them, and wash the few dishes from lunch and cooking dinner while she waited. She ran the water until the stream became almost too hot to touch, then she slipped each dish from the stack in the left side into the foaming bubbles on the right.

She hated doing dishes by hand and missed the dishwasher she had often complained about having to fill while growing up. One nice thing about this place, the monthly rent covered all of their utility costs, except for the phone, cable and internet. She let the cold water run into the other side of the sink as she washed each dish then dipped it under the stream to rinse before placing it into the rack on the sideboard. The sound of the water drowned out the noise of the racing game, a noise that drove Stephie almost mad with its incessant screeching tires and revving engines.

Dishes done, she dried two plates and a glass and set them at the butcher block that served as their kitchen table. The timer on the stove buzzed just as she was finding forks in the silverware drawer.

"Shut that thing off!" Phil yelled over the roaring engines.

Stephie raced to the stove and twisted the dial on the timer. *How did he even hear that over his game?* The buzzing stopped, but the car noise did not. Maybe she just didn't understand men, she worried. She and her mom had lived without men since her dad abandoned them for a new life in California—a life that included a new wife and children, and no room for the old.

She used hot pads as she lifted the baking dish from the oven, remembering to set the dish onto the cutting board she had placed on the countertop. She didn't want a repeat of the lecture she had gotten from Phil about the security deposit and not ruining the surface of the counter because of her stupidity. Stephie had spent an entire morning, trying every cleaning product they owned, hoping to fade the light brown circle that had been left in the laminate. Was it her fault that her mom had done all of the cooking and hadn't really taught her only daughter the things she should know about working in the kitchen?

After removing two cans of Phil's favorite soda from the fridge and taking them to the table, she opened the door and said, "Dinner."

Phil seemed to ignore her, so she returned to the kitchen, getting a glass from the cupboard and filling it with cold water from the tap. She had already served herself a portion and sat down before silence hit the living room. Stephie knew Phil had only put the game on *pause*, planning to return to it as soon as dinner was over.

22

The second he entered the kitchen, Phil started in on her. "Macaroni and cheese *again*? Don't you know how to make anything else?"

"I haven't made it in a week," Stephie said as tears sprang into her eyes.

"Oh, that's right," he said as he dolloped an oversized portion onto his plate. "What was that concoction you made yesterday supposed to be anyway?"

She decided his question didn't deserve an answer. Phil had already critiqued that meal to death last night. No use bringing it back up again this evening.

He looked around the room, as though he expected something else to be waiting to take its place on his plate. "This is *it*? You didn't make meat, or green beans, or something to go with this?"

"No," she said, her voice almost hidden in the heaviness of the air between them. "I didn't have much money this week when I went to the grocery store. I thought . . ."

"You thought. That's the problem!" He let the plate bang against the table top and he sat down, picked up his fork, and started shoveling food into his mouth.

She wondered if he ever spoke to his students or colleagues this way. His friends would give the same attitude right back at him, but Stephie couldn't see herself treating him the way he treated her. She wanted to stay silent, to ignore his rude behavior, but there was one thing she still felt sure about. If she was ever going to save this marriage, she was going to have to stay close to her faith. "Phil?"

23

He looked up at her, a glare of contempt in his furrowed brow. He continued to chew as he waited.

"The prayer? The food hasn't yet been blessed."

He swallowed what was in his mouth before saying, "Yeah. You'd better bless it, or else it might kill me." He closed his eyes but didn't put down his fork.

Stephie didn't care. She went on without him. "Our Father . . ." Once she was done, she managed to take a single bite before Phil inhaled the rest of his serving, dropped his dirty dish into the remaining dishwater, and returned to his waiting game.

She washed the dishes, put the leftover casserole into the fridge, and quietly passed through the living room and into their bedroom. The room should have been a sanctuary for the still-newlywed couple. Instead, it was Stephie's refuge, a place away from Phil and his gaming systems, Phil and his volatile temper, Phil and her fantasies of what should have been.

She lay on the bed and picked up the card that had arrived this morning from Utah. Lisbeth's bridal shower was only days away, and Stephie knew there was no way she could attend. And she was positive she didn't want to. She didn't want any of her friends to know how miserable she was. She didn't want them to know how miserable the entire institution of marriage could be.

Let them dream their dreams, she thought. Lisbeth will find out soon enough. *If only I'd been smart like Jenny, smart enough to avoid this whole marriage thing altogether.*

4

Jenny didn't know if she'd been lucky or cursed. The entire day had passed without her once seeing Mr. *Tall-Dark-and-Handsome* that Tiara had raved about when she had gotten to work this morning. She didn't mind. Her promise to give up on hoping was still too fresh to let herself worry over a non-meeting of a guy that Tiara had picked out for her. Besides, she had too many other things to think about— like what would be expected of her as maid-of-honor.

She knew that Lisbeth said not to worry about her responsibilities, and that her mother would let Jenny know before the shower started. But Jenny didn't want to be blind-sided in front of a group of people in case there was something really awful she would have to do—something like arrange for her own date at the wedding breakfast. Tamlyn had talked about that before her wedding, but luckily Randy had a groomsman who wasn't married or seriously dating either, so Jenny had been paired up with him. He was a nice enough guy, but far too young for her to even consider developing a relationship with him, not that he was interested.

She had been a bridesmaid too many times, but this was her first commitment to be a maid-of-honor, and she didn't

25

have any idea of what that actually meant. Who could she ask? Jenny glanced at the computer sitting on the desk in front of her. She could go to the internet. She was sure to find information there, but that seemed so cold, so impersonal.

Her friends were an option, but two of them were busy being pregnant, and one was still a newlywed. She didn't want to bother any of them. She thought about calling Stephie, but realized she didn't have a new number for her now that she'd moved. Stephie had cancelled her cell phone for some reason, probably money if the truth be known. So, that counted out all of her friends.

Unfortunately Jenny knew what she had to do, whether she liked it or not, she'd call her own mother and ask for advice. *Mothers always know what to do about things like this, don't they?*

Logging out of her computer, Jenny took her purse from the desk drawer, turned off the switch to the daylight lamp she kept on her desk—even if she didn't make it into the sun very often she needed the special light to fool her brain—and walked toward the front of the office, glad she didn't run into Tiara or the mystery man on her way.

A light rain began to fall the minute she left the building. By the time she had walked across the street and neared the parking lot, she felt like she'd taken a shower with her clothes on.

"Care to share my umbrella?"

Jenny wiped a wet strand of hair away from her eyes and looked at a man she didn't know. The fleeting thought passed through her mind, *Is this Mr. Tall-Dark-and Handsome?* She certainly wouldn't have minded if he were, *if* she had wanted to give romance one more chance, that was. He was very good looking—in a Christopher Reeve-sort of way—dark hair, strong chin, somewhere over six feet tall. She could imagine him in a Superman costume for sure.

"No, no. That's all right," Jenny said. "My car is right here." She stopped next to the silver Cavalier she had been so proud of when it was new, almost ten years ago. Now it needed a paint job, the engine leaked oil, and the seat spring had started to poke through, sometimes snagging her pantyhose, making a run that showed beneath the hem of her skirt.

"At least let me hold this over your head while you unlock the door." His voice was deep and rich, like that baritone she had once heard at the opera. His eyes sparkled and a smile crinkled his cheeks into tiny dimples.

Suddenly, Jenny realized what she must look like, all wet and scraggly, like a drowned cat. She ran her hand across her forehead again, hoping to smooth any damp hair that was out of place. "Thanks." She fumbled in her skirt pocket, searching for the car keys she was certain she had stored there. When her hand came out empty, she opened the snap at the top of her purse. "Must have dropped them in here," she said, embarrassed that she was taking so long. *Nerves?*

"Take your time," the man said.

Jenny noticed that the rain was pouring off the umbrella and falling on his back. "Oh, you're getting wet." She reached her hand tentatively toward him, as though she intended to adjust the umbrella, but he waved her off.

"I'm okay. Rain does tend to have that effect now, doesn't it?" He chuckled—a warm and friendly sound—and Jenny relaxed, knowing he really was okay that she was taking this much time.

"Do you work around here?" he asked.

"I'm at Tech Aide," she said, then wondered why she had bothered to tell him. She knew he was just making conversation while he was waiting. Maybe she felt guilty about making him stand in the rain while she found those darn keys. She heard a jingle then pushed her hand into the lining of her bag. "Success," she said as she pulled the wad of keys from the purse.

"How did you ever lose a set like that?" He took the carabineer from her hand and hefted it up and down as though he were testing its weight. "And such a delicate piece of fine jewelry, too."

He laughed again as he handed the keys back to her, and Jenny loved it. *Why couldn't someone like you have been around back when I hadn't given up yet on men?* Yesterday.

She unlocked the door, and slipped into the front seat, tucking her skirt under her legs so she wouldn't be more embarrassed. "Well, thanks again."

"Anytime," the man said then with a wave of his hand and a tip of his umbrella, he was off across the lot and out of sight.

"Darn! I didn't even think to ask his name," Jenny said to no one. She inserted the key into the ignition and gave the starter a grind. *One. Two. Three.* At last the engine took hold and she pumped a little gas into its system. "But then, why should it matter? I'll never see him again, and I've given up on men—remember?"

***

Twenty minutes later, Jenny was home, peeled out of her wet clothes and lounging on the bed, trying to work up the nerve to call her mother. When she was a girl, talking with her mom had always been one of Jenny's favorite things to do. They had so much in common—books, music, and movies they both loved, needlework and crocheting talents they shared, and a *joi de vivre* that kept them involved in many activities together as though they were best friends instead of mother and daughter.

But all that seemed to change as Jenny got older and still remained unmarried. At first it was the questions—"Are you dating anyone? Whatever happened to that nice young man your aunt Debbie introduced you to? Have you met Mrs. Harmony's nephew? He's staying with them this semester while he goes to school at Snow."

The years ticked by and her mother seemed even more nervous about Jenny's dating and marriage prospects than

29

she did. By her thirtieth-fifth birthday, her mother's tactics had changed a little.

"What's wrong, Jenny? Are you being too picky? Do you know the difference between dating and just hanging out? I can send you the link to an article about it. Too many boys think it is okay to just hang out, you know."

Jenny knew, but she didn't need to read an article about it. Her singleness was humiliating enough in her small hometown community. It was a lesser factor now that they lived in Salt Lake, but the memories of innocent questions still remained.

Lately, her mother had stopped asking altogether. Jenny didn't know which was worse, the barrage of unanswerable questions, or the stilted silence. And now, to have to call her mom and ask about being a maid-of-honor for her last single friend's wedding. It was like rubbing salt into an already too tender wound.

Jenny punched in the numbers then waited as the phone rang several times. Her mother didn't answer as quickly as she used to. Like it or not, Jenny had to admit her mother was getting old, and the last thing she wanted to do before her life was over was see her only daughter get married. All four of Jenny's older brothers had gotten married young, while Jenny waited, and waited, and waited.

Jenny heaved a great sigh just as her mother's thin voice came across the connection. "Hello."

When had her mother started sounding so old? Was it

30

since her seventieth birthday, or had she been failing long before then and Jenny had been so wrapped up with her own woes to even notice?

"Hi, Mom. This is Jenny."

"Jenny! It's so nice to hear from you. How long has it been, dear?"

Leave it to mom to cut right to the chase with the guilt. Jenny decided to ignore the comment and dig in. "Mom, what are the responsibilities of a maid-of honor?"

"Maid-of . . ." Her mother sucked in a gasp of air that Jenny could hear clearly through the phone. "Why do you need to know . . . do you *need* a maid-of-honor?"

There she goes, turning this around into thinking that at last the miracle had occurred, and Jenny was getting married. She tried to keep the frustration out of her voice but knew she wasn't really successful. "No, Mom. I don't need a maid-of-honor. I've been asked to *be* one."

"Oh. I see," Mrs. Grant said, the disappointment evident in her reply. "Who's getting married *this* time?"

"Mom, you know Lisbeth is the only one of my friends *left* to get married." Jenny hated that she had to mention this fact to her mother, as if her mom didn't already know that her only daughter was destined to live the rest of her life alone. "She's asked me to be her maid-of-honor, and I don't know what will be expected of me. It's different from being just a bridesmaid."

"Will you be in charge of the shower or has someone else already planned that?"

31

"I think her mother did," Jenny said, glad that her own mother had settled into answering her question without a comment about Jenny being the last of her single friends. "I got an invitation already, and Lisbeth said for me to come a few minutes early to check in with her mom."

"Is it a *couples* shower?"

Her mother sounded liked she knew what she was talking about, but Jenny had never heard of such a thing. At the risk of sounding stupid, she asked, "What's a couples shower?"

"Oh, they can be a real mess, let me tell you." Mrs. Grant was off and running. "It's sort of a new thing actually. Peggy Daily gave one for her daughter a couple of weeks ago. Suzi and her fiancé, what's his name again? Tom? Terry? No, it's Terrance. Whoever heard of such a thing to call your child *Terrance* in today's world?"

"Mom." Jenny hoped to bring her mother back to the subject at hand. Once Mom got going, Jenny knew she could be there all night, listening to her rattle on like she needed to spill every word she had stored in her head before she could stop to take a breath.

"I'm getting there. Anyway, a couples shower means both the bride and the groom can come, and everyone brings the whole family. Kids running around like playtime at the daycare, and anyone who isn't married brings along a date, like some big family reunion and he's being introduced to the entire family all at once."

"Date?" Jenny's heart sank. She was right back to the feeling she had before Kira's wedding breakfast. No date for Jenny. Surely the invitation would have said something if it was a couples shower, wouldn't it? Or Lisbeth would have told her. She couldn't have forgotten something that important, even if she were getting ready for her own wedding day. Surely she wouldn't expect dateless-Jenny to come up with a date to bring to the shower. If she did, then Jenny's life as a maid-of-honor was sunk.

***

All evening long James had been kicking himself. Who was she? He hadn't been struck with interest in a woman this quickly for a long time. Why now, and why didn't he ask her name? He'd noticed there was no wedding ring. At least he had thought to ask her where she worked. *Tech Aide.* She'd said she worked at Tech Aide. Well, for the next two days, so did he.

He had to get out of the file server room tomorrow—*if* he could stay away from that Brinkerhoff woman. Maybe he'd be able to find out who the lady in the rain was. Would he recognize her without that sexy strand of wet hair curled against her forehead? The only other clue he had about her identity was the fact she drove a Cavalier much in need of a paint job. How many women at the company would fit that description? He loved the way she'd gotten flustered as he waited for her to find her keys, and with a keychain the size of his fist, it was funny that she'd lost it at all. He hoped she realized his laugh had been friendly.

James smashed his pillow into a more comfortable wad and propped himself against the wall that served as a headboard. The mute button was blinking to remind him why he didn't have sound from the television. Some booted *American Idol* contestant was chatting with Piers Morgan. James didn't care what they had to say. He tried to replay his brief conversation with the woman while they stood under the umbrella, basking in the rain. Well, he was basking in her presence at least, although she didn't look like she enjoyed the getting-wet part.

Anytime, he had said. And somehow he meant it. *What makes her so different?* James couldn't put words to his feelings, but something inside told him to pay attention. Was this the reason why he'd come to Utah? And was this woman the reason why he had been called to work at Tech Aide? *No.* Surely he was here to make another big breakthrough in the world of computer technology. That was where his passions really lie, wasn't it?

He'd spent years avoiding the prospect of meeting a woman, falling in love, and getting married. They all seemed so shallow that he didn't want to waste his time. He couldn't suddenly change his whole purpose in life now, could he? But maybe he should try. Maybe that really was the reason he was drawn here, to Utah, to Tech Aide—to meet a woman. Not just any woman, but the right woman. And for no apparent reason, this woman had drawn him in, and he'd found her in a parking lot.

It seemed like he was having a midlife crisis when he thought about the last few months, giving up his successful company and moving hundreds of miles away—to meet someone? And at a little company like Tech Aide. *I'm too young for a midlife crisis!* There had to be something more—burnout, dusting off old dreams, getting away from the California expectations. But he'd loved his life there, except for the part about being alone.

He knew the Lord had sent him places for lesser things—like the time he had been transferred to Lillie, in northern France, and met the little girl outside the Cathédrale Notre-Dame-de-la-Treille. She had been crying and barely able to state her name. *Annette.* They had located her mother who had been separated from the child as a flock of passing school children swept the girl away. The conversation that followed had been in his broken use of the French language, but the spirit had been strong, and James had known that this little girl was the reason he had been sent there, sent to Lillie, and it had proven to be true in the end when her mother became member of his church.

Had he been sent to Salt Lake for a similar reason? Was he here to find a girl—a woman? Was it possible that the one he had met today in the parking lot was his new *Annette?* Of course, this time he hadn't thought to get her name. But he knew where she worked, and that alone was a Godsend. *Two whole days.* Two days was all the time he had left at Tech Aide to find her. And in that same amount of time he had

35

to learn everything about her. He didn't understand why. Nothing had really changed, yet something inside kept prodding him, telling him he needed to know more about the woman in the rain.

But first he had to start by learning her name.

**

It took Jenny over an hour to get the rest of the information she needed from her mother. Most of it sounded simply awful—well, probably not if she hadn't been so frustrated about the whole idea of getting married. Or *not* getting married. Actually it sounded like much of the work had been done.

Lisbeth and Gary were in the midst of addressing their wedding invitations, and she had at least considered possible colors and styles for the bridesmaid dresses. The shower was planned, scheduled, and people already invited, so all Jenny had to do was show up mid-morning on Saturday, and she could check that off her list of things to do.

Her mother did mention that the maid-of-honor might plan games for the shower. Jenny hoped she didn't have to do that. Shower games were the worst part of the event as far as she was concerned, yet everyone else seemed to love them. These mix-and-mingle ice breakers seemed such a waste of time and energy. In all the showers she'd attended, Jenny already knew the people she wanted to know, and the ones she didn't would never be in her life again anyway, so who cared if she got to know them? Besides, the games always led

36

strangers to ask her more uncomfortable questions, the same ones over and over again.

"Are you married?"

"Are you dating someone?"

"When do you think you'll be getting married?"

She thought the questions were almost as intrusive as those people who insisted in touching the belly of a pregnant woman. Too intimate to share with people you hardly know.

At least with the shower already happening, Jenny was fairly certain she wouldn't have to hold a bachelorette party. None of their close friends would be likely to attend that anyway, with pregnancies, new grooms, and too many miles between them keeping the rest of their group away. Lisbeth was too shy to have many other friends who were close enough to invite to such a party, and she was certain that anyone Lisbeth knew from work would be invited to the shower, if they were close enough to be called her friends.

She'd find out tomorrow if Lisbeth needed help with arranging anything for the reception, which was probably the most important responsibility she would have as the maid-of-honor, at least until the day of the wedding.

Her mind somewhat settled, Jenny thought she'd do okay as the maid-of-honor. A glance at the clock told her it was well past time to go to bed. She had an important meeting in the morning at work, and she wanted to be alert and ready to listen to the presentation Rick Myers was sure to have. Rick always opened his meetings with a presentation. Jenny used to think it was great, a sign he was organized, but after three years of watching them, she now found it boring—just like she had found Rick. Her mother had had high hopes for that one, but Jenny got over any such notions about him quick.

Mom. Tonight her mother had been helpful, and actually seemed to know what she was talking about. But Jenny still worried about all the times lately she hadn't, those moments when mom had been confused and unable to explain what she was talking about. *Maybe I should call the doctor again,* Jenny thought, but there really was no reason why. No new changes, nothing much to tell him. Maybe she'd run over to see her tomorrow. Until then, Mom would be fine.

Jenny wondered if she could say the same thing for herself. The questions about being Lisbeth's maid-of-honor had kept Jenny's mind busy all night, but once she climbed into bed she found herself thinking about the dark-haired guy in the parking lot. He had sure been handsome—those twinkling blue eyes like a clear spring day. He'd come to her rescue like a Boy Scout—helpful, friendly, courteous, and kind. She didn't know yet how he compared to the rest of the traits the organization tried to instill in young men, but she imagined they were an ingrained part of him. Why did she have to find everything about him so darn attractive?

She could kick herself for not finding out anything

38

more about him. *Don't let yourself go there, Jenny!* Why hadn't she at least asked his name? *Because you're over men.*

No excuse. Of course, he hadn't asked hers either. But she'd managed to blurt out that she worked at Tech Aide. And what did that matter? Lots of women worked at Tech Aide in one department or another. Was he going to come snooping around the building in an effort to look for her? No. And why would he? He probably had a gorgeous wife at home. *But I didn't see a wedding ring.*

She tried to block the train of thought from her mind. He was just a nice guy who stopped to lend his umbrella to a woman in a parking lot. That was it. No reason for contemplation. No reason for obsession. No reason to even let the thought of him continue to cross her mind.

Then why couldn't she get the man out of her head?

5

Yesterday's rain storm had done something to Jenny, but something worse to her car. After a series of cranking the starter, a turn of the key only resulted in a click. No grinding, revving, or anticipated sound of the engine taking hold and running. *Maybe if I let it sit for a few minutes . . .* But Jenny's patience wore out long before enough time could have passed for the battery to recharge, if that was what the problem really was.

One last try resulted in nothing. Not even a *click* this time. If there had ever been a time she wanted to swear in frustration, this might be it, but she restrained herself. She pulled the lever to release the latch then stepped from the car. Lifting the hood, she stood staring at the engine, hoping the problem would magically appear, so obvious that even someone as automobile-challenged as she was would know exactly what to do.

The interior parts all looked innocent enough, unless that little stream of grease running from the doohicky to the whatchamacallit meant something more than a messy mechanic had filled the oil at some time. "Great. Second morning in a row I'm going to be late, and there's that meeting with Rick about the system upgrade."

40

She unfastened the brace holding the hood open and let it drop back into place. Slipping her phone from the pocket of her slacks, Jenny punched in the auto-dial for Tech Aide. It took three rings before Gretchen answered the line.

"Tech Aide. How may I direct your call?"

"Hi, Gretch. It's Jenny."

"Hey, Jen. What's up?" Gretchen still sounded too young to be manning the phone lines for anything but arranging a group sleepover at her house after the school dance.

"Car trouble."

"Bummer." The snapping sound of gum came through the phone lines.

Jenny made a mental note to mention it to Gretchen's supervisor. She didn't want to get the girl in trouble, but being professional didn't allow the receptionist to sound like a teeny-bopper gum-chewer either. "Gretchen, I've got that ten o'clock with Rick and the team, but I'm not sure how long it will take for the automobile club to send someone, or if the problem is even repairable at this stage. Is there anyone . . ."

"Hey," Gretchen said before Jenny could finish her question. "We've got that temp guy working again today. I don't think he's been assigned yet this morning. I'll send him out to . . ."

"No! No, that's okay, Gretchen." Jenny could see it now. If this was the temp that Tiara wanted her to meet, the

41

woman would be after her all the rest of the day to see how the ride into work went. Jenny couldn't afford to meet the guy, let alone have him come to her apartment, even to the nearby parking lot, to pick her up.

But it was obvious Gretchen wasn't listening. "I just buzzed for him to come down to the front desk. I'll give him your address, and he should be there in about fifteen minutes. See you in a little while."

The phone went dead in Jenny's hand.

She stared at the cell for a minute, debating whether to call Gretchen back. But by now the temp worker might already be on his way, and she did need a ride to work or Rick would be furious at another delay in the project.

Might as well get something done while I'm waiting, she thought. Jenny punched in the number for the auto club she subscribed to. She hating paying the fee each year, but days like this made it worthwhile. Single women were often at the mercy of their cars, and she couldn't afford to take the entire day off to get the car repaired.

The service line picked up after a single ring. Jenny explained her problem, and the woman at the other end said she'd have someone there shortly.

"Thank you. If he's here in ten minutes, I'll be standing by the car. Anything longer and he'll need to check in with the landlord's office in my complex."

She gave the woman details the service tech would need, snapped her phone closed, then sat in the front seat of the

42

car, keeping her eye out for a lost soul who was coming to pick her up. *I feel like some stupid damsel in distress*, she thought, as she inserted the key and gave it one more twist.

Still nothing. Like it or not, she was stuck, and meeting this temp worker was now her destiny.

***

James read the address Gretchen had written for something like the fourth time. "I thought Brigham Young laid this city out so you could find anyplace without getting lost?" Well, that hadn't worked too well on this one. 850 South Lake Street. *Where in the heck is Lake Street?*

He'd followed the directions, or at least he thought he had. South Temple east to 71 southbound, down to 800 South. Turn left and Lake was about a half a block on the left. Or was he supposed to go past 8th South then turn left?

Suddenly his scribbled instructions didn't seem right at all. He had just crossed 13th East, so he knew he had already gone too far. Like it or not, he was going to have to turn around, but the man in him said he'd give it one more try before he stopped to ask for directions.

12th, 11th, 10th, 9th, 8th, 7th, 6th. "Dang!" He spat the word like a bad taste from his mouth. He made a left onto 5th East and another left onto 900 South. Checking every street sign as he passed Liberty Park, he nearly missed the small green sign that said *Lake*. If that Cavalier hadn't almost ploughed into him just as his car swerved to avoid the mutt that had entered his lane.

"Wait! A Cavalier?" James pulled into a driveway and turned the car around, heading back toward Lake Street, but a half a block ahead, he saw the Chevy make a right turn, headed north on 700 East, Highway 71, the way back to Tech Aide.

"No, it can't be," James said. "Wrong color." He shook his head, as if to wipe the idea from his mind then turned into the road he had at last found. The building at 850 South Lake was easy to find, now that he had the right road. An apartment complex sat at the end of the street, a dozen or more cars parked on the asphalt next to it. A tow truck marked A+B Towing pulled out of the drive just as James pulled in.

He parked the car then stepped out to look around the lot. No damsel in distress. No car that looked like it wouldn't start. He glanced at his watch. He was twenty minutes later than he thought he would be. Had she given up? He looked toward the apartments, but Gretchen had failed to give him the unit number. He pulled his cell from his pocket and turned on the screen. Nothing. Blackness.

"Stupid." How could he have forgotten to charge the phone, especially since he was working? Too much on his mind last night, too much time wondering about that woman.

James turned off the ignition to his Altima before taking a walk around the parking lot, doing a quick check to make sure *this* mysterious woman—Jenny Grant—wasn't just

44

waiting in her car for him. No such luck. Or maybe it was. Jenny Grant was the name of the woman the matchmaker had wanted him to meet yesterday. Perhaps he was simply avoiding the inevitable.

As James returned to his car, a dark-haired man bounded out of the complex, a garment bag flung across his shoulder, the bag and his body almost running into James on the way to his own vehicle.

"Whoa!" The man stopped short in front of James. "Sorry 'bout that."

"Yeah."

"Dry cleaner's waitin'," the man said as he tucked the bag into the back seat, attaching the hanger onto the hook above the window. He jumped into the pick-up, pulled the door shut, and turned the key in the ignition. "See ya."

James suddenly came to life. "Wait!"

The guy rolled his window farther down and stuck his head out so he could hear past the noise of his engine. "Need somethin'?"

"Jenny Grant. I was sent down here from Tech Aide to pick up Jenny Grant. Have you seen her?"

"Jenny?" He opened the truck door and stood on the running board, looking around the parking lot. "I don't see her car anywhere. You sure you're supposed to pick her up here?"

"What kind of a car does she drive?" James wondered if he had passed her after all along the way.

The man's voice had a hint of distrust as he said, "Cavalier. How long have you known Jenny anyway?"

A Cavalier? It couldn't be. Not wanting to raise any more suspicion from this guy who could possibly help him, James said, "Haven't met her yet."

"Oh, really? Well, her car's not here and in that case, I guess you'd better be on your way." Despite his earlier hurry, the man stayed standing on the running board, waiting for James to leave. "I'll tell her you came by."

"Thanks," James said. "Thanks, a lot." He knew where he wasn't wanted, and he was happy to oblige. Besides, he really wanted to get back to Tech Aide. He was certain if he could get a chance to work with the computers the boss would see how much help he was and offer him a regular job.

And a job—not Jenny Grant—was exactly what he needed.

6

Stephie stared at the little blue line, hoping—no, praying—her eyes deceived her. But the plus sign remained the same, even after she shut her eyes tight then opened them only enough to peek through the slits under her lashes. "No, no, no, no, no!" *How did this happen?*

But she knew the answer. Despite the fact that Phil had formed a relationship with the control paddle on his gaming system, she and her husband *were* still newlyweds. She'd do anything to try to regain that spark of romance the two of them had felt before the wedding, before the move to Boston, before the hours of mindless video games had sucked her husband away from her.

She'd do anything, except maybe this. *Thirty-four years old, living thousands of miles from my mom, and pregnant.* She looked into the mirror at the sad eyes that gazed back. "I don't even have my best friends to comfort me in my time of need," Stephie whispered. "I don't have *any* friends here." The apartment door slammed. "Good-bye, Honey. I love you too," she said to no one.

Phil was gone and wouldn't be back until it was time for dinner. For once, she was glad he hadn't popped his head in to see what she was doing, to ask if there was anything she

47

might need. She wanted to be alone at this moment, to consider what the result of her test might mean, not only to her body, but to her marriage as well. *This is all we need.* But she wasn't convinced if she meant that as a good thing, or if a baby would be the final straw to break the proverbial camel's back.

Stephie checked the pregnancy test one more time. No change in the results. She shoved the white rod into the opened wrapper, surrounded it a couple of times with toilet tissue, then dug into the bottom of the waste basket so she could cover the evidence like a dog buries a bone. No use in letting Phil suspect they were going to have a baby. Not that he would unless the evidence was staring at him. There was too much tension in their relationship right now as it was without adding this to the mix.

She finished her morning routine, grabbed the wet towel Phil had left on the floor, and tossed it into the wicker basket waiting to be taken downstairs to the laundry. She stood in front of the opened refrigerator door for all of three seconds before she decided breakfast was out of the question. The nausea should have tipped her off earlier than the late period—she was crazy-irregular anyway—but Stephie just thought she was upset about Phil's drastic change in behavior. The anger, his obsession with gaming—both drew him farther away from her and their marriage.

She hadn't really thought about getting pregnant. Not so soon. Maybe that was naive. Before the wedding, everyone

48

had told her not to expect an easy path to motherhood, not at her age. She knew they were right about the path not being easy, but according to the test strip, getting pregnant didn't seem to be a problem. They hadn't even tried, and here she was, expecting their first baby as easy as a teenager who had no plans to get married.

Now that Phil was gone, and she'd had a few minutes to think about the test strip sitting in the bottom of the trash can, Stephie wanted to talk to someone—anyone—about the things she was feeling, but Phil would have taken their only cell phone with him—he never let it out of his possession—and 7:00 a.m. was too early to visit any of their neighbors anyway, even if she had known them well enough to make a surprise visit.

The doorbell rang less than five seconds later. *Who on earth can that be?* She pulled her robe closed and padded across the kitchen to the front of the apartment. The distorted view through the peephole only told her a woman stood in the hallway.

"Who is it?" Stephie asked, not certain she would recognize a name, if one were given.

The woman turned around to face the door, as she called out, "I'm your new neighbor. I heard your husband leave already, and I thought maybe you'd like some company."

Stephie couldn't decide if the woman—girl, maybe from the sound of her voice—had read her mind about wanting

49

someone to talk to—a gift from God—or if she was just plain loco for visiting someone she didn't know at this time of the morning. It took her too long to consider whether she was ready to open the door to this stranger.

"Oh my gosh! This *is* where Stephie Harris lives, isn't it?" The young woman's voice sounded frantic, as though she'd made a serious mistake and suddenly knew it. "I'm so sorry, I . . ."

"Wait!" Stephie pulled open the door. "I'm Stephie Harris." She ran her hand across the top of her hair, self-conscious about the fact she'd done nothing to improve her looks since she had jumped out of bed this morning. The only thing that had been on her mind then was rushing to the bathroom to use the pregnancy test kit she had sneaked into the house with the groceries the day before, and since Phil wouldn't let her get a job, it didn't really matter if she stayed a mess all morning.

"Hi." The young—yet obviously pregnant woman—stuck her hand out. "I'm Rachel Leeds, your next-door neighbor." She patted her hand against the top of her belly as she continued, "And this is Jeffrey. He's due to make his debut in about a week."

"I should hope so," Stephie said before she could stop herself. The woman's belly was gargantuan. She was glad to hear the roaring laugh that burst immediately from Rachel, but she began to wonder how the girl knew her name.

"That obvious, huh?" The smile that crossed Rachel's face was broad and genuine. "Mind if I come in?"

"Please. Please do. I'm sorry. I was just startled by the doorbell ringing this early . . ."

Rachel's face suddenly looked crestfallen.

"No, I mean . . . it's okay . . . I was just thinking I'd like . . ." She gave up trying to explain and opened the door wide. Did it matter how Rachel knew who she was? She wanted to talk. She'd been sent this young woman, far more knowledgeable than she about carrying a baby, at least judging by her current condition. Stephie thought somehow her wish had been heard, and the answer was standing before her.

"Thanks," Rachel said as she maneuvered herself into the living room that suddenly shrunk in size through her presence. She waddled to the couch and pointed. "Safe?"

"I hope so," Stephie said. "It came with the place, so you never know."

Rachel lowered herself onto the cushions. "Hey, this one's better than the one in our place. Wanna trade?" She fidgeted around until her back was supported, placing a throw pillow under the arch for added comfort.

Stephie could feel the smile on her own face, a gesture that had been sadly lacking for too long, at least since the move to Boston. "Would you like something to drink?"

"Nah, I'm fine. Thanks." Rachel looked like a Buddha

51

perched atop the soft couch. The contentment on her face seeming like she had reached the pinnacle of nirvana was heightened by her worship of the perfectly round bundle of unborn baby she held in her arms.

Not sure what to say, and almost afraid to disturb the reverence of the moment, Stephie waited, hoping her visitor would break the ice. But Rachel just sat, taking in a series of deep breaths reminiscent of the cooling-down process following an aerobics workout.

After a few more moments, Stephie asked, "You okay?"

Rachel nodded before speaking. "Lamaze. You know, breathe, two, three, four . . . ?"

Stephie made an O with her mouth and shook her head like she understood perfectly what Rachel was talking about, but in truth, she wasn't really sure why the girl was breathing Lamaze at this moment. There was no way she was going to ask her. Rachel continued her deep breathing as Stephie studied her face. Despite her pregnancy, she didn't look old enough to be married, let alone have a baby coming any day. Her auburn hair was pulled into a ponytail and her cheeks were rosy like a portrait of Santa.

"Oh," Rachel said. "He kicked me." Her smile widened, although Stephie wouldn't have thought it was possible.

"Yeah, I feel that way sometimes, too." The words slipped out without her meaning to say them.

Rachel gave her a strange look. "I never would have known you were expecting."

52

Stephie was startled. How did Rachel know? She touched her abdomen before realizing there was nothing there to show. Then she figured it out. Rachel thought she meant a baby was kicking, not the way Stephie felt lately about the way Phil ignored her.

"I . . . I . . ." Embarrassed by her own gaffe, Stephie finally said, "I guess I was actually referring to my husband."

Rachel started to rise from the couch, her hand held out toward Stephie. "Your husband? He kicks you?"

Stephie was quick to correct her second mistake. "No, no. He doesn't kick me."

Rachel sighed and lowered back into the couch. "Well, then what did you mean, if I may ask?"

Stephie debated for a moment. Did she want to tell this young, pregnant girl all about the woes of her marriage? Did she want to spoil that bubble of happiness that Rachel seemed surrounded by? She had prayed for God to send her someone to talk to, but Rachel wasn't exactly what she had in mind. Or was she? Stephie had long known that the Lord delighted in answering prayers in the oddest ways. And a teenage mommy, ready to pop at any time, was definitely the strangest answer to her prayers she had ever seen, but God must know what He was doing.

"Things have not been that great since Phil and I moved to Boston," she began her story.

7

"Distributor cap." Jenny would have to remember that. "The distributor cap has to be dry inside." Yesterday's rainstorm had been a drencher. At least the mechanic from the towing company had recognized exactly what the problem was and fixed it before Jenny was late for the scheduled meeting.

She pulled into a parking slot, glanced at the dashboard clock—9:53—and grabbed her purse as she removed the ignition key. Locking the door, she slammed it shut and headed off in a run across the street toward the building that housed Tech Aide.

"Hi, Gretchen," Jenny said as she rushed past the startled receptionist.

"Jenny? Where's the temp I sent to get you?" Gretchen followed her halfway to her cubical, where Jenny only stopped briefly to grab a packet of file folders.

"Didn't see him," Jenny said. "The auto club people got there, started my car, and I came to work. Sorry," she called over her shoulder as she hurried into the board room where the planning meeting for the system upgrade was ready to begin.

Rick Myers was tapping his finger against the surface of

the interactive whiteboard. He already had two servers open when Jenny stepped into the room.

"Good morning everyone," Jenny said as she slid into a seat at the board table, near the back of the room, arranging her file folders into a neat stack before her. She automatically tucked a few stray hairs away from her face and behind her ears, hoping to improve her appearance. Old habits died hard.

Jenny had once done everything in her power to impress her boss, wishing he would take notice and ask her out. She joined the gym, lost twenty pounds, and took up tennis, keeping an eye on the nearby courts in case Rick was playing at the same time she was. A lasting relationship with him had been another one of her pipe dreams, and her mother's, left unfulfilled despite the efforts Tiara had added to her own. Tiara the matchmaker had failed. And Jenny was still alone.

Rick didn't seem to care about her then, and he certainly didn't respond to her now. An automatic slide presentation was underway, and his full attention was turned toward it, admiring what was likely his own work. Boring, as usual.

"Hey, Jenny. Just get in?" Nathan Greenly leaned across the table toward her, his position almost threatening and his tone insinuating.

She chose to ignore him and glanced around the room for a more friendly face.

Melinda Stanton was positioned near the whiteboard—and Rick—prepared to respond if he needed anything. "Do you want water, before we start?" Melinda took a lens cleaner from her pocket and wiped it across the computer laptop screen, as though the effort would make the presentation more focused on the whiteboard.

The door opened and Isaac Richards entered the room. "Hey, guys. Sorry I'm late. Grace wasn't feeling too well, and we were afraid it was time to get to the hospital and welcome a baby." He slid into the empty seat next to Jenny, patting her arm like they were best buds in the whole world.

Actually, Jenny guessed they might almost be that very thing. After all, Isaac had married one of her best friends when he married Grace, and he and Jenny had worked together at Tech Aide for a good three years.

"So, did you have to take her to the hospital?" Jenny could hardly believe she had to actually ask.

"Nah! This time it was just plain indigestion. You should see the strange foods that woman craves! We thought she'd left this stage a long time ago, but no." He laughed for a minute at his own memory. "Just this morning, she had an ice cream bar, a bite of a powered sugar donut, a half jar of salsa and a handful of chips, a banana and four dill pickle spears, yet she said none of it satisfied what she was hungry for. It was almost enough to make me gag, and I have an iron stomach."

He patted his belly which, Jenny noted, had grown a

56

few inches in the time that Grace had been expecting. "Oh, that's what you call that." Jenny couldn't help from teasing.

"Hey!" Isaac said, drawing back to give her a fake punch on the arm.

Rick turned to give them an executive stare-down.

"Oops!" Jenny said, drawing Isaac's attention toward their fearsome leader.

"Sorry," Isaac said. He pulled himself up stiff like a repentant student, ready to listen to the wisdom of the ages being delivered by a strict school teacher.

Jenny stifled a chuckle before opening a notepad, ready for writing, or drawing pictures if Rick's presentation was too boring.

"Now, if I may begin . . ." Rick pointed a finger toward the light switch, and Melinda immediately flicked it to *off*, leaving the office lit only by the projection onto the whiteboard and a series of dimmed canister lights around the edge of the room. The automatic series of slides that had been flickering across the board stopped, and the Tech Aide logo appeared.

Leave it to Rick to think he needs to impress us like we are a bunch of potential investors. Although Jenny doubted investors would be able to sit through the droning of Rick's presentation for very long. She'd only been here a few minutes, and already she was having trouble not falling asleep.

Jenny jumped like she was shot when the office door flew open.

"Has anyone seen . . . Oops!" Tiara stood halfway into the room, her eyes opened wide like Betty Boop, only without the mascara to complete the effect. "Sorry. I didn't mean to interrupt."

Rick had moved back into stare-down mode. His voice was clipped as he asked, "Who did you need, Tiara?"

"Umm." The hesitation wasn't like Tiara's usual self. She glanced around the room until her eyes stopped on Jenny. "Can I . . . can I see you a minute?" Tiara shrugged her shoulders and gave Rick another look of apology before waving her hand for Jenny to follow her immediately.

Rick's expression told Jenny she'd better do something fast, or his quick temper would likely explode. She stood and followed Tiara from the room.

Once the door was shut, Jenny turned toward the woman who was now fanning herself like she was in the middle of a hot flash. "Tiara, what was that all about?"

"He's here. He's working on the floor today." She gulped a breath then continued, although Jenny struggled to make sense of what Tiara was trying to tell her. "I don't know where they had him hidden yesterday, but I saw him come in the front door a few minutes ago. Gretchen sent him to help Val with something in the back cubicle. You can't let him stay back there with her. You know she'll do everything she can to get her claws into him, and he's perfect for *you*."

At last Jenny caught on to what Tiara was talking about.

58

"It's that man, isn't it? The temp you wanted me to meet from yesterday."

Tiara's head bobbed up and down, sending little ringlets above her ears bouncing like coiled springs in an earthquake. "Yes, and you've got to hurry." She stepped behind Jenny, so she could put her hands flat against Jenny's back, and tried to exert enough pressure to get her moving, buy Jenny would have none of it.

Breaking free and placing her hand onto the knob of the office door, she nearly hissed out the next set of words. "Stop it. I know you think you're doing the right thing, and I know you believe this man is perfect for me, but I'm not interested. I'm not going to crash into Val's cubicle on a wild goose chase over some man you think I need to meet, and I'm not going to lose my job because you have a reputation as a matchmaker to keep."

All the color, except the brush-on blush, had drained from Tiara's cheeks. "Well, I never . . ."

"That's right, you *never*. You never stop to think. You assume because you're so all-fired sad you never married that everyone else feels the same way." Jenny couldn't believe the words coming out of her own mouth, but she couldn't seem to make them stop, either. "I've had enough of men, and I've had enough of *you*, Tiara. Take care of your own life and leave me be."

Jenny yanked on the knob then realized she had to turn it before the door jerked open. She gave a spiteful final glance toward Tiara, entered the room, and slid into her vacated seat. She tried to ignore the fact that both Nathan and Rick were staring at her. Melinda cleared her throat as though she were hoping to divert the extra attention away.

Only Isaac showed his concern by placing his hand against her arm and asking, "You okay?"

Jenny shrugged his hand away. "Fine." She hadn't meant to sound snippy with Isaac, but she knew she did. She couldn't bring herself to look at him, or anyone for that matter. *What got into me? I never treat people like that.* She could feel the heat in her cheeks from the embarrassment. She refused to think about what everyone in the office must have heard or thought about the way she had spoken to Tiara.

Darn that Tiara Brinkerhoff anyway. If it hadn't been for her, none of this would have happened. Jenny wouldn't have offended Grace's husband. She wouldn't have interrupted Rick's precious meeting.

And she wouldn't be wondering just what this new temp worker was like, and if he really was as perfect for her as Tiara thought he was.

***

James was in his element. Odd as it might seem, he loved solving computer programming problems. All those numbers and code marching down the screen entranced him like the words of a fine novel. Then this woman—Val. *Was that her name?*—had mentioned to Gretchen that her station computer was feeding her garbled messages, James had been in the right place at the right time.

"Let me take a look at it," he had said. At least he would earn the money the company was paying him, and not feel his time was wasted like it was when he went to pick up the non-existent Jenny Grant at her apartment complex.

"Can't hurt," Gretchen had said. "Besides, Mr. Myers is in a meeting, and he didn't leave any specific assignments for you yet this morning."

"Let's go," Val had said as she led him to her cubicle toward the back of the office.

James tried to keep his eyes from straying to the hem of her sassy skirt as she walked in front of him, almost impossible with the way she swung her hips. He was sure it was on purpose. He reminded himself he was here to find a new position in the computer field if that's where the Lord wanted him, not to flirt with the office staff—especially if he wanted to become one of them. Although he did plan to keep an eye out for the mysterious woman he had met yesterday in the parking lot, even if he didn't know why.

Less than ten minutes and Val's problem was solved. "Wow! We've never had a tech who could clear up a code error that fast," she said. Her voice was almost a *coo*, soft and enticing. She placed her hand against his shoulder and ran it gently down his arm, stopping with her fingers tickling across his wrist, but James pulled away, ignoring her obvious come-on. He could tell she was the kind of woman who considered flirting an extreme sport.

61

Before he could say anything—or even move away—another woman popped her head into the cubicle. She was older, her hair streaked with silver, and her clothing tailored. "A tech who can clear up error code? Let me at him. And Val, you're late for Rick's meeting."

"On my way," Val said.

James pulled his wrist out from under her fingers. He didn't miss the quick glance the older woman gave him, proving she knew what the younger woman was doing. "Lead on, Mc Duff," James said.

Something about this woman said she should be trusted, while Val should have had flashing warning signs across her forehead: *Danger! Watch out!*

"Come back anytime, James," Val said as she leaned against the prefab wall that separated her workspace from the aisle, seemingly in no hurry to get to her meeting.

"So, James," the older woman said as she led him away from Val and toward her own office. "You've survived your first encounter with Val the Flirt, I see." A wide grin and deep dimples marked the older woman's mirth. She stuck her hand out as she said, "My name's Marie Davis."

"James Cox."

"My computer's in here," Marie said, ushering him into an actual office, not just a cubby like the others he had seen so far.

A gold nameplate on the woman's desk said *Marie Davis, President of Research and Development.*

62

At last. James was relieved to see this woman was someone who might recognize he was more than just a temp worker. Impressing her could be what he needed to get his foot in the door. At least she didn't seem to be like the other women he had met so far at Tech Aide. He could only hope the men were more stable.

Five minutes later, the problem with Marie's computer was fixed and she was ushering him down a hallway at the back of the building and into another office. The placard on the door said *Personnel*. A middle-aged man, with his tie a bit askew, sat working at his computer in the center of the room. He rose from his chair as they entered.

"Cory, this is James Cox." Her tone was brisk but friendly. "I've just hired him. Fill out whatever paperwork he needs to start work full time today. Take his picture, get his name badge going, everything."

"Sure thing, Marie," Cory said as he stuck his hand out toward James. "Cory Savage."

James gave the man a firm shake then sat in one of the seats as Cory indicated he should.

"Buzz my office when everything's done, and I'll come back." Marie started to move away from Cory's office, but turned toward James for one final comment. "Welcome to Tech Aide, James. It's good to have you."

"Thanks. It's good to be here," James said, proud that his skills had gotten him a new job, no matter what department he'd be working with. Then she was gone.

Cory opened his desk drawer and pulled out a sheaf of papers. "Let's start with an application, work history. Just formalities, you know." He placed the stack of papers onto a clip board, slid a pen onto the board and handed them to James.

"Thanks." James scanned the first page then started to write.

"Had much experience with computers?" Cory seemed genuinely interested.

"Some," James said. "Ever heard of Info-Systems Technology?"

"Of course." A chuckle escaped Cory's lips. "Who hasn't? Did you used to work for them?"

James couldn't help but smile as he thought about the company he started. The company he loved, and the one he had sold for a small fortune the week before he moved to Utah. "You might say so."

***

Jenny rushed from the room as soon as the meeting was over. Rick had dragged it on forever, and she hadn't thought she'd be able to tolerate sitting there another minute. But at least it was through, and the time was close enough to lunch that she could take a break from the office for a while. She needed a walk in the fresh air to clear her mind.

Dropping her file folders onto a heap, she promised herself she'd straighten her desk when she got back. She grabbed her purse from the lower desk drawer and headed toward the front of the building, nearly crashing into Tiara on her way. She couldn't make herself say anything to the woman, not after the tirade she had laid upon her earlier.

She couldn't explain why she had been so mean. Tiara really didn't intend any harm in her matchmaking ways, and Jenny knew that. Usually she was patient and kind by listening to Tiara's descriptions of the men she thought Jenny would like. On occasion, some of them even sounded interesting, but years of nothing working out had worn on Jenny's patience, as well as her peace of mind. And now with Lisbeth getting married . . . *Glad to be free*, Jenny stepped onto the sidewalk and turned toward The Gateway. There was still a shower present to buy.

And the matter of being maid-of-honor.

Was that her problem? Was it the coming wedding of her last single friend—of her *best* friend—that had made her respond to Tiara the way she had? If so, the problem really belonged to Jenny, not to Tiara, who had simply gotten in the way.

Poor Tiara. She was actually a few years older than Jenny herself, and Jenny knew she'd never been married either. How could she make all those perfect matches and not manage to find one for herself? Everyone Jenny knew at the company who married because of Tiara seemed to be happy. What about Tiara though? Had Jenny been right when she accused her of being sad because she was single?

Sad was a good way to describe how Jenny felt about

singleness herself. Maybe she was more like Tiara than she had realized. But, no. Not anymore. Last night she had decided. She liked being single. She liked the freedom it offered. And she liked the opportunities she would have by never having to worry about pleasing a man enough to make her his wife.

Still, the look in Tiara's eyes bothered her. *Is she* really *like me?*

***

Tiara looked like a deer in the headlights, James decided as he exited Cory's office. The woman was pressed against the wall, eyes open and staring toward the exit. Her hair was disheveled as though she had scrunched it with her hands in an effort to pull her thoughts together. He'd seen men do that before, but didn't think a woman would ever risk her hairstyle.

Before he could say anything to Tiara, Marie arrived at his side. "Ready?"

"You bet." James glanced back toward Tiara, finding it odd that this woman who seemed so filled with words was now so silent, almost as though she were frozen in time.

Marie must have noticed something was wrong as well because she stopped, placing her hand against the woman's arm. "Tiara? Everything okay?"

The spell was broken. Tiara shook her head, as though clearing cobwebs from her mind. "Oh . . . yes. Yes, I'm fine."

James wasn't sure he believed that. Her eyes looked

puffy, as though she'd been crying. Her voice sounded flat, not at all like the exuberance he had heard from her yesterday at their first encounter. Even the shine was gone from her eyes, and the redness on her cheeks was nothing more than make-up.

"If you say so," Marie said.

James could sense that she was ready to let Tiara deal with whatever her problem was on her own. He would follow Marie Davis's lead, and hope that Tech Aide would be just the place he needed to be.

"Your cubicle is this way," Marie said as she turned toward the location where he had seen Jenny Grant's name on a cubicle earlier.

He glanced into Jenny's empty office space before realizing Marie had stopped and was pointing at the slot directly across the aisle. "This one's yours. I'll have Gretchen send your starter supplies—you know—pens, pencils, note pads, paperclips, et cetera. Did Cory give you a computer pass code?"

James nodded. "Got it right here." He patted the pocket on his shirt.

"Good. Spend today getting to know our system, setting up your office, meeting a few of the other employees. Monday is soon enough to get you started with program creation and solving problems." With a wave, she was gone.

James sat in the chair, spun it around once and decided it would do. He checked the desk drawers—empty except for

67

a couple of stray paperclips and a left-over blank sticky note. He placed his fingers against the desktop's keyboard and pretended to type—*Welcome home* would have been his message across the screen. No one was there to respond, no one to say, "Hello to you too."

He slid his chair so he could look into the empty cubicle across the aisle. Based on how much time she'd spent in her space so far, he figured the elusive Jenny Grant would remain missing in action, and he'd have no one but his computer screen to talk to anyway.

That was okay by him. He and his computer had long been best friends, and until he figured out why he'd felt inspired to sell Info-Systems Technology and leave California, and the stress of being CEO, he and the computer could continue to work together like a happy couple.

8

Jenny's afternoon had been crazy—what else was different in her life lately?—and she didn't make it back into the office. What she intended to be a leisurely lunch—an hour away from the office, Rick's meetings, and Tiara's romantic advice—started just as she planned. As a single, it was easy to get a seat at Biaggi's Ristorante. She loved the Farfalle Alfredo, even if it was a little spendy for lunch. But she never treated herself out to a dinner alone, and now that her friends were all married, or soon to be, evenings out would become an even rarer occurrence. One she deserved to give herself, especially today.

Just reading the menu's description—*grilled chicken, bowtie pasta, roasted peppers, crispy Italian cured bacon, sautéed red onions and peas tossed in our Alfredo sauce with asiago cheese*—made Jenny feel she was far away from her worries, almost like she had taken a trip to Tuscany. She sipped on a glass of grape juice while she waited for the meal to be delivered.

Then her cell phone rang. Jenny looked at the incoming number before she answered. Her mother. "Hi, Mom."

"I hope I'm not bothering you, Jenny. I know it's late."

What on earth was her mother talking about? It was just barely noon. "No, Mom. I'm just waiting on my lunch to be served."

69

"Lunch? Lunch?"

The panic in her mother's voice confused her. "Is something wrong, Mom?"

"No, I . . . Is it only noon, then? Hee hee . . . Sorry. I just couldn't imagine why the light was so bright coming through my shutters at midnight."

Uh, oh. Jenny realized her mother was having another moment of confusion. They had been coming more often in the past year, but the doctor still hadn't detected anything to be worried about. He told Jenny and her brothers to keep an eye on their mom, but her tests all indicated everything was working properly. "All systems go," he had reiterated when Jenny called to double-check.

"It's the middle of the day, Mom. A bright, sunny day." Jenny tried to keep her tone assuring. She didn't want her mother to become even more upset if she thought her daughter was mad at her. Jenny wasn't mad, just frustrated that the doctor couldn't tell them something to do to help her mom to not have these episodes. They didn't seem serious enough to indicate Alzheimer's, and no one had mentioned dementia either. She prayed it wasn't something as horrendous as a brain tumor. That would be a bigger concern than having her forget what time of day it was.

"Well, in that case, have a nice lunch, dear. I'll talk with you later."

The phone went dead before Jenny could say good-bye. She made a mental note to check back in with her mom

70

later, and ask the doctor about the possibility of a tumor as well. The waiter approached with the steaming hot plate of pasta as Jenny slipped her phone back into her purse. The aroma smelled yummy, and the waiter wasn't bad looking either, although much too young for her. *If* she was interested, which she no longer was. Would she have to keep reminding herself she no longer was interested in men? *Get over it, Jenny.*

He set the plate in front of her and offered garlic bread from the basket. Jenny took a slice and put it on the saucer next to her half-empty glass. Paul—that was the name on his uniform tag—picked up the carafe of grape juice from the ice bucket and poured in enough of the dark purple liquid to fill her glass to the top.

"Thank you," Jenny said, wishing there were something wittier she could say to this handsome young man. *Young* was indeed the word to describe him, but she couldn't stop herself from at least looking, despite her earlier self-reminder.

"Anything else I can get for you?" Paul said, a smile crossing his lips. But Jenny noticed his eyes were roaming away from her, looking instead around the room like he expected someone to call out to him or need his assistance.

If he were only ten—no make that twenty—years older, she would have plenty more he could do, *if* she hadn't given up on men. But she had, and he wasn't the least bit interested in her. *As if . . .*

71

"Nothing right now. Thanks," she said as he moved away.

She was on her second bite when the cell phone rang again. *Drat!* She placed her fork on the platter and grabbed the purse strap from the floor where it had fallen. Four rings and the call would go to voice mail. With one to go, she found the phone in a fold near the bottom of the bag.

"Hello," she said, still chewing the bite of chicken she had placed into her mouth at the first ring.

"Jenny? It's Lisbeth."

"Oh, hi, Lisbeth." Jenny discretely finished the chicken then took a sip of the grape juice to wash it down. "What's up?"

"Big problem." Lisbeth sounded rushed, but when hadn't she sounded like that, ever since she and Gary had gotten engaged.

"How can I help?" Jenny figured it was her job as the maid-of-honor to at least offer her services, even if there was nothing she could do. She could only hope the problem wasn't something that had come between her best friend and Lisbeth's fiancé.

"It's the flowers. My mom forgot to order the flowers for the wedding as soon as I decided which ones I wanted. Now the florist isn't sure he'll be able to get them here in time for the wedding." Lisbeth sounded crestfallen, but Jenny was relieved it wasn't something more serious than flowers. "Why did I have to choose Hawaiian orchids anyway?"

Jenny knew exactly why. They were Lisbeth's favorite flower, an acquired taste from her friend's time spent on the big island. "Let me make some calls for you and see what we can do."

"Oh, Jenny. Would you really? My mom's so busy getting everything ready for the shower, and I'm still trying to address invitations."

Jenny was sure that task alone could take days. Lisbeth was one of those people who accepted everyone she met as a friend. Even if she was shy, she loved people and wouldn't want to hurt anyone's feelings by leaving them out of this special occasion, especially by accident.

"Who's your florist? I'll start with him and see where we need to go from there."

"The Rose Shop on South Temple. Do you need the number?"

"No, I've got it. My mom orders flowers from there." Jenny hoped all those dollars her mother had spent would somehow open the windows of heaven, or at least the deliveries from Hawaii, in time to benefit her friend. "Leave everything to me."

"Thanks, Jen. You're the best."

"That's what everybody tells me," Jenny said. It was hard to hold back the chuckle that rose in her chest. "Go get busy on those invitations. I'll talk with you later." She clicked the phone shut, but this time decided to leave it sitting on the table in case another emergency call came through before she was done eating.

The pasta had cooled, but her stomach told her she was still starving so she finished it off anyway. She was sure dinner would be nothing spectacular. She'd probably just make a peanut butter and jelly sandwich, and the toast from this morning was long gone. She signaled for her waiter to bring the check, paid the bill, and was halfway across the mall, trying to convince herself it was okay to go into Victoria's Secret for a shower gift, when she remembered she had left her phone sitting on the table at Biaggi's.

One final glance at the skimpy garments on the window poster and a look at her own body told her there was no way she was going in that store anyway, shower present to buy or not. If she'd been as skinny as the model on the advertisement, maybe she *would* have gone in to buy something for herself, but she wasn't, and she figured Lisbeth would die of embarrassment if she opened a gift like that in front of the guests at her shower. Jenny opted for Bath and Body Works instead on her way back across the mall. She entered the store and headed directly toward the scented lotions and bubble bath. *If Lisbeth wants orchids, then orchids I'll get her. The more the merrier!*

Her bank account significantly dinged from her purchases, Jenny stood at the cashier's desk of the

74

restaurant, two bags filled for Lisbeth's shower hanging from her arm. Paul, the waiter, must have seen her from the far end of the place. He strode forward, her silver phone waving with his hand above his head. She nodded and gave a thumbs-up in his direction to let him know she'd seen it.

Someone bumped into her from behind. "Oh . . ." She turned around in time to see a man walking away from her. He was about the same height as the man she'd met in the parking lot yesterday, his hair nearly the same color. *Maybe,* she thought. If the waiter hurried, perhaps she could see where the guy went. If it *were* the man from yesterday, she could thank him again for his kindness, helping a woman be protected from the storm. And find out his name.

But luck wasn't with Jenny, not this time. Paul got stopped by a customer asking for a drink refill, and by the time he reached Jenny and handed her the cell phone, the stranger was gone.

"Que sera sera," Jenny said. *Oh great! Now I sound like my mother.*

Walking across the plaza, she kept her eyes open, but the man who had bumped into her was nowhere. Jenny glanced at her watch. It was already past 1:30, but she had promised Lisbeth she'd follow up on the flower situation, and the day was beautiful. It wouldn't take her more than a few minutes to walk the couple blocks from The Gateway to The Rose Shop. The bags she carried were a little awkward, but she could manage.

Once she arrived at the shop, Jenny was glad to see the owner was working. She had met him a time or two when she came in with her mother, although she couldn't remember his name. Fortunately he remembered hers.

"Miss Grant, how are you this fine day?" He looked past her, as though searching for someone. "Your mother isn't with you?"

Jenny was a little surprised by his question, but then she realized it was her first time in the shop alone. "Actually, I'm here to help a friend with her wedding. You're doing the flowers for Lisbeth Connor."

"Ah, yes. The Hawaiian arrangements. We're having a little difficulty securing enough—"

"Enough? You mean you can get *some*? You'll have some of the orchids?" This might be easier to solve than Lisbeth thought.

"We have the bridal bouquet, attendants, and the main serving table covered." The man pulled a file from under the counter and flipped it open, glancing over a chart sketched below the order information. "It's the additional tables that are causing the problem. We can't get enough for the centerpiece arrangements . . ."

Jenny sighed. Problem solved. "Will you have a few extra flowers, even some stray petals?"

"Of course."

"Then let's go with the look of a luau. Sea shells, strings of shell necklaces, some confetti, a pineapple or two, with

76

loose petals thrown in it's perfect," Jenny said. She'd never made decisions like this for a wedding before, but a problem solved was easier than letting Lisbeth worry about a detail that could be fixed so easily. "I'll let Lisbeth know, but she will love it. She spent almost two years in Hawaii, and I know she attended several luaus. She'll feel right at home."

"Perfect. I have just the adornments to make it look complete." The shop owner looked proud, as though he had thought of the solution himself.

"Is there anything extra we will owe you?" Jenny reached for her wallet, but it wasn't where she thought it should be.

"No, no. This will be less expensive than the original bid," he said. "The bride's mother and I will work out the details on the final billing, and I'm sure the groom's parents will be happy with the lower price. Bridal clients are always shocked by how much flowers cost."

Jenny had placed her purse onto the counter as he spoke, and she continued to move the few items around in the bottom, searching for her missing wallet. "Hmm . . . I had it at Bath and Body."

"Is something wrong, Miss Grant?"

"I seem to have misplaced my wallet." Jenny set the shopping bags next to her purse and sorted through the items in each bag. "I must have left it back at the mall. I'd better run and see." She gathered her belongings and only hesitated at the door long enough to say, "Thank you."

"Thank *you*, Miss Grant," the shopkeeper said. "And tell your mother I said hello."

Hurrying back toward the mall plaza, Jenny let her mind replay the last time she had seen the wallet. She was sure she had placed it into her purse when she left with her purchases, then she had gone back to the restaurant to pick up her phone and headed the few blocks to the flower shop. Her purse had been unsnapped when she put it on the counter there. Maybe her wallet had fallen out as she walked.

Jenny retraced her earlier path, her eyes scanning the sidewalk for the lost wallet. She stopped in at Bath and Body but they hadn't seen it. Then the memory struck her at the doorway to Biaggo's. The man who had bumped into her, the one who looked like the helpful guy in the parking lot during the rainstorm . . .

A terrible though planted itself in Jenny's mind. That guy at the restaurant hadn't just bumped into her on accident. He had done it on purpose to distract her from realizing he had stolen her wallet. She suddenly hoped he *wasn't* the guy from the rainstorm. He had seemed like such a nice guy.

***

James felt good about the afternoon spent in his new cubicle. A tray filled with office supplies had arrived not long after he took possession. It hadn't taken but a few minutes for him to arrange everything, and now he sat, logged into the desktop, scanning over the company

78

templates. "Simple programs." A soft chuckle escaped his throat. "Especially since I designed most of them." The layout and coding interface that were not part of the Info-Systems Technology he had designed seemed easy enough to navigate. He saw a few places he might easily tweak, which would make the system run a little smoother, but he knew better than to get started late on a Friday afternoon.

Although he could hardly wait for the chance to once again work in familiar territory. Of course, the contract he had signed with the new owners of Info-Systems tied his hands when it came to making improvements upon and then repackaging his old programs, but James didn't plan to use those anyway. He'd had several new ideas he wanted to develop and didn't have the time for because of maintenance packages for the old ones. Now he'd have the time he needed, he was certain. He opened a notepad application and entered the places he wanted to modify into a to-do list, knowing they would keep until he started as a fulltime employee on Monday.

"Busy?" Val leaned against the opening of his cubicle. Today she wore slacks, much more modest than the skirt she'd had on yesterday.

"Just making a few notes before heading out for the weekend." He didn't dare ask about her plans. She'd likely take it as an invitation.

"Hmm. Big plans for the weekend?" She had no problem asking him though.

79

Val was fishing, and James knew it, but he refused to bite. "No."

"There's a party going on down at Murphy's on South Main," Val said. "Everyone's invited."

"Thanks," James said. Somehow he couldn't imagine *everyone* going. Gretchen was probably too young. Tiara was too old. And Jenny had never come back to work after she left for lunch. He wasn't much of a party-goer himself, and Murphy's sounded like a place that didn't match with his lifestyle. "I'll have to skip it tonight though. Have a good time."

He glanced as his watch as though he had someplace to go in a hurry. He didn't want to know anything more about Val or the party. He wanted to slip away before she tried again to get him to come by making him feel guilty.

"Find everything you need, James?" Marie Davis stood in the doorway.

James stood and offered the chair opposite his desk to the woman who was responsible for his being here. He hadn't done the same for Val. "Couldn't be happier."

Marie stepped into the cubicle and took the seat across from him.

"Sorry you can't make it," Val said, apparently taking the hint it was time for her to go.

"See you later," he said, not adding that he'd be back on Monday. Val probably knew that already anyway.

"So . . ." Marie looked around the tiny space as though

80

she were taking in every detail of its compact nature. "Cory tells me I hit upon a goldmine today." Her tone was playful, teasing as though she expected him to play along too.

"Maybe silver." James entwined his fingers at the back of his head and leaned comfortably against the back rest of his chair.

The older woman crossed her ankles and rested her left hand on the corner of James' new desk. "I thought it was too much of a coincidence, same name and all. Do you mind telling me why you're here?"

James took a deep sigh. In the business world, it was hard to say how much he could speak about the influence his faith played in his day to day life. This was Salt Lake City, but would Marie Davis understand that a man could sell a multi-million-dollar business, move thousands of miles away from his home, and seek work as a temp because the Lord told him to? James decided to give it a go. If he was meant to work here, she might as well know the truth. "Ever heard of the golden question?"

Now it was Marie's turn to laugh. "I thought we were talking about silver here, or did you mean 'What do you know about the Mormon church'?"

A roll of his eyes and a sheepish grin preceded another chuckle. "Sort of both, I guess."

The woman settled back into her chair, obviously in no hurry. "I'm all ears."

"I wish I knew myself exactly why I'm in Utah," James

81

began. "Life was great in Southern Cal—beaches, warm sun, and a company that kept me away from all of that." He could tell Marie was working to stifle a guffaw. "Well, yeah. I guess I was kind of married to the office." He reached out and patted his computer monitor. "These little babies have a way of sucking you right into their screens, you know?"

"Unfortunately. I've seen it happen all too often." Marie glanced at her watch, before continuing. "That's why I keep a strict rule around here. We close at 6:00, and everyone—and I do mean *everyone*—is to be out those doors by 6:15. I will not let Tech Aide be the reason any employees have marriage problems because they are getting home late from work."

"I'm afraid that kind of problem might never affect me." James hadn't meant to let it slip that he wasn't married, at least not to his boss. He guessed Tiara had already figured it out from the way she chased him down the first couple of days. And he couldn't forget Val. *What had Marie called her? Val the Flirt?* For all he knew, even the elusive Jenny Grant knew he was nearing forty and never married. And the fact that he didn't wear a wedding band only made it more plain—especially in Utah.

"You're not alone, you know."

James tried to reel his thoughts back toward the conversation he was having. "I'm . . . I'm sorry." He shook his head and brushed his hand across his face, as though clearing cobwebs from his eyes.

82

"I said, you're not alone." Marie lowered her face and brought her left hand toward her own eyes in a mirror of James' gesture.

He couldn't help but notice. Her ring finger—the one on her left hand—was empty. And from the looks of things, never had a ring adorned that finger for any period of time. No mark, no tan line, no permanent indent from a long-worn piece of jewelry. Marie Davis looked to be nearing sixty, and yet he knew she had always been alone.

"I'm . . . did . . ." None of the words that came to his mind seemed like the right thing to say. He didn't want to be hurtful. He didn't want to tread places he didn't belong. He'd had too many people try to go there with him and he knew how painful those questions could be.

"Water under the bridge," Marie said, her tone becoming more cheerful as though she realized her comment had taken them both into a place they didn't want to go. "Take a look at that clock, son. Fifteen minutes and you'd better be out of here and on your way home. No way your life can change if you're married to your computer." She stood abruptly and took two steps toward the door. "Next time we chat, you can start again with that golden question."

She was gone before James could speak. If he was her goldmine, was it possible that she needed him to ask the golden question? Why hadn't this woman ever married? James thought she was strikingly attractive, even for a

83

woman of the age he attributed to her. Had her business been her entire life—the sin that James himself sometimes felt guilty of? Had the Lord sent him here to see his own life reflected in the loneliness of this woman, because he knew that was how she felt. He sensed it, like her inner voice spoke through his own heart.

He logged off the computer and flipped the switch on the desk lamp before leaving his cubicle, where he almost ran smack dab into Tiara Brinkerhoff. "Oh, sorry," James said, truly concerned that he had flustered the woman. Her eyes looked puffy and her cheeks were red, just like the last time he had seen her this morning. Had she been crying again?

"No, no. It's *all* my fault." Tiara looked at him, but her face drained to white like she had seen a ghost. She clutched a stack of file folders to her chest and backed into the cubicle wall, as though trying to make more space for him to pass.

James started to walk away, but something inside told him he needed to make an effort to start a conversation, even though before now he had wanted to stay far away from Tiara and her reputation for matchmaking. "Are you okay, Ms Brinkerhoff?" He was surprised by his own words. It was nothing like him to interact with other employees when he didn't have to. Even when he was head of the company at Info-Systems Technology, he kept mostly to himself, comfortable at spending time alone.

"Tiara. Everybody calls me Tiara," she said. She stayed huddled against the wall, her eyes downcast as though she was in a supreme war to avoid looking at him.

He had to do something. "Here, let me carry those papers for you," he offered. James reached his hands toward Tiara and the folders.

At first she shied away, like his fingers were flames of a candle drawn too close to her body.

"Really," he said. Turning his palms face up to accept the stack.

After another moment, Tiara placed the folders onto his outstretched hands. "Thank you." Her voice was almost a whisper, nothing like what he had heard from her the past two days.

"Where would you like these to go?" James asked.

Tiara didn't speak, but she did begin to walk toward the front of the building and the exit door. *Good*, he thought. *At least we're going the right way if she goes completely bonkers and I need to make a quick getaway.*

"Gretchen will take them," Tiara said once they reached the receptionist's desk.

James set the folders on the counter in front of the younger woman, making sure they were situated so they wouldn't fall off. That would be all he would need, to have them spill and he'd be stuck here sorting through files all night. Actually, that would have been more like his old life rather than interrupting anything, but he still hadn't figured

85

out what brought such a drastic change in Tiara, not that he was sure he really wanted to know.

"Thanks," Tiara said. "See you Monday morning, Gretchen."

"Hope tomorrow is a better day, Tiara," Gretchen said as the woman turned to go. She too was standing now, obviously ready to head home.

"Me, too," Tiara said, as she left the building.

James watched her through the double doors until she turned left and headed toward the TRAX station.

"See you on Monday, as well," Gretchen said.

"Thanks," James said.

As he pushed the glass doors open for himself, he saw a woman across the street. She looked familiar and her steady gate had a natural swing that he had seen before. It only took him a moment to realize it was the woman from the rainstorm. She looked to be in a hurry, and James knew there was no way he could catch up to her.

Besides, what would he have to say to her anyway? *Hey, I got a new job today?* What would she think about someone as old as he was getting what looked to be an entry level job at a computer company? *At least it's a step up from working as a temp.* Yes, but a definite step down from the owner and creator of the company. And that step was the one he needed to sort out before James felt he could proceed with anything that might help him know where his move to Utah could lead.

9

Stephie's day had been the best since she moved to Boston. Since they had moved across the country, she had been so bored. She wasn't sure why Phil refused to let her work after their marriage, although she had her suspicions he wanted to take complete control of her life and the money. He'd shut down her cell as soon as they'd arrived in the East, kept his phone and the set of car keys where she couldn't use them without feeling like she needed to beg permission—something she refused to do from her own husband—and gave her a strict allowance for food. No wonder she felt like she was becoming a prisoner in her own life. Maybe she was more than bored, she considered. *Maybe I'm a little scared, too.* Stephie pushed the thought from her mind, choosing to focus instead on this morning, and the new friend she made.

A morning spent with Rachel made the hours fly by, and her chores were all done before noon. Folding clothes and washing dishes didn't seem like such drudgery with a good mix of conversation poured in. And, despite the fact Stephie felt a little guilty for divulging her secret woes about Phil and their marriage and the initial shock of the pregnancy, talking with Rachel had left her burden somehow lighter.

Having friends did make life easier, Stephie decided. And she and Rachel had bonded like sisters. The affinity of being newly married and pregnant far overshadowed the differences their age and current happiness levels might bring.

Even the afternoon alone again in the apartment didn't seem so bad once Rachel had gone. Stephie found herself humming, the words to a favorite song running along in her head in time with the rhythm. Determined to make a favorable impression on Phil, she pulled a cookbook his mother had given her from the cabinet. Mrs. Harris had put big red stars next to several dishes and told Stephie at the bridal shower, "These are some of Phil's favorites."

"Chicken Perkelt." She scanned the ingredients, but the combinations of onions, mushrooms, and paprika made her stomach do a flip. "Too rich for me. Ah, this looks good. Pesto Pasta with Green Beans and Potatoes."

A quick check of the recipe and she thought she could pull it off, although she'd have to substitute regular potatoes for the red. She wasn't sure what *pesto* was—although she had heard the word mentioned at Italian restaurants where she had eaten. Surely she could leave it out without Phil noticing. Pasta was pasta after all.

She set a pot of water on to boil for the pasta and a smaller one for the potatoes then dug around in the cabinet for the other ingredients—a clove of garlic purchased for a chicken recipe she'd backed out of trying, olive oil, and processed Parmesan cheese. The canister was almost empty, but she hoped she had enough to give the casserole a good flavor.

A few peeled potatoes later, she warmed a bag of frozen green beans, getting them ready to drop into the pot with the potatoes once the time came. In nearly no time, the kitchen began to fill with the aroma of her cooking. Stephie halted when she came to the next ingredient—plain yogurt. "Plain?" She knew she had never bought plain yogurt before. She rummaged around the fridge and the only yogurt she could come up that was even close was vanilla. *At least the color will be right*, she thought. "It has to be better than using the cup of Black Cherry Cheesecake."

While the potatoes and water for the pasta boiled, Stephie sliced two juicy red tomatoes and arranged them onto a saucer. She mixed up a jug of frozen grape juice and put it in the fridge to stay cold. She dropped the pasta and beans into their respective pots at nearly the same time. If Phil kept true to his usual arrival time, the meal would be ready to serve right when he got home.

Placing a pair of white tapers into the candle holders saved from their wedding reception, Stephie surveyed the table she had set. "Perfect," she whispered, hoping that the evening would indeed be perfect, like they used to be, before their marriage.

She couldn't have asked for better timing. The pasta was tender, and the potatoes browned—just like her mother-in-law's recipe called for—the minute Phil opened the door to their apartment. Stephie had lit the candles. "Hello, Sweetheart," she called to him as she placed the drained penne onto a platter then poured the green bean and potato sauce over the top.

"My mother's recipe?" Phil smiled as he came over to check out the meal she had placed onto the table. "Smells a little different."

A flash of worry ran through Stephie's mind. "I . . . uh . . . we didn't have any . . ."

"Looks good though," Phil said, as if he hadn't heard her stuttered beginning of an explanation. He dropped into a chair, waiting.

She pulled the grape juice from the fridge and poured glasses for each of them.

Phil used the serving utensils to toss the pasta and sauce together then served himself a generous portion. "This is one of my favorites, you know."

Stephie smiled, more to herself than anything. "I know," she said, praying the change in yogurt would be alright. She hadn't bothered to taste it, figuring she wouldn't know the difference anyway.

Before she could join him at the table, Phil jumped up and pulled her chair out. "Let me get that for you." He waited until she was ready then slid the chair with her in it closer.

Stephie couldn't remember the last time he had offered

to help her into her seat. *If all it takes is a little pasta to bring back my husband, then so be it.* A recipe from his mother's cookbook every night might help him remain the man she loved. She looked up at him, a smile on her face. She could almost feel her eyes twinkle.

Her happiness must have been irresistible because Phil leaned over and gave her a gentle kiss, their first in several days.

"Hmmm. Nice," she said, keeping herself from adding the words *I've missed you.*

Phil sat down and immediately crossed his arms. "Ready?"

Stephie nodded and Phil offered a short, but appropriate prayer. A rush of warmth poured through her. Maybe her husband was back after all. Tonight might be the perfect time to share her news from this morning. She practiced in her mind. *Phil, honey. I have wonderful news. We're pregnant.*

But before she could say them, Phil let out a horrible sound, nearly as bad as retching.

"Phil? What's wrong?" Stephie rose from her seat, and reached her arm across the table toward him.

A glob of Phil's pasta hit the plate in front of him. "What *is* that stuff? Are you trying to poison me?" He spat into the mess then grabbed his napkin to wipe the residue from his lips. He took a swig of grape juice and moved it around his cheeks like a morning mouthwash then stood

91

and hurried to the sink where he spit again, getting rid of the juice as well. He turned on the tap and leaned over to let water rush into his mouth. After a minute, he spoke. "What on earth did you do to my mother's pasta recipe?"

The gentle moment was long gone between them. Phil's harsh voice was back, and Stephie couldn't stop the tears that had popped into her eyes a minute before. "I . . . I . . . the only yogurt we had . . . and I don't know what *pesto* means . . . and . . . and I tried my best."

Phil returned to the table long enough to pick up the glass of juice. "This stuff okay to actually drink?" He looked at the liquid for a moment then decided it must be. He gulped down the remainder from the glass, set it into the sink then moved to the doorway. "Don't wait up for me. And get rid of that stuff. It could kill a horse."

The door didn't slam behind him, but it might as well have with the way Stephie felt.

She thought about taking a bite to test out the pasta for herself, but her stomach was already too sensitive, and she didn't dare take the chance. "I'm such a failure." She slumped back into her chair, and looked through the tears in her eyes at the ruined attempt for a special meal. She let her hand rest against her abdomen, hoping the comfort of knowing a baby was growing there could soothe her hurt feelings. It didn't.

She suddenly felt more alone than ever. Phil was gone for who knew how long. Her mother was miles and miles

92

away, as were her best friends. The idea of the baby was so fresh she didn't know what to think about it. Then she remembered—Rachel. "I wonder if Rachel would like to have company?"

It wouldn't hurt to at least go and see, Stephie decided. But before she left the apartment, she had some cleaning up to do. The garbage disposal took care of the pasta-mess and everything else got put away. The last thing she did before closing the door behind her was to force a great big fake smile onto her face.

This has been my best day ever in Boston, and no one, not even my grumpy husband and his mother's pasta recipe is going to spoil it for me.

10

The police had arrived shortly after Jenny called. Completing the reports and giving a description of the possible perpetrator had taken much longer than she anticipated. It was nearly six o'clock when they had finished, and Jenny figured going back to the office was a wash. She walked—no, stormed—across the plaza, barely listened for the safety clicks at the crossings, and into the lot where she parked her car.

What a day this had turned out to be. At least it was the weekend. She still had her bags filled with packages for Lisbeth's wedding shower draped around her wrist, and the alterations were made for the wedding flowers like she'd promised.

She didn't look forward to an evening of calling credit card companies and leaving messages with other vendors to report her stolen wallet, but even that might be better than having to look joyful at Lisbeth's wedding shower for an entire afternoon. *Stop it!* Jenny warned her inner voice. *She's your best friend, and you're happy she's getting married.*

Jenny knew it was the truth, but she needed a good reason to feel sorry for herself after the way her day had gone—at least she tried to convince herself that was so.

She reached the car and fumbled for the keys. Once again, they had fallen somewhere into the netherlands of her purse. *Why don't I just put the darn things in the pocket?* The loss of her wallet and the long interview with the police officer hadn't helped her mood any from the way she had flown off the handle at Tiara earlier in the day.

Poor Tiara, Jenny thought. Although Tiara was sometimes annoying, especially when it came to her matchmaking, she didn't mean any harm. Actually, Jenny decided, it was sort of sweet that Tiara wanted everyone married, like she was the mother of the office, only trying to protect her young from the big bad world of loneliness.

"Ouch!" The sharp key edge told Jenny she had found what she was looking for. She pulled the fob from the bottom of the purse and shoved the correct key into the lock, glad to see that the knob popped up just the way it was supposed to after she turned the key. Sometimes it didn't, being just as stubborn as she herself could be. She opened the door, tossed her purse into the passenger seat, and slid behind the wheel. Leaning over the center console, she placed the packages on the adjoining floor mat, trying to position them so they wouldn't fall over, dumping their contents on the ride home.

She started to turn the ignition then realized she didn't have the keys. "What the . . . ?" A quick glance around the car's interior told her she hadn't merely set them down someplace. Suddenly she remembered. The car door.

Seconds later, she had the keys, the car was started, but she felt only a little better when she peeled the tires against the asphalt in an effort to leave this horrible day behind. Jenny swerved the car just in time to avoid a dark-haired man who was entering the parking lot as she exited the gate.

***

James unlocked his car and got in, trying to forget the woman from the rainstorm. If he were dating, Marie's edict about leaving work by six-fifteen might mean something, but since he wasn't—and he didn't intend to suddenly start—this would be just like any other night. He'd stop somewhere, probably fast food then head to his apartment to watch TV. He didn't like most of the shows on regular TV, but the specialty channels—Discovery, Nat Geo, The History Channel, or A&E—occasionally had something he thought was worth his time. And if they didn't, he always had a book he could read. He was fascinated by history and politics, and spent a great deal of time learning about those topics. A biography or two also made it onto his stack of current reading materials. He knew about the lives of many people, except the people he usually worked with.

He didn't used to be such a loner. When he was in high school he had participated in several sports—basketball, track, and even a spring season of baseball born from his childhood in Little League. He'd loved after-school clubs that got him involved in two school plays and took him on a summer trip to Hawaii, and the annual Christmas Toy Drive that required a lot of his time around Thanksgiving. But once he had reached college and started working on his true passion, computer programming, he'd found it easier, and often more satisfying to just say no when people invited him to do things. *Just like tonight.*

He started his car, put it in drive, and headed toward the parking lot exit, considering his life for once the way his mother had always tried to get him to do. She worried about him. "When are you going to find a nice girl and get married?" she asked almost every time they spoke on the phone. "You know I've always wanted to be a grandmother."

He always gave her the same response. "No pressure, Mom. I'm not ready for a relationship. I'll get married, I promise." But he'd do it in his own time.

Years had gone by and the time never seemed to come. The girls he dated were shallow, only wanting to rush a friendship into an engagement ring. He'd seen his high school buddies all get married, and he wanted that too for himself someday. Just not *this* day, or the next, or the next, or the one after that, and the months, then years had slowly dropped away.

Now he was thirty-five and still unmarried, and certainly with no prospects. *Well, unless I pursue the woman in the parking lot.* James had no idea why that idea had popped into his head and he chastised himself for thinking about her, especially since he didn't even remember to ask her name. *Stupid!* He wasn't going to spend another night kicking

97

himself for not following through on something that would likely go nowhere anyway. If the Lord wanted him to be here for a woman, then the Lord would take care of getting the two of them together. *Wouldn't He?*

The one thing James knew had been right about his move to Utah was his chance to work at Tech Aide, and Marie Davis had sensed it too. Why else would she have hired him so quickly? He wondered if somehow he could find a way to develop another new product, just like he had done when he owned Info-Systems Technology. When it came to computers, he knew where he wanted to go, and what he hoped to accomplish.

When it came to women, he could only pray that one day he would know the same thing.

11

It only took a half-second for the door to Rachel's apartment to fly open after Stephie rang the bell. A tall man—blond and maybe all of twenty-two—grabbed Stephie's arm and yanked her into the room. "Thanks for coming. Her water broke and the pains are coming quick."

"Rachel?" Stephie was trying to keep up not only with the information the man was giving her, but also his hurried pace across the room and into the bedroom where Rachel was attempting to close an over-packed suitcase.

"No!" the man shrieked. "We don't have time for that." He dropped Stephie's arm and moved to his wife's side, gently lifting her wrist as though it were broken, touching his other hand to the small of her back, and guiding Rachel past Stephie and into the living room.

"Wait a minute," Stephie said. "What's going on?"

"Oh, hi Stephie," Rachel said the minute she saw her. "Honey, this is the woman I told you about." Her conversation sounded like she hadn't a care in the world.

"Yes, yes, yes. I know," Rachel's husband said, still concentrating on getting his wife out of the apartment door and into the hallway. "The baby's new neighbor."

"No, silly," Rachel said then she let out a shriek of her

99

own. "I think I'm gonna have this baby right here and right now!" She doubled over as much as she could, with the little Buddha bundle protruding even more than this morning.

No, you can't have the baby now, Stephie thought, then added aloud, "I don't know what to do!"

"Grab that suitcase, would ya?" Rachel's husband said as he moved his precious cargo toward the elevator doors and started punching the button.

Stephie rushed back into the bedroom, wrapped her arm around the too-full case to hold its contents in place, and met them at the elevator just as it arrived.

"Come with us," Rachel pleaded as she reached out to touch Stephie's arm. "Please. I need you."

Stephie couldn't imagine why Rachel needed her. *What can I do? What can I do?* She looked around as though the answer would be written somewhere in the room. It wasn't like she knew anything about giving birth to babies, but Stephie knew now was not the time to tell Rachel that. She wouldn't be Prissy informing Scarlett O'Hara in the middle of Atlanta burning down around her and Miss Melly in the throes of childbirth, 'I don't know nothing 'bout birthin' no babies.'

She was quoting movies when this girl needed her, and needed her *now,* whether she knew anything or not. "Of course I'll go with you," Stephie said. She noticed the look of relief that passed across Rachel's husband's face as well as the soon-to-be mother's.

"Thank you so much!" he said, as he attempted to move his wife more quickly toward the elevator door.

They were both so young. Stephie suddenly knew she'd do anything to help them.

A new baby. How would she feel in a few months when she herself was making this trip? She knew she would be just as nervous as Rachel, and she could only hope that Phil would be as supportive as Rachel's husband when the time came. After months of practically no interaction with Phil, Stephie needed this time with Rachel almost as much as the girl needed her.

They had reached the main floor of their apartment building, and Rachel seemed at ease for a minute. The earlier pain that had caused her to cry out had either subsided, or she was holding back from screaming in public.

"Where's the car?" Stephie readjusted the suitcase under her arm then stepped forward to help support Rachel, whose husband looked around as though he had no idea where his car was, or if he even had one. Stephie suddenly realized she didn't know this man's name. At least her asking might be a distraction. "By the way, Rachel. Do you think now would be a good time to introduce me to your husband?"

"David. His name is Daaaaaaaaa . . ." Once again Rachel was bent over, her hand jammed into her side as she panted. "One . . . two . . . three. . . Oh, why didn't they tell me it would hurt this bad?"

101

Stephie could think of a million reasons why, but this wasn't the time to share them. Instead, she took charge of the situation. "David, go get the car. Pull it up right here in front of the sidewalk. I'll stay with Rachel, and you *hurry!*"

The final word was a signal, and he was off like a track star determined to win the biggest race of his life.

"Breathe with me, Rachel," Stephie said. She sensed that structured breathing would at least give Rachel something to concentrate on, other than the pains that seemed to be shooting through her in a regular rhythm.

The two of them were only on their second set of counts when the two-door faded black Honda, definitely an older model coupe, screeched to a halt in front of them. The car had to be older than either Rachel or her husband, Stephie decided. She looked at the vehicle with trepidation. Rachel would obviously require the front seat, and David would drive. That left the tiny square called a backseat for her to squeeze into. Maybe she'd be better off climbing in the hatchback.

Rachel let out another moan that rivaled any in the best horror thrillers Stephie had ever seen. David had abandoned his seat and rushed around the car to his wife's side. Stephie had no choice but to get into the car. There was no dignity in the way she sprawled herself across the half-bench touted as a backseat. She was barely situated when the front seat crashed onto her legs, pinning her once Rachel was in the car.

"I can't get the seatbelt on," Rachel yelled as she yanked against the strap attached to the floor. "David, you must not have installed it right. Did you ask the mechanic like I told you? The seatbelt won't reach across to the clasp."

David had returned to the driver's seat, the hinge creaking in a painful way as he pulled the door shut. "Honey, I think it's okay. They don't make a shoulder belt for this old of a model, so we had to improvise. You should be safe though. You're wedged in there pretty tight . . ." He popped the clutch, sped across the parking lot, glancing over his left shoulder as he pulled into the lane of traffic. "And I'm not sure the length of the belt is the problem."

Don't go there, Stephie thought, as if she could will him not to mention the size of his wife's belly at the present moment.

"Come this time tomorrow, the belt should fit your waist just fine." His smile said he was trying to be funny. It was obvious Rachel was not in the mood.

"Are you saying I'm FAT?" She turned her face toward her husband, and Stephie was able to see the rage implanted there. In a half second, it was gone, replaced by pain.

"Hey, Rachel," she said, hoping to pull her mind away from the ill will the younger woman was feeling toward her husband. "Time to count. One . . . two . . . three . . . Come on, join me." She kept her voice light, wanting desperately to avoid having Rachel turn on her as well. "One . . . two . . ."

103

"Three," Rachel managed as the car came to a halt at the emergency entrance to Brigham and Women's Hospital.

Stephie had read the sign as they roared past the entrance. *Well, Brigham. You certainly get around. I thought all your roots were currently tied to Utah.* Stephie chuckled at her own private joke.

The hospital's emergency doors slid open, David ran into the building, and, in what seemed seconds later, a group of hands reached into the car door, extracting Rachel from the seat like a rescue expert pulling someone from a wreck. Before Stephie could sit up, David had slammed the door, returned to the driver's seat, gunned the engine, and maneuvered the car into a parking slot.

"Hey, wait!" she called as he ran across the parking garage toward the hospital entrance. Stephie was stuck. Not only could she not get her feet onto the floor to sit up, she knew she wouldn't be able to open the door and flip the latch on the seat so she could get out of the car by herself.

And that was only half the problem. She had no way to get home once she got out of the car, and she wasn't sure she knew Phil's cell number anymore so her husband could even come and get her. His number had been auto-programmed into the phone she no longer owned. Had he changed it to a Boston number without telling her?

Like it or not, it seemed she was here for the duration of Rachel's delivery. As she settled back down into the seat, trying to find a comfortable spot to place her head, she thought a nap might be just the thing she needed to work off the last memories of the failed dinner.

She could only hope Rachel's baby didn't take more than the rest of the night.

12

After rubbing her eyes, trying to sort through the puzzle in her mind as to why she'd set the alarm for a Saturday morning, Jenny reached over and flicked the alarm switch, ending the beeping noise. Then she remembered today would be busy, weekend or not. It was Lisbeth's shower, and Jenny was not in the mood for another celebration of marriage.

The previous evening spent on the phone with credit card companies, trying to understand the heavy foreign accents of the customer service agents, had actually passed quickly. Calls to the bank and license bureau resulted in pre-recorded messages telling her operation hours that didn't do her any good. She could only hope the guy who'd taken her wallet didn't drain her dry in the meantime.

"Crum," she said, flopping back on the bed, wishing she could pull the covers over her head and hide out until Monday.

At least she'd slept like the dead. That was one good thing about emotional exhaustion. She ran her tongue across her teeth then tasted the leftover *yuck* from last night's binge. She'd needed something to get her through the stress. Two bean burritos, a week-old tub of homemade beef stew, and even the half carton of her favorite ice cream, Cherry Cheesecake, hadn't made her feel any better about the way the day had gone. How stupid could she be to lose her wallet?

Stolen, Jenny reminded herself. Not *lost.*

Confident she'd done everything she could before Monday to minimize the repercussions; she decided she needed to deal with the more pressing matters at hand—maid-of-honor. *What did I agree to do this for?* And what would she have to do as a maid-of-honor during today's bridal shower party?

She headed toward the bathroom, hoping the steamy hot water would melt the fuzz from her brain. She'd need her wits about her to get through this day without saying something stupid to Lisbeth and ruining her excitement. Not good to make the blushing bride cry, especially when the problem really belonged to Jenny.

Fifteen minutes later, hair washed and body wrapped in a fluffy robe, Jenny glanced at the clock. She had an hour before she needed to be at Lisbeth's, even with promising she'd come early to discuss the duties she would take on as the *honorable* maid. *Why can't I even use the right title?*

Jenny ran her fingers through her hair to pull out as many tangles as she could. No use filling her brush with damp strands when her fingers were just as effective. She tucked the robe tighter around her waist before rummaging through her closet for something to wear. No matter what

107

she chose, nothing would make her feel pretty, not on this day. It really didn't matter though. This was Lisbeth's day. Heck, it was Lisbeth's *month*, for crying out loud. *It certainly isn't mine.* And no month would ever be.

"Cut out the pity-party," she said right as her cell phone rang. Jenny grabbed it and flipped the handset open. She had almost expected it to be her mother, but it wasn't. The number showed long distance. Maybe one of the credit card companies was calling her back.

"Hello?" She almost hung up when she heard nothing but dead air, then she realized she had accidentally pushed the *answer* button one too many times. She hit it again, hoping to find a caller on the other line instead of the call-waiting service she had gone to.

Nothing. She supposed the caller thought she had hung up on them. *Oops.* Whoever it was would call back, if it was important. A glance at the screen told her she'd missed four calls. She scrolled down to retrieve the numbers, but the screen went dark. *Dead battery.* She knew there was something she'd forgotten to do last night before she fell into bed.

She plugged the cell in to charge, then went to her closet, finally settling on an outfit. The dress was black, but the airy green jacket looked like spring. Still wrong for so early in the season, but it would do. A dash of make-up, a final brush of the hair, and Jenny was ready to face the music—"Here Comes the Bride." She went into the kitchen and popped a piece of bread into the toaster. Sure, there

108

would be food at Lisbeth's shower, but she imagined it would be mostly sweet punch, cake bites, and mints like the last four bridal showers she had attended. She was already brooding enough over the loss of her wallet and her status of *last woman single*, there was no way she needed to add a sugar rush to her foul mood.

Toast eaten, Jenny grabbed her purse, thinking about how light it felt without her wallet, said a silent prayer that she wouldn't get pulled over for something stupid on her way since she didn't have her driver's license, and headed toward the parking lot and her car.

One piece of luck was with her—the Cavalier started just fine, and she was on her way across town to Lisbeth's parents' house. Traffic was light, and it only took her ten minutes to drive into North Salt Lake. Even if she hadn't known how to get to the house, she would have had no trouble finding it. Someone must have had a good time setting ribbon and balloon decorated stakes into the ground for five blocks, pointing the way to the Connor home.

She pulled into an open space in front of the house next door and checked her face in the rearview mirror.

"You can do this," she said aloud, an effort to convince herself she really felt that way.

After getting out of the car, Jenny opened the back door and grabbed the wrapped presents. She shook her head, hoping to ward off the negative thoughts that could easily settle inside her mind. *Not now. Not today.*

She rang the doorbell then opened the door anyway, letting herself in, calling in a false cheery voice, "Hey! I hear there's a party going on."

Lisbeth's younger sister, Kari, appeared from the direction of the kitchen, swooped the bags from Jenny's arms, and said, "I'll take those. Mom's out in the kitchen and Lisbeth . . . she's still upstairs, getting ready."

"Thanks," Jenny said. "I'll just go out to see if I can help your mom."

"Good choice," Kari said as she headed toward the family room. "I'm afraid Lisbeth would drive you crazy. 'How does this look? What should I wear? Can you help me with this, or that, or whatever?' The entire family is about insane from all this pre-wedded bliss."

Jenny didn't have a chance to respond before Kari was gone, but she already understood how the younger sister felt.

She pushed the swinging door open and popped her head into the kitchen. "Anybody home?"

Mrs. Connor was moving around the kitchen like an Iron Chef in the middle of a competition. The timer on the oven beeped, sending her flying toward the stove. "Jenny, I'm so glad to see you. Can you give me a hand?" She hit *cancel* and the sound stopped, but Mrs. Connor didn't. She put on a set of oven mitts, opened the door, and pulled a tray of cookies from the oven.

"Let me grab something to set those on," Jenny said, pulling the chopping board from underneath the counter and making a space between the punch bowl, already filled with pink sparkling slush, and the canapé tray.

"Hot, hot, hot!" Mrs. Connor said as she placed the baking sheet onto the wood surface then fanned her worn mitts as though her hands were on fire. She slipped the mitts off and rested the palms of her hands against the outside of the iced punch bowl for a minute. "Ahhh! Much better."

"It certainly looks like you've been busy," Jenny said. Cooling racks contained at least four different types of cookies. China platters displayed the perfectly rolled canapés. Finger sandwiches were arranged several inches high on a silver platter, a cellophane-wrapped toothpick protruding from the center of each. "What can I do to help?"

Mrs. Connor picked up the punch bowl. "Take this to the table in the backyard. Kari will tell you where it goes."

"Sure," Jenny said. *Keep me busy, and maybe I'll forget what I'm here to celebrate.* She doubted it, but at least she could hope.

***

James woke up much earlier than he had hoped to, but he hadn't been able to sleep late on a Saturday since he couldn't remember when. Not that he didn't attempt to sleep in, but his body just seemed to pull him from a deep sleep five minutes before his normal alarm would have gone off anyway. This morning he tried to make himself go back to sleep. The sunshine already pouring through his bedroom window had another idea.

111

He climbed from bed and paused just long enough to say a quick prayer. He was truly grateful this morning for his blessings—a new job that seemed to have some prospects for product development, a boss who already liked his work, and a new city that he would at least find interesting to explore. He knew a lot about Salt Lake City, mostly because of his reading and research about the important members of his church. The only time he'd ever been here though was when he'd been dropped off at the airport, ready to fly to France where he would serve for two years as a missionary for that church.

Maybe today would be a good time to find out more about the city. He showered and dressed, grabbed his car keys and was on his way. It was still early enough that McDonalds was serving breakfast at the drive-thru, so he ordered his favorite—a bacon, egg and cheese biscuit with an orange juice—and munched away as he drove toward the heart of the city.

The wide streets and directional grid made it easy enough for James to keep track of where he was most of the time. Only trying to find Jenny Grant's apartment on Lake Street had given him fits. He turned left on State Street and headed north, surprised at how run down some of the areas seemed in contrast to what he expected them to be. This was Salt Lake, for crying out loud. It was the capital of the entire state. You'd think the shops and houses would have better upkeep, he mused. But then he remembered how Los

112

Angeles also had areas of decay that didn't seem in keeping with the wealth that surrounded the homes hidden behind iron and stone gates. Cities were cities, and it took all kinds of people and structures to make up the place.

Paris had been the same. Of course, some Europeans still tried to blame their decay on the wars, but how long did it really take for a city to recover? It had already been over sixty years. James would have thought reconstruction would have been long over. His drive today though made him consider that perhaps decay was a continual thing. While one building decays, another gets replaced.

That was certainly the case once he reached the center of the city. A huge new library, spacious and beautiful, almost drew him inside. A few relics from the 2002 Winter Olympics reminded James of seeing the venues on television back when he was first starting his business, hoping to someday have the kind of success experienced by Mitt Romney, who had been called in to save their skin. In the center of town, James realized the LDS Conference Center was much larger and more impressive than he had imagined from watching on the screen at his own chapel every six months.

He found a parking lot next to that building, paid the necessary money, and decided to walk around the area known as Temple Square. He crossed the street and entered the gates, leaving a couple of dollars in the outstretched hand of the homeless man standing outside. He figured the

113

guy probably made as much panhandling as anyone who had a job at a fast food restaurant on an hourly wage, but at least James wouldn't feel guilty if the guy really was having trouble getting a job, and what did a few bucks mean to him anyway? His company buyout had set James up for life, if he played it right. He chuckled, thinking he guessed he had reached his goal of becoming rich someday, just like Romney.

The noise of the city seemed to disappear once he was inside the grounds surrounding the temple. The dark gray edifice towered over the spot where James stood, yet he knew that the other buildings outside of the gate stood even larger. Yet, the temple was the building that drew his attention. He walked along the back side and turned toward the front of the building where a group of kids, dressed like they were ready for church, seemed to be playing. Wondering what was going on, James continued to move toward the street he knew was North Temple. He hadn't entered the square through the easternmost gate because it had been jammed with so many people.

And now James knew the reason why. A beautiful bride, dressed in her white wedding gown and carrying the dress train across her left arm, smiled and laughed as her new husband leaned down to whisper something to her. His arm tucked tight around his bride's waist, the groom was young, probably in his early twenties. James stepped back, not wanting to intrude upon their moment of privacy.

How young they seemed. How in love they looked.

James wondered what his life would have been like had he found a bride and married that young. He was certain his business wouldn't have taken off like it had, if only because he couldn't have spent the time that he did these ten plus years to make it so successful. But when it came to love, did the success of a business really matter? Or was it the other way around? Did love really matter when what he had wanted was the success of a business?

Obviously not. He'd had a successful business, one that would take care of him well. What did he need a wife and a bunch of kids for anyway? As the couple leaned once more toward each other, James almost felt the tenderness of their kiss. An arrow shot through his soul.

"I have to get out of here," he mumbled, looking around to make sure no one had heard him.

He retraced his steps, back through the gates, across the road, and into the lot where he again climbed into his car. He didn't know where he was headed as he started the car and drove north, out of the city, away from the temple and the center of Salt Lake.

Soon the road took him into an area that was more residential. It didn't matter. Maybe he'd look for a home for sale, one with a reasonable price. He could afford it, and if he was going to stay at Tech Aide, it would be more comfortable to live in a house instead of an apartment.

It took him a couple of blocks to sort out what the series of stakes with the ribbons on top meant. He was unconsciously following them, trailing behind several other cars that seemed to be doing the same. A wedding, or one of those parties for the bride-to-be, was the reason behind the decorations that had drawn him along. The bevy of women, all carrying wrapped packages as they headed toward the door proved his guess was right and served as the signal for James to turn his car around and make his escape.

He'd had enough of weddings for today. Heck, he'd had enough of weddings for the rest of his life. Or at least that's what he tried to convince himself as he drove away.

13

The Honda weaved into the apartment complex parking lot and settled into a spot. Stephie was glad they'd made it. Neither she nor Rachel's husband had gotten a wink of sleep. Not with Rachel in the delivery room until nearly seven in the morning, and Stephie cramped into the back seat of the hatchback, trapped behind the seat with the broken latch and a door handle too far away to open.

"You gonna be okay returning to the hospital?" Stephie asked the tired father. He had slumped onto the steering wheel and looked like he was already asleep.

His head popped up when she spoke, and he looked around, disoriented for a second. Then he visibly relaxed. "I'm a father." A lopsided grin split across his face and his head collapsed forward again for a second.

"Yeah, you're a father," Stephie said. "Hope you enjoyed that nap. It might be the last sleep you get for a while."

"What nap?" David shook himself awake and opened his car door. He moved to her side, unfastening the broken seat latch so she could at last escape the cramped quarters where she had spent the night and half of the morning.

Every muscle in her body was stiff and sore from the

117

uncomfortable night without sleep. Stephie had to unfold herself to get out. Her clothing was disheveled, and her hair had to be a mess. The sun was already pounding down full force, and the humidity was high judging by the dampness that coated her face. Shaking off the last recesses of her immediate need for sleep, she stretched her back, hoping to work out the kinks well enough that she could walk.

"Thanks for the ride," she said.

"Thanks for being there to help, and sorry you were stuck in the car all night," David said, reaching out to give her shoulders a hug before running back to his opened door and climbing into the car.

Stephie shut her door and stepped out of the way as David peeled the car out of the lot and down the street. She shook her head and started toward the entrance to the apartment building, walking next to the car she shared with Phil. She wondered what her husband had thought about her being out all night. Did she want to go inside and find out, knowing he was home? She glanced toward their apartment window, but the sun's reflection blocked her from seeing anything inside.

"Let him think whatever he wants to," she mumbled, trying to convince herself it didn't matter. He'd been so rude toward her lately that he deserved to worry about her for once. *As long as he doesn't hit me.* He'd never done that before—words yes, but physical blows, no—but lately she wasn't sure what he might do.

She didn't have to wait to find out. He stood at the open apartment door, waiting for her to make the final steps before he lashed into her. "Where have you been all night? Who was that guy who dropped you off in the parking lot?"

Stephie slipped her way past her husband, stepping into the apartment and hoping he would do the same so they could close the door. There was no use in everyone in the complex hearing the false accusations she felt were yet to come. "Phil . . . honey?"

"Don't you try to sound all sweet." Phil shut the door before turning toward his wife. "I want to know who he is, why he was hugging you, and where you've been."

An instant wave of exhaustion passed over her. "Let me sit down first." She moved toward the couch. Phil dogged her every step, but he didn't sink into the couch beside her.

"You're *my* wife. I sat up all night waiting for you to come home. You should have called. And I *still* don't know who that guy was and why you were with him."

Stephie doubted he had stayed up to wait for her—likely to obsess over his games, although he looked too well-rested to have done that either. She tried to stifle a yawn before answering. "I couldn't call, Phil. *You* had the cell, and I was stuck in the back seat of the Honda."

"I'll bet you were." The sarcasm was evident in his voice, but Stephie chose to ignore it.

"While David was in the delivery room with his wife, Rachel."

119

Phil pulled himself taller, leaning forward toward Stephie as though he were a snake ready to strike. "Who the hell is *Rachel?*"

"The young woman who is our next door neighbor," Stephie said. "I stopped by to visit her after you left last night, and the next thing I knew, I was on my way to the hospital with the two of them. She was in labor, and David could hardly even think."

"You know the people who live next door?"

"Yes . . ." Stephie wondered if he was going to make a huge deal out of the fact she'd made a friend without his permission.

Phil eyed her as though he wasn't quite sure her story was legitimate. "You were in a hospital. You could have called."

Maybe not. "Actually, I was stuck in the back seat of the Honda," she repeated. She sighed, hoping to keep herself from yawning yet another time, and praying her natural response would alter his mood. "With a broken door latch and a seat stuck against my legs."

Phil's anger seemed to cool. Although he could blow up at a moment's notice, he usually backed off an argument, preferring to run away instead. Stephie was surprised he hadn't stormed out of the apartment the moment she came in.

"I've been awake all night, waiting on David—or someone—to discover I was stuck there." She held her hand over her mouth to stifle yet another yawn.

"And that's all? Nothing *else* happened?" The sarcasm was lighter now, more like frustration over an errant child.

"That's all." Stephie stood and started toward the bedroom. "And now I'm really tired. I'm going to bed." She stopped to glance at her husband before exiting the room. For a moment, he reminded her of who he used to be, when they had first married. Before the anger, the controlling behaviors, and the gaming had taken over his life.

Then Phil clicked on the television and the video consol, before settling in on the couch she had just vacated. The intro music started, harsh and metallic. She heard the first shots fired as the bedroom door clicked behind her, and her new husband was back, in all his glory.

***

The Monday morning alarm found Jenny still in a foul mood. Although the bridal shower had gone well, she had to face more aggravation of dealing with her stolen wallet this morning. The inconvenience alone was enough to upset her again, and the license bureau and banks wouldn't open until nine, so she dressed and headed into work.

"Morning," Gretchen said as Jenny passed the reception desk.

"Whatever," she mumbled, refusing to look at the girl who had no way of knowing why she was being rude.

Jenny tried to shake off her bad mood. What did it matter? It wasn't like anything in her life was about to change. She bumped into someone, startling her, but not

121

enough to utter an apology. She glanced back to see a dark haired man, someone she didn't know. He seemed familiar—too familiar. Could it be?

"Sorry," he said.

For taking my wallet? She couldn't stop her mind from jumping to the conclusion. There was no way, but she gave him a closer look. Same build, same dark hair. The words flew from her mouth before she could stop them. "Did you steal my wallet?"

James pointed toward his chest. "Are you talking to me?"

Jenny stormed toward him, wishing she could make herself stop, knowing her accusation was insane, but every frustration she'd had the last few days had built to a head inside her and insisted on coming out. "Give it back!" She could feel her nerves kick in, but she had to know. "I've already cancelled the credit cards, so they're no good anyway. But I'd like to have the wallet back, and to have the satisfaction of seeing you hauled off by the police." She had stopped a half-step in front of him, and her finger poked him in the chest, accentuating her final word. Immediately, she knew she was wrong, but how could she take back her words now? *But what if I'm not?*

"Look, lady," James said. "I have no idea what you're talking about. I didn't take your wallet. I've never even seen you before."

Jenny realized she had done more than cross the line.

The man's face was going red and his voice had become louder with each word he spoke.

"Now, if you'll excuse me." He turned on his heel and headed away from her, farther into the depths of the office.

Jenny knew she had seen *him* before. Then it hit her, the man with the umbrella. Her Superman with every Boy Scout trait etched upon his actions. The man who had been on her mind the entire night after she met him, keeping her awake as she justified the million reasons why she had promised herself she would give up men.

But was he the same guy she was sure had taken her wallet?

"Who is that man?" Jenny said, hovering over Gretchen's desk like a teacher scolding a student who had misbehaved.

Gretchen popped her gum a couple of times before she answered. "James. James Cox. He was a temp, but Marie fell in love with him after he fixed a couple of glitches in the system computers, so she hired him. He's full time now, and his new space is right across the aisle from your cubicle."

"You have got to be kidding," Jenny said, her voice suddenly sounding more tired than angry. This was Mr. Tall-Dark-and-Handsome, who now worked at Tech Aide full-time, and she had insulted him like he was a common criminal. She slumped her forehead into the palm of her hand, elbow resting on the counter in front of Gretchen.

She had to be wrong. *Could anything else go wrong this week?* Jenny decided she didn't really want to know the answer.

A stolen wallet, totally offending *two* co-workers, and a mother who couldn't keep the hour of the day straight. It was a good thing Lisbeth's bridal shower was over, at least, and that she'd hadn't made a fool of herself there, or made her best friend upset because of her own harsh feelings about men and weddings. Yet now, she had brought that anger into the workplace.

Grr! Men! Jenny headed back toward her cubicle, careful to not look toward the right, which would give her a view of *him*. Why did they all have to look so much alike? Oh, she knew in general men didn't look that much alike, but all she could see lately was tall men with dark hair, and that Superman chin. She couldn't seem to tell them apart, no matter what situation she was in.

She wished she had a door to shut—no, a door to slam—but her cubicle didn't offer that luxury. Another reason why she needed to work harder, find a way to move up the company ladder and into a real office. That was something she would continue to work for, but right now she had calls to make. Losing her wallet had made her angry, and she was ready to take her emotions out on everyone and everything that got in her way. She needed to get herself under control or she wouldn't have a friend left in the world.

Jenny put her purse away in the bottom drawer of her

desk, although she didn't know why it was necessary since there was no wallet inside it. She'd call the bank about getting a new ATM card and the insurance company about getting a replacement card. She flipped the phone open and punched in the first set of numbers. Her head propped up again in the palm of her left hand, Jenny took a deep breath, hoping to make herself calm and ready to deal with the problems before her. Straightening out her misfire at James Cox would have to come later.

14

James slapped his hand hard against his desk. *That woman is out of her mind!* Of course he *had* seen her before, but how dare she accuse him of stealing her wallet, especially since he had been nice enough to stand in the pouring rain, holding an umbrella over her head in an effort to keep her from getting soaked. He'd been hoping to run into her ever since. But not this way, not with her ready to rip his face off and fling such an accusation at him. Forget the fact he had more money socked away from the sale of his company than she had probably seen in her entire life. The thought of him stooping so low as to steal her wallet would have been hysterically funny, if she hadn't made him so mad.

Punching the power button on his computer, James dropped into his chair, letting the force of his emotions propel the chair away from the desk, nearly ramming him into the cubicle wall behind him. He jammed a foot against the floor mat and sent his chair back toward his desk, hitting his left knee against the handle of the lower drawer in the process. "Ouch!"

A matching "Ouch!" came from directly across the aisle that separated his cubicle from the one that belonged to Jenny Grant.

126

A glance toward the opening in the partition gave him proof of the information he had suspected all along. The woman standing in the rain in the parking lot, the one who drove the gray Cavalier, the woman who had accused him of stealing her wallet—all of them were the same Jenny Grant who would be working directly across the aisle from him. James lifted his eyes toward the ceiling, shaking his head as he felt the rage drain out of him.

The sliding of another chair in Jenny's cubicle brought the scrambling sounds of wheels gone out of control, then a thump, before a loud groan.

Good, he thought. *I hope she hurt herself. I hope she hurt herself enough to make something bleed.* As soon as the thought ran through his head, James regretted it. Sure, he was mad, but that didn't give him an excuse to be nasty. There had to be some sort of misunderstanding—unless the woman was just a raving lunatic.

He supposed that could be a possibility. Tech Aide seemed to be filled with women who had issues. First, Tiara Brinkerhoff the matchmaker. Then Val the flirt, who he wanted to avoid almost as much as he did now with crazy-Jenny. Even his boss, Marie, had problems with a non-existent love-life that had kept her married to her business.

Is that the reason I'm here? Am I supposed to see my life from the women's side? But what purpose would that serve? He wasn't anything like any of them.

Except—every one of them, James realized, because just

127

like them, he wasn't married. *Don't tell me it's one of them I'm supposed to marry.* From what he had seen so far, that would be cruel and unusual punishment.

***

Jenny picked herself up from the floor where she had unceremoniously landed when the chair tipped as the wheels spun out from underneath her. Her fall hadn't done anything to quell her seething frustration, until she started to cry. The whole weekend she had fought against her emotions, and only part of the battle had to do with Lisbeth's upcoming wedding.

No, her emotions had swirled out of control this morning because she had let them stew all weekend. The man who had helped with her car door, the one who had stood patiently in the pouring rain, surely couldn't be the same man who had stolen her wallet. Yet they looked so much alike. Or at least she had thought they did.

Now that she'd seen James Cox up close again she wasn't so sure. She grabbed a wad of tissues from the box hidden in her desk drawer and dabbed her eyes. *Is it possible that I'm wrong?* Somehow she hoped so. Their brief encounter in the rain had seemed so . . . romantic! And now she had accused him of stealing her wallet. She definitely owed him an apology.

But she'd never been any good at telling people she was sorry. As much as she wanted to believe she'd found the culprit and that her wallet would magically appear back on her desk after her bold accusation, she knew deep in her heart she didn't want that to be the case at all. She wanted to believe in the innocence of her rainstorm hero.

Stop it! Jenny chastised herself. *You're making him sound like some character in a romance novel.* And romance needed to stay as far away from her mind as the idea of marriage would ever be. Now that she'd decided to stop worrying about finding that perfect someone, it seemed the men she met all were vying in her mind to become possibilities. Well, she'd had enough of it, and James Cox was not going to worm his way into her too-long list of failed dreams, no matter how good-looking and kind he might be.

Waiting for a program to open on her computer desktop, Jenny noticed an icon that said she had a new email. The sender's name was Tiara, the other person Jenny knew she owed a big apology to. She had totally screwed up the past two days at work, and the years of friendly working relationship she'd had with Tiara might have been ruined at the earlier loss of temper she'd allowed herself to have. *What's wrong with me anyway?*

She knew what was wrong with her. Lisbeth was getting married, and Jenny was the maid-of-honor. *Always the bridesmaid, never the bride.* The words her mother had repeated all too often stung just as strong when Jenny thought them as they did when her mother said them, and she always said them at the most inopportune times. Like in front of Kevin, the best-looking guy at the company picnic

129

last summer. Why had she thought it would be fine to bring her mom along to a work-related event anyway? And then there was the dinner at The Olive Garden in South Salt Lake. Her mom had practically asked the waiter to marry her daughter after giving him a run-down of all the times she had attended her friends' weddings in the past few months. Jenny cringed at the memory.

None of that was really a reason for her to snap at anyone though, even Tiara with her romantic meddling. Jenny had to admit, the woman had been successful at pairing up many of their co-workers, both on the job and through the people she seemed to know in the community. And some of the matches she found had not only been good-looking, but several seemed to be made of money. Not that money was something that would sway Jenny into changing her feelings, if she had ever found someone that Tiara suggested even the least bit to her liking.

The blinking mail icon was driving her crazy. It was almost as insistent as Tiara herself, and the only way to stop it was to turn off her computer, or to open the message to see what Tiara had sent her. Jenny had already lost too much time at work the last few days between this morning's anger, last Friday's lunchtime fiasco with Lisbeth's present and flowers, then losing her wallet.

I might as well open the darn thing and see what she's sending. Jenny hoped it wasn't an apology. She felt guilty enough about owing one to Tiara without having her beat Jenny to the gesture.

The message wasn't an apology. As a matter of fact, it wasn't even really a message from Tiara. Rick was calling for a special meeting in his office for the entire development team. That included Jenny. The message was marked *Important.* And the time stamp told her she only had a few minutes to pull herself back into focus.

It was hard to say what was going on, or why Rick would call another meeting a single business day after the last one. She could only hope she hadn't messed up anything else that she wasn't aware of. That's all she would need was to have Rick out to get her for some missed opportunity.

She couldn't afford to have someone else upset with her.

At least Lisbeth wasn't mad at her. That was one point in her favor on a day she needed all the friendships she could manage to save. If she could avoid James Cox the rest of the morning, that too would become a point in her favor. Luckily, she heard his fingers drumming against the keyboard when she slipped from her cubicle and headed toward the meeting room not far away.

***

James wondered why he was already getting an email from Tiara. It was the only email that had come through the Tech Aide system and the new account he had logged into on Friday. He clicked on the message, which opened immediately.

131

He scanned through the short note, which was actually a forward from Rick Myers, who James realized was their supervisor. He was calling a special meeting, something important that everyone on research and development was expected to attend. *Everyone.* That meant that Jenny Grant would also likely be invited. James took a deep breath. No getting around it. If he was going to find his niche at Tech Aide, he was going to have to work with her.

James picked up a brand new pen, scratching it against a yellow notepad to make sure the ink actually worked. He popped the pen into his breast pocket, lifted the notepad, and also picked up the electronic tablet he had brought from home. Time to raise the level of computer technology above the supplies Gretchen had made sure were delivered to his cubicle on Friday. He was ready to tackle whatever challenge Rick Myers had for him.

If he could also tackle the problem that was Jenny Grant, life at Tech Aide would be all that much better.

15

The house was quiet. Stephie understood that newlyweds shouldn't feel relief when their spouse was gone, but that's exactly how she felt all the same. Their honeymoon had been fun, a week-long cruise of the Caribbean into Mexico, with stops at Grand Cayman and Cozumel. Even the months after the wedding, when they had lived in Salt Lake while Phil finished the school year teaching high school history had been tolerable, although somewhat lonely on the weekends when he preferred to hang out with his friends. But at least he'd been home and attentive to her during the weekday evenings, and she'd had her friends to help fill the loneliness.

It had been so much fun attending bridal showers for Tamlyn and Kira before she and Phil moved to Boston. She wished she could be there for Lisbeth's shower and wedding, and to see the baby Grace was going to deliver soon. Stephie touched her abdomen, thinking about her own baby nestled inside. How would Phil react to the news she was pregnant? Would there ever be a perfect time to tell him? She didn't want to think about it, not now. Not when he did everything he could to avoid spending time with her, preferring his online games every morning, evening, and weekends too. At least he wasn't yelling directly at her when he yelled at the people he was playing against.

Stephie cleaned up the dishes Phil had left from his breakfast, made the bed, and picked up the few stray pieces of laundry to put into the hamper. She'd vacuumed the carpets and mopped the square of linoleum in the kitchen the day before, so neither of those chores needed doing. On Saturday, she had wanted to get some sleep after the restless night spent in the back of the Honda in the hospital parking garage, but Phil's noisy version of gaming had stopped that from happening. *If only I had some earplugs.* Thank goodness he hadn't stayed home long after she arrived. Of course, she wondered where he had been the rest of the weekend, but she didn't venture to ask him when he stopped in this morning to change his clothes and grab something to eat.

Mid-morning. Monday. Phil was gone, and she had nothing to do. When she'd been in Salt Lake she worked at Tech Aide, but Phil threw a fit when she mentioned the idea of a full time job when they moved. He said he didn't want her riding public transportation, but she had used TRAX in Salt Lake, so that wasn't the reason. Phil wanted control, and he'd been successful when it came to controlling the money. He got all of it; she got nothing. Well, that wasn't completely true. He gave her a small allowance, enough for groceries, but nothing for her personally. Not that she needed much since the only time she left the house was to buy food. She hadn't even been to church more than a few times since moving. It wasn't fun to go alone, and Phil had become so involved in his Sunday morning gaming that he refused to go with her.

It was one more way he kept her from making friends, and in a sense, from feeling needed. The sound of a door closing in the outside hallway reached her, and she wondered if it might be David. Had Rachel and the new baby come home yet from the hospital? *How long did she have to stay?* Before Stephie could even consider an answer, someone knocked on the door to her apartment.

She hurried to look through the peephole. David stood on the other side, a grin spread across his face like the one he had worn Saturday morning, but this time he looked more rested, more put together. He was dressed in a pressed white shirt and khaki-colored slacks, a tie pulled up to his collar and his hair combed from the dishevelment she had seen then.

Stephie pulled open the door and said, "Good morning, Daddy."

David's grin got even wider, although Stephie wasn't sure how that was possible.

"Oh, good. You're home," he said, sounding a little breathless. "It's Stephie, right?"

"Yes, that's right," she said. "How's the new Mommy doing?"

"She's great, just great," David said.

"And the baby?"

135

"Jeffrey David Leeds."

"A wonderful name," she added. "Did you get to bring them home yet?"

David relaxed a little, as though they had finally gotten to the reason he was standing in the hallway outside of Stephie's apartment, and now he could move forward. "Yes, we've been here since yesterday, but my boss just called, and I'm needed at the office. A big meeting with an important client, and I can't afford to miss out on this one. I hate to leave Rachel and the baby home alone, and I was wondering . . ."

"If I could come over and spend some time with her until you get home? I'd love to," Stephie said before David had time to finish the point he was making. "Let me just grab my house key, and I'll come right with you." She moved to the arch between the kitchen and living room, grabbed the lanyard hanging there on a nail, and joined David at the apartment door. "I'm ready."

"I can't tell you how much I appreciate this," he said as the two of them stepped into the hallway, Stephie pulling her door shut behind her and checking the knob to make sure the door was locked.

"Not a problem. It'll give me someone to talk to," Stephie said. "With Phil at school and work, I get sort of lonely during the day."

David opened the door to his apartment and let Stephie enter first. "I'm not sure how much talking you'll get done

136

with Rachel. She is pretty exhausted, and when I left a few minutes ago both she and the baby were sleeping."

Stephie felt a little disappointment, but spending a few hours at Rachel's apartment at least meant that she was out of her own, and the possibility of being able to help out this new mother was better than sitting at home alone all day. "No problem. I'll try to keep quiet so she can get some sleep."

"Thanks. Help yourself to anything around the place that you might need," David said. "There are leftovers in the fridge, maybe even a soda or two, hard to say what you might find in the pantry, and you probably know your way to the bathroom."

A smile rose to her lips as she assured him with a nod that she was capable of locating the bathroom.

"Here's my number in case you need me," he said as he scratched the numbers on a notepad sitting on the end table by the sofa. "I'm not sure when I'll be able to leave the meeting. I'm supposed to have a few days off for the birth of a new baby, but sometimes clients don't care what's going on in your personal life, know what I mean?"

"Yeah, I used to work with those same kinds of people," she said. "I'm free today for as long as you need me and if I need anything you don't have, my apartment is right next door."

"Oh, yeah," David said, with sort of a chuckle in his voice. "I guess that's right. Well, I'd better get going."

"See you later, and congratulations again on the new baby," Stephie said as she watched him head down the hall toward the stairwell.

She closed the door behind him, and looked around the apartment. The layout was the same as hers, a small living area where she now stood and had visited with Rachel, a slightly larger kitchen area off to the right. She could see dishes and a couple pans stacked higher than the rim of the sink. With the baby coming so quickly, Stephie doubted Rachel had had time to straighten up, and it looked like Phil hadn't thought to do so. At least washing those dishes would give her something to do while she waited to be of service to either Rachel or the new baby.

A new baby. If she had calculated correctly, she'd be holding a new baby of her own in a little over six months. Would Phil be as worried about the two of them as David was about his wife and new addition to their family?

She could only hope.

16

The board room was already filling up when Jenny made it to Rick's emergency meeting. Rick and his secretary Melinda Stanton had taken their usual positions at the head of the long oval table, the customary slide show opened on the whiteboard above them, a Tech Aide logo dancing across the page. It seemed everyone who was anyone in the company was crowded into the room already—Marie Davis, Cory Savage, Rob Archibald, and Michele Lyon among them. Marketing, personnel, Research and Program Development were all represented in spades.

The chairs along both sides of the table were packed tight, and as far as Jenny could tell, there were only two of them unoccupied—a chair on the left between Tiara Brinkerhoff and Nathan Greenly, and one on the right between Isaac Richards and James Cox. Val had wedged herself in as tight next to James as she could possibly without sitting on his lap, and Jenny hated the idea of sitting next to the man she had so thoroughly insulted an hour ago, but the idea of sitting next to Nathan and having him make lecherous remarks to her during the meeting was more than she thought she could face this morning. At least she would have Isaac there to talk with should the need for interaction arise. James had the decency to look uncomfortable with the way Val was trying to garner his attention. *Maybe he isn't such a bad guy after all.*

Jenny hurried to the empty seat, sliding into the chair just as Sarah Moore took the final place that was vacant. "Shut up, Nathan," Sarah said, taking control of the moment before the meeting got formally started.

Jenny didn't know what Nathan had said to cause Sarah to make the statement, but she could guess. She wished she'd thought to be so bold any of the numerous times he'd said something crude to her. His face now looked like he'd been dashed with a cold cup of water, and Jenny sort of liked it. Not his face, but the reaction Sarah had so effectively gotten.

"Thank you for coming in on such short notice," Rick said, obviously anxious to get the meeting started.

He clicked the slideshow behind him one frame forward, and a picture appeared of a mainframe computer like those first used in the 1960s, the ones Jenny had seen on TV, the ones that looked like the entire system on the Starship Enterprise.

"For years it has been technology's dream to store more data on the smallest unit possible, and today we have come to this." He clicked another slide and a computer chip and a ruler flashed onto the screen.

"Come on, Rick," Rob whined. "Get to the point. We already know the history of the computer and the chips that store its data."

"I know, I know," Rick said. "But you haven't seen this." A third slide had another data chip, smaller than the last in comparison to the ruler, and three dimensional."

"What is it?" Michele asked.

"A new concept in data storage," Rich said. "A multi-level, multi-platform data chip, capable of keeping layers of information one on top of the other, as well as allowing a single chip to save information from various interfaces, including Mac and PC, without one piece interfering with the other. It will revolutionize the computing industry for both homes and businesses, and we here at Tech Aide will be getting in on the ground level."

A buzz of questions and comments surged around the table as everyone wanted to be heard. Jenny realized some of the ideas Rick had just shared were similar to platforms that were already in use, but she also saw the vision of how even more could be done than programmers were already doing, and she wanted to be part of that advancement.

"I've brought you all together to issue a challenge," Rick continued once he got the talking back under control. "Be the team to put together a set of programs that can play nice together, who can allow the other programs to function as they are intended while sharing their playground, as you will, with each other on the same microscopic data chip, and not only will there be a significant bonus in your paycheck, but you could also be promoted within the company. Of course, you'll also be doing the world, and our company, a favor by moving the industry ahead by leaps and bounds."

A raise and a promotion? Both sounded great to Jenny. She could always use more money in her paycheck, especially if she was going to work toward traveling to more exotic or historical places, now that she didn't need to think about finding a husband and getting married. She only allowed herself a half-second's glance toward James. Yep, money meant freedom, and to a single girl like her, the faster she could make it, the quicker she could find adventures that would be more fulfilling.

***

A raise and a promotion? Neither of those things excited James as he considered Rick's proposal. No, it was the thrill of the chase. The process of creation that got his creative juices flowing. He already had a dozen ideas of ways he could interface the programs he had himself developed, and he thought he could work on those without crossing the restrictions of the contract he had signed when he sold the company. That would be a great place to start, and a platform with which he was already intimately familiar.

"I've put together a set of teams," Rick was saying. "Melinda will hand those lists out."

Rick's secretary was making her way around the room, leaving a sheet of bright yellow paper in front of each of the people sitting at the table. James would have been perfectly happy working on this project alone. No one knew him, or his skills yet, and of course, no one knew his history in programming, or the programs he planned to work on again for himself, at least not like he did. He scanned the list and found his name under the heading Team C.

It was the other names he found there that brought him to a halt. He hadn't expected to recognize anyone among them, but there they were: Tiara Brinkerhoff and Val Paterson—better known as Val the Flirt. A quick glance her way told James she too had noticed they would be working together. She had sidled up even closer to his chair, as if that were possible, and positively beamed when he looked her way. He gave her a false smile, and looked back again at the final name he recognized on the list.

Jenny Grant.

Forget Murphy's Law, God must have something out for him.

***

You have got to be kidding me, Jenny thought when she saw the list of names that had hers among them. Working on a project with Val always meant issues anyway just because her personal agenda got in the way when it came to male clients, or men who happened to be on the team. Then with the way Jenny had treated Tiara on Friday, she still felt the sting of shame, and although she knew she should apologize, she hadn't made the time to do so.

Along with James Cox, whose name headed the roster.

She forced her hand to not smack herself in the head when she read his name a second and then a third time. Why couldn't she have been on Isaac's team? She *liked* Isaac.

143

Heck, she had liked him well enough to introduce him to her friend Grace. Chalk that up to one case of matchmaking that Tiara couldn't claim for herself. Jenny started to wonder if she could do a little re-matching when it came to the composition of the teams that Rick had put together.

"Hey, how's your team looking?" she learned toward Isaac and touched the list to show him the group she was talking about.

"Not too bad, but not as talented as yours." The sound of a text message pulled him away from her for a minute. "Grace isn't feeling well again this morning."

"Is everything going okay?" Jenny said, suddenly thinking that some things were much more important than their project and the team she'd been put on.

"Yeah, she will be fine," Isaac said. "She talked with the nurse last night on the phone, and she knows it's nothing that isn't to be expected as her time gets so close. I'm just hoping I don't have to leave early and take her to the hospital." He pulled his eyes away from the phone screen and looked at Jenny, winking as though to let her know he was kidding. "Especially now that we've got this great project to work on."

Jenny smiled and nodded. The project did sound great to her, but she understood that all Isaac had on his mind were Grace and the baby.

"Anyone have any questions?" Rick said, back in charge of the meeting. "No? Then team leaders listed at the top of the column, please gather your people and get started. I'll check in with each group individually as the week goes on. Thank you." He strode from the room.

Team leaders at the top of the column. Jenny remembered without even checking that James Cox was at the top of her list. Well, not really, but he *was* at the top of the team list Melinda had dropped in front of each of them. *Great! My team is being led by a guy who was nothing but a temp last week.* No promotion would be waiting in the wings for her and no bonus either, Jenny was afraid, unless she could get herself moved from this team and onto another. Rick would never go for it. He wouldn't just let team members switch around. He was too much of a control freak, but Jenny decided she should at least try. No one ever got anywhere if they didn't make an attempt to change the things life, and controlling bosses, threw at them. Isaac would be the perfect team leader, and she approached him before he packed up his stuff to leave the meeting.

"I sure wish I was on your team, Isaac," Jenny said as she gathered her notebook and pen.

"Are you kidding me?" Isaac said. "Do you know who your team leader is and what his credentials are?"

Jenny wasn't anxious to consider her team leader, but she suddenly had a sinking feeling that Isaac knew something that she didn't about James Cox, the man she most wanted to avoid. *Needed* to avoid after this morning's confrontation. She noticed that James had already moved

145

toward the exit, probably looking for a way to avoid her as much as she wanted to avoid him. Or could it be Val he was trying to avoid? She was dogging his every step as he made his way through the door and onto the main floor of the office.

Turning back to Isaac, who was again checking the messages on his cell phone, she asked, "What kind of credentials does he have any way that you think makes him so important?"

"He's the guy who started Info-Systems Technology. Ever heard of it?"

"Who hasn't?" The sinking feeling suddenly was stronger than before and Jenny's hopes for a promotion followed right behind it. Info-Systems Technology was Tech Aide's biggest competition, and Jenny had heard the name James Cox as well, but she hadn't connected *that* James Cox with the James Cox who was now her team leader and working from a cubicle across the aisle from hers. And she'd accused him of being the person who stole her wallet.

***

If James was a swearing man, he'd think strongly about doing it now. It wasn't the project that worried him—his mind was swirling with ideas about how he could start with his own systems from Info-Tech and let them "borrow" data in a way that would decrease the size of storage, and probably marry the interfaces so they could share programming data. No, it wasn't the computing challenge

146

set out before him; it was the members of his team that would offer him the greatest challenge.

He had practically been molested by Val Paterson from the minute he'd entered the board room for the emergency meeting. A half a breath closer and she would have been sitting on his lap. As it was, her hand strayed a little too often to his knee, and he had to keep jerking away, hoping she would get the hint. She didn't. Of course, he knew already to watch out for her moves and advances. She'd tried to cuddle up too close when he had made the error of stepping into her cubicle last week and fixing a coding error for her. This morning was only an extension of that moment, and no matter that he'd tried to ignore her, she didn't care to take the hint that he just wasn't interested. If he could think of a way, he'd suggest she watch that movie about guys who aren't that into you, but she would likely think he was just the bartender and end up with him anyway.

And then there was Tiara Brinkerhoff. Sure, she'd been subdued since midday on Friday, when he caught Jenny giving Tiara an earful, but who knew when the matchmaker side would again take over and she'd be back in full force, with a string of questions about his non-existent love life. James felt sorry for her. Would her changed mood affect her ability to work as part of the team? Was Jenny Grant the underlying problem?

Jenny Grant, with her false accusation. It nearly made

147

his blood boil again just to think about what she had said. She had no idea who he was, or how much he could add to the success of this team. And because she hadn't made those details connect, she would only get in his way as he tried to lead this project.

James decided she needed to know, and that she would know soon enough. He'd make sure she understood that on this team, he was the leader, and that he had every right to be.

He wasn't sure why Rick Myers had put the four of them together. Since he'd given him the leadership position, James figured Rick at least knew who he was and what he was capable of doing. But Val, Tiara, and Jenny would soon find out what sort of powerhouse programmer had just hit them.

He didn't need the promotion. He didn't need the money. But he did need to put Jenny into her place, one way or another, and perhaps this challenge would provide the perfect venue for him to do just that.

17

Stephie spent the next two hours in Rachel's kitchen. First she hand-washed the sink full of dishes, the pots and pans proved her earlier suspicion—Rachel didn't feel well enough after dinner the night Jeffrey was born to do them, and probably dishes from her lunch as well. Plus the plates and glasses David had used in the meantime were added to the pile. Stephie hadn't heard what time the contractions had started on Friday, but Rachel had either ignored them, or the baby was quick in coming, because it wasn't that late when David appeared at her apartment door, asking Stephie to come with them. She hoped her own delivery would be quick and easy, once the time came.

Dishes done, she stepped back into the living room, but nothing seemed to need tending there, and she didn't want to use a vacuum cleaner and possibly wake either Rachel or the baby. She went back to the kitchen and opened the fridge. There wasn't much inside, but she noticed a few spills that could stand to be cleaned, so she found a dish cloth, filled a bowl with warm water then sat before the fridge and carefully wiped each shelf, feeling good about finding something helpful that she could do.

The chore didn't take much time, and soon she found

149

herself again looking for something to occupy her hands, and keep her mind busy and far away from her own troubles at home, when the tiny cry of a fussing baby brought her to the door of Rachel's bedroom. *What a sweet sound.* She stepped toward the bassinette near Rachel's bed, reaching out a finger to stroke the fuzz that lined the baby's scalp.

"He's beautiful, isn't he?" Rachel leaned up against her elbows, raising her head in an effort to get a better look at her baby.

"Beautiful indeed," Stephie said. "Do you want to hold him?"

"Oh yes," Rachel said, struggling to sit up, using her pillows as a prop against her back. "He's probably hungry. How long have I been asleep?"

"I'm not sure," Stephie said, as she slipped her hands under the tiny baby and lifted him from the nest where he'd been sleeping. He smelled of lotion, and powder, and newness. The aroma was heaven to her senses. "David came over a couple of hours ago and asked me to keep an eye on the two of you. He had to go in for an important meeting."

"It's always an important meeting." Rachel took the baby from Stephie and nestled him against her breast. "Oooh, you sweet thing. I'm so glad you're finally here."

Stephie wondered if David was gone from home as much as Phil was lately. Maybe her situation wasn't so different from anyone else's after all. Maybe all husbands sort of forgot about their wives and returned to the way their life was *before* they were married. She hadn't had a dad at home to show her anything different, and although Isaac, Randy and Ben didn't seem to abandon Grace, Tamlyn or Kira to hang out with their own friends, maybe she just didn't know what was happening. *Just like they don't really know what's happening to me.*

Rachel continued to coo and talk with her baby, and Stephie suddenly felt out of place. "Do you need me to help you with anything?"

Fussing with the buttons at the top of her gown, Rachel said, "No, I'll be fine. They taught me how to breast-feed before I left the hospital. I'd bet little Jeffy is hungry. Yes, you're probably hungry, aren't you baby?"

"Okay, I'll just head to the other room then," Stephie said. "Call me if you need anything."

"Okay," Rachel said as she continued to prepare to feed her baby.

Stephie realized that it was after noon, and that she herself was hungry. She figured Rachel had a good chance of also being hungry, so she decided to see if she could put together a sandwich for each of them. Maybe they could talk for a minute when Rachel was done feeding the baby, but before Stephie was finished, David walked through the front door and peeked his head into the kitchen.

"Hey, I'm home. Sandwiches?"

"Rachel's awake, so I thought she'd be hungry," Stephie said. "Right now she's feeding the baby." She placed both sandwiches onto the same plate and held it out toward him. "Here. Why don't you go have lunch with your wife and new son?"

"Thanks," he said. "Thanks again for coming, and for the sandwich, and your help on Friday."

"Not a problem," she said, deciding it was time to head back to her own apartment. "Just let me know if you need me again, for anything. Anything."

And she meant it. She needed to be needed, and it was becoming more and more obvious that Phil wasn't going to be there for her. Was it time she was no longer there for him?

***

Jenny wanted to find a way to apologize to Tiara, but the public forum of the team meeting was not going to provide that opportunity. Tiara hadn't really done anything that warranted the way Jenny had lit into her, nothing different from what she had always done. But the last of her friends getting married, being asked to be a maid-of-honor, and all of the emotions connected with it, had been enough to force her over the proverbial edge when Tiara had been so certain she had once again found the perfect man for her. The perfect man—James—was now standing at the head of the table in front of her. He had taken over the smaller of the two meeting rooms, the one next door to the room they had just left. Tiara had been right about one thing—he was handsome, and he had an air authority about him that Jenny found intriguing.

152

She hadn't had any trouble finding him, or, should she say, the team? Val's laughter was loud, and probably fake, like the blonde hair she wore piled upon her head. Jenny was tired of working on projects with Val, and the way the woman was acting now was exactly the reason why. *Pushy* was the best word for her when it came to men, yet it suddenly struck Jenny as funny that that attitude hadn't done anything more to get Val closer to being married than she was herself. Was there a secret to making the perfect romantic connection? Was it something she should have learned as a teenager from her mother, or her best friend? For a moment, Jenny was glad she wasn't taught how to chase guys the way Val had obviously learned at some point in her life.

I'd rather be alone forever than be like Val. And since that was what she had already decided to do, she didn't have to worry about following in Val's footsteps. Right now, her biggest problems were being a member of the team with the two women who most drove her crazy, and accusing James of stealing her wallet. If she didn't work hard, he could end up stealing her bonus and her promotion as well, and where would that leave her?

With no other choice before her, she entered the room and took a seat. Probably tired of being followed from spot to spot, James also sat then pushed his chair away from the table where Val sat down beside him. Jenny couldn't be certain, but it seemed from the look on his face, he wasn't any happier to have Val on his team than she was.

Actually, the entire team looked like a pretty sad case, and the idea of them not only coming up with a great idea, but being able to pull it off was less than certain. *Bye-bye bonus. And bye-bye promotion.*

James opened the team meeting with a call for ideas. "Anyone have anything that came to mind while Rick was talking?" He picked up a marker and stood so he could write on the whiteboard behind him.

The silence was deafening. Jenny couldn't make herself focus on the task in the midst of this company. She was impressed that James had asked for their ideas first. Many of the men she had worked with in the past dictated the way a project would run based on their own ideas, but James seemed interested in hearing from his team. Even if nothing would come from it. Val rarely had a fresh idea of her own, although James had no way of knowing that. And Tiara still looked like she was afraid to speak in front of Jenny.

Tiara didn't have on as much make-up today as she normally wore. Her eyes looked puffy—*had she been crying all weekend?* Jenny felt responsible, although she would have hoped that Tiara had gotten over the harsh things she had said to her. She had been cruel, reminding Tiara she spent her time as a matchmaker because she couldn't set her own wedding date. Jenny didn't know the truth behind why Tiara was single yet had a good guess why she hadn't been able to snag a man, but pointing it out in the office, where half the people in their department could hear, was simply unacceptable. She had to apologize, but again, she knew the time and place was not here. She'd keep her eyes open though, and when the time was right, Jenny needed to let Tiara know how truly sorry she was.

And as for Jenny herself, ideas were in short supply right now. She was still feeling the sting of embarrassment over her accusations toward both Tiara and James.

James waited another minute before he sighed, turned to the board, and started writing his own list of ideas. "In case you haven't heard, I started a company known as Info-Systems Technology. I'm no longer the owner of that company, but that doesn't mean I don't still know a little bit about their programming and the methods of information storage I saw in its future. If you're interested, I think there are some ways we can use that knowledge to move our own project forward."

Of course she had heard of Info-Systems Technology. *Who hadn't?* It had been one of the fastest growing computer tech companies since the dot com boom. And James had been the owner. She put the links together in her mind. If James had started the company, that meant he not only developed the initial technology, but when he sold it, he must have gotten rich. Wouldn't he? Or did he go bust when the bottom fell out of the market? He was no longer the owner. Did that explain why a man as old as James Cox was looking for work as a temp, and why he would be excited to be offered a fulltime job for another computer

155

software company? He needed the job? He needed the money?

All the same, he had developed the software that became Info-Systems Technology. Maybe he really could be an asset to their team and their company. Maybe his ideas were worth listening to, considering. Maybe, as a part of his team, she still had a chance for that promotion and a raise.

Unless, he really is a thief. Not only taking her wallet, but to steal ideas from within her company. *No, he couldn't be.*

***

James was still frustrated by Jenny's earlier accusations, but he wouldn't let that stop him from moving forward with his plans to develop the kind of software he'd wanted to ever since he had started his own company. As a matter of fact, he probably would have been farther along the process of having a multi-level, multi-platform data chip already in production if he hadn't felt so strongly that he needed to sell the company and move to Utah.

And months into being in Salt Lake, and a week at Tech Aide hadn't given him a definitive heads up as to why he was supposed to be here. At least, not until now. This project could be the exact reason, the opportunity he needed to take the computing world by storm.

Maybe the move had nothing to do with his being single. He'd sure not found anyone in the time he'd been here that would answer that question, unless he counted Jenny. Strangely, despite her accusations and attitude, he felt

156

himself attracted to her. The moment he spotted her standing in the rain, he had wanted to come to her rescue, be her knight in shining armor. When he'd seen her at Tech Aide, he thought he'd been given a second chance, although he wasn't sure why he had wanted to, even before she had accused him of stealing her wallet.

It wasn't his usual habit to approach women—strangers—and see what he could do to help, and he rarely wanted to see them again after an initial encounter. Of course, too many of those initial encounters had been arranged by well-meaning women like Tiara, hoping to match him with some other lonely-heart single, no matter that they shared nothing in common. But this time was turning out to be different. Not only did he and Jenny now work at the same company, they were teamed together on a project that could be interesting, if not downright exciting. *If* she stopped working so hard to offend everybody. He wanted to understand the reason why.

She had appeared flustered when she entered the room and saw Val Paterson standing beside him. *Did it bother her that Val is flirting with me?* Or was Jenny just annoyed to have been teamed with him so soon after her accusation?

Whatever the case, James hoped they would be able to work together. He was excited to begin this project, and he hoped the women would catch his vision and help him build upon it. To be fair, James opened the floor to the three of them to add their own ideas to the list of possibilities.

What he got was nothing. Absolutely nothing.

Val hung on his every word like she was listening to the greatest orator in the world. He found her attempts at flirty admiration annoying, fawning all over him like a cat that couldn't get enough of being petted, despite the fact he was as unresponsive as possible. He hated women who threw themselves at men. Didn't they have any self-esteem?

And Tiara. Tiara looked like she'd been beaten—*I wonder what happened after I last saw her on Friday?* She had been confident about herself as a matchmaker, even if she wasn't so confident about herself now. She had been more than eager to introduce him to Jenny, and to introduce Jenny to him. If only that had worked out a little better. If he'd seen her *before* Tiara made such an issue over them meeting he might have been more willing to have an introduction, but nothing had gone right in his getting to know a thing about Jenny, other than that she was just as anxious to avoid him as he was hesitant to know her.

He couldn't quite decide about Jenny. She was a beautiful woman—golden hair, bright blue eyes, and a dimple when she smiled added to her looks, and yet she was still single in her late thirties. Had she been married and divorced? Or was she more like Tiara and Val, single because she drove men away? There had to be a good reason.

It didn't matter. He was letting himself consider a romance that had no chance of developing, not that he was in the market. He was here to develop new product, to reach

158

a new pinnacle of success in the world of computer programming. *I don't have time for women.* Not for Val, or Tiara, and certainly not for Jenny Grant.

Since not one of them had any ideas that would benefit the team—or at least that's what he assumed their silence implied—he decided to start at the basics.

"In case you haven't heard, I started a company known as Info-Systems Technology . . ."

18

Jenny made it through the team meeting and the rest of the day, but she could hardly wait to be gone. When six o'clock rolled around, she was the first one out of the building. With the appearance of James Cox, work had suddenly become more stressful than ever.

If he weren't so good looking, and smart besides . . . *Stop it*, Jenny told herself. She couldn't help it though. Just like Tiara had told her before she had actually met James, he *was* tall, dark and handsome. The ideas he had presented during their first team meeting had proven he was brilliant too. How had one person ever come up with the concepts he had developed for Info-Systems Technology? And now he was taking those ideas far and above anything she had ever imagined. He was already mentally programming how the systems would work together on a multi-level, multi-platform data chip, integrating circuits and solving problems on the whiteboard as though there was nothing the least bit challenging about the work that lay before them.

But she couldn't think about the project, or about her new team leader. James would have to be put on hold until tomorrow, longer if she could help it. The project would be her top priority in the morning, but right now, she had

160

more pressing things to do than to think about James, his great idea, or his good looks. Lisbeth had texted her an hour ago, with a message, "Call me ASAP. We need to talk about the bridesmaid dresses, and bachelorette party???" Not what Jenny needed to think about with work and James on her mind.

She'd hardly had a free moment to talk with Mrs. Connor at the shower the family threw for Lisbeth over the weekend, but she had hoped she wouldn't need to put together a bachelorette party—this brought a giggle to her throat as she considered the new meaning that word had taken on with the hit TV series of the same name. *Sick!* She didn't know that she could pull it off anyway, especially since even the thought of attending one more such event was making Jenny wish she'd never agreed to being the maid-of-honor in the first place, let alone, being in charge!

She got into her car and started the engine. A few raindrops had started to fall, and she hoped it didn't make the roads slick. Sometimes the pavement and her worn tires didn't get along, especially when the road was wet.

The first thing Jenny needed to do was call the Rose Shop and make sure the Hawaiian orchids and the other flower arrangements were on schedule. Although the wedding was still a few weeks away, she knew from the experience her own mother had had organizing events that the flowers could be the most difficult of all the details to pull off.

161

She headed away from the company parking lot as the phone rang once, twice, and a third time before it was picked up. She knew she shouldn't talk on her cell while she was driving, and the new laws said she'd have a huge fine if she got caught, but she excused herself with *everybody does it*, as the ringing stopped.

"The Rose Shop," a gentleman's voice said.

Drat! Jenny recognized him right away as the owner, but she still couldn't remember his name. "Hello, this is Jenny Grant."

"Ah, Miss Grant. It's so good to hear from you again. How is your mother?"

There was no way Jenny was going to tell this nice man the truth. "Fine. She's doing fine." She didn't have time right now to worry about her mother.

"So good to hear. Please give her my regards."

"I'll do that." This was the second time he had told Jenny to say hello to her mother. She'd have to remember to do that the next time she spoke with her.

"But now, you have called to ask about the orchids." The man's voice was now all business.

"Is everything still on schedule for their delivery in time for the wedding?" Jenny turned left, heading around the block toward her apartment complex, aware of a dark blue Altima following a little too close behind her. She tried to remember where she had seen it before. In the Tech Aide parking lot? Or maybe the one at her own apartment? She

162

couldn't be sure, and guessed it didn't really matter. She flipped on the left turn signal of her car as she waited to cross into the parking lot to her complex. "Just following up for the bride."

"The date of the wedding—still scheduled for June?"

"The fifteenth."

The sounds of screeching tires pulled Jenny's attention toward her rearview mirror, as two cars swerved far to the right lane and around her. The dark blue of the car she had noticed earlier sat at an angle to her back bumper, the rain coming down heavier now around it.

"What was *that* all about?" Jenny felt her heart pounding hard against her chest.

"I'm sorry, Miss Grant?" the shop owner said.

"Oh, nothing to do with you," Jenny said. "Someone almost crashed into the back of my car." She took three deep breaths, trying to slow her heart rate and keep her mind working properly at the same time.

"Are you alright? Do I need to call the police?" he said, worry evident in the tone of his voice.

Jenny continued to look toward her mirror, seeing the blue car edge out and into the lane to her right. "No. No. Everything is fine now."

Although she wasn't sure about that completely, she was no longer fighting to catch her breath from the fear of nearly being hit. Instead, she fought to keep her wits about her because of what she had seen, rather than what she had just

163

experienced. She recognized the driver of the dark blue Altima, and she thought the truth was a little disturbing.

"I'd better go," Jenny said.

"Yes," the florist said. "Take care."

The phone connection went dead in her hand, but Jenny's mind was swirling with conversation. James Cox was driving the car that had almost crashed into her. Why was he following her to her apartment? Had he done so deliberately and been behind her all the way from the Tech Aide parking lot? He'd been so helpful there when she first met him after work on Thursday. And today, despite the way she had accused him of stealing her wallet, he had included her in the discussion of his ideas during their team meeting.

So why was he following so close behind me? And why was he in the turn lane heading into her apartment complex? Did he try to hit her on purpose? *No. Stop grasping at straws here, Jenny.* But she didn't convince herself.

Did her new team boss have something out against her? Was he trying to make her life miserable?

And if not, then what on earth *was* he doing?

***

What on earth had he been thinking? James didn't know why he had decided to follow Jenny once he saw the little gray Cavalier pull out of the parking lot at Tech Aide. He certainly hadn't meant to follow her all the way across town to her apartment complex. He must have been blinded by the rain that had started to fall—or something—when he

164

failed to stop with plenty of room between them as she waited to turn left. He could only count himself blessed, or extremely lucky, that he hadn't rear-ended her when he came to his senses and realized how the short distance was rapidly closing between them. He had slammed on the brakes, hoping the wet street wasn't slick, listened to the squealing tires, and prayed as hard and as fast as he could that his car would stop before he ran into her.

It had worked. God had seen fit to answer this prayer, this time. Why hadn't he been there all the other times James had prayed for a miracle? Cars honked as they passed the two of them. James pulled down his visor, hoping to keep his identity hidden from Jenny. *How embarrassing!* He checked the lane to the right of Jenny's car and nosed his vehicle away from her bumper and into the stream of traffic, praying for one more miracle—that she wouldn't look over and recognize that it was him.

But this time, luck wasn't with him, and God seemed to have another idea in mind. James glanced in Jenny's direction only to find her looking straight at him. He'd always known God had a warped sense of humor, but did He have to prove it right at this very awkward moment in time? James gunned the accelerator, and peeled his way down the busy street and away from Jenny Grant.

Crap! Crap! Crap! Jenny had almost been nice to him after the team meeting, and now she would have another reason to blow up at him tomorrow morning. She seemed to

165

be over the accusations at the loss of her wallet, and she had actually participated in the meeting, adding strong ideas to his rough outline of where they might be able to go in the development of the new software. He was pretty sure she wanted to apologize, but she hadn't taken the opportunity, likely not wanting to bring it up in front of the other two women who would never let her live it down.

And now he'd given her one more open door to tell him off for nearly smashing into the rear end of her car. Why would she think he was there, anyway? Would she be concerned that he'd been following her? He hadn't really been. It was some subconscious thing. He hadn't looked for her or for her car when he'd pulled out of the parking lot, and it hadn't really registered that she was driving a few cars in from of him. At least not at first. But when he did, it was like he had no control over the steering wheel. He was drawn to her, like flies to a piece of spoiled meat. No, not that. It was more like the way a butterfly was drawn to a blooming flower. Like a moth was drawn to a flame—and like that moth, he was almost burned in its attraction.

Thank Heavens he hadn't actually run into her.

Since the near accident, James had safely made it back across the busy downtown area of Salt Lake City, and into the parking lot of his own complex. Resolute, he headed toward his apartment, sure that he had just hit upon the one thing he needed to do. He needed to thank his Heavenly Father. Sense of humor or not, God had sent him here and put him in this place. James still wasn't positive this was why he was in the city, but his passion for life had come back full force with the introduction to this project.

And like it or not, Jenny Grant was part of those feelings. If only he could keep his head on straight and worry about the project and not about the woman. At least he was certain that dating and relationships was not the reason he'd been sent here, and for that, he could be thankful.

***

Like so many other times, Stephie spent the evening alone. Phil didn't come home after his classes or work, she didn't dare touch a thing on his gaming system so she could watch television, and she felt she'd already overspent her welcome at Rachel and David's place, once David came home.

Phil had been upset when she was gone Friday night and almost refused to believe that she was at the hospital parking garage while Rachel was inside the building, giving birth to her baby. But maybe that emotion was good for him. It was the greatest reaction she'd gotten from Phil in weeks for anything more important than the botched job she'd done at his mother's recipe. At least Stephie knew he still *could* react to real things, not just the action on the television screen as he lost yet another man in the world of virtual reality.

How could she bring him into their actual world of

167

reality? The reality she had discovered when the blue line appeared on the pregnancy test strip. How could she tell Phil that she was pregnant?

Stephie ran through a set of scenarios in her mind. *Hi, honey. Guess what? We're pregnant.* No, too forward. A note with a photo of a baby placed tenderly against his pillow? He'd just think it was trash and throw it away. A whispered message in his ear? When was the last time she'd gotten close enough to him to try that one? Every idea she came up with had an immediate reason why it would never work. Talking to Phil lately had become impossible. It was no wonder she was lonely.

She paced the area between the living room and kitchen a dozen times, wandered into the bedroom, and made a quick stop in the bathroom—she'd already noticed the number of times she needed to go had increased in just the few days she'd known she was pregnant. Was it a figment of her own imagination, or had the baby already grown to a size it was pressing against her bladder? Whatever the case, she doubted Phil would notice the number of times she went, before she was ready to tell him about the baby.

Of course, that would mean he actually had to *be* home to notice, and not gaming. Not a given since the video game screen was much more important than she seemed to be.

By eight o'clock she thought she'd go crazy if she didn't get out and do something. She needed to talk to someone, anyone who could help her feel like she was still important.

168

Digging through the couch cushions, Stephie came up with a dollar and a quarter. The pocket of Phil's jeans netted four dollars, and the dresser drawer where he dumped anything extra had another five and some change. Suddenly she felt wealthy.

She'd never get over her loneliness here in the apartment, and she knew it. There was a coffee shop the next block over. She could get a cup of hot chocolate and maybe a danish. And if she was really lucky, they might have a pay phone. She'd call her mother.

No, Mom wouldn't make me feel any better. Instead, she decided she'd call Jenny. Just talking to a friend who seemed to have life all together would make her feel better. And Jenny was the perfect one. Jenny, who knew better than to rush into marriage just for the sake of getting married. Jenny, who didn't care that she was nearly forty and had never been married. Jenny, who stayed at Tech Aide and was working her way up the corporate ladder, headed for a lifetime of career success.

Jenny Grant was the perfect woman in Stephie's mind, and at this moment, she missed her more than anyone else in her life. Even if she didn't have much money, a phone call with Jenny was exactly what Stephie needed.

***

Thank goodness that crazy fool didn't run into me, Jenny thought as she parked her car. *What on earth was James doing following me home anyway?* It sort of creeped her out to think

169

that James had followed her all the way across town from Tech Aide and ended up right behind her in the turn lane to her apartment complex.

She was certain he didn't live there. No new neighbors had moved in, and the next person she knew would be moving out was Gary Page, Lisbeth's fiancé. The two of them were already planning to move into an apartment in his parents' basement, maybe not the best of circumstances for someone like Lisbeth, who was used to having a great bedroom in her own parent's house for all these years, but a couple needed to start somewhere. She had told Jenny that they would have an outside entrance, which afforded them more privacy than her bedroom, and the rent was cheap.

"We'll be able to save enough to own a home of our own in no time," Lisbeth had said, in her usual bubbly optimism that she saved for her very best friends.

Maybe some of that optimism was just what Jenny needed this evening. She threw her purse onto the coffee table once she entered her apartment, stepped out of the shoes she had foolishly been wearing—what had possessed her to wear high heels to work today?—and allowed herself the luxury of flopping across the couch, feet resting on the pillows piled on one end. If she didn't think a nap right now would keep her up way too late into the night, Jenny might have drifted off.

But she knew there were things she needed to do. A load of laundry was waiting in the basket by the washer, and she really did need to call Lisbeth—*bridesmaid dresses and bachelorette party*—and see what *else* she expected from her as the head of the bridesmaids. There she went again, refusing to call a spade a spade. *Maid-of-Honor*—something more than just a plain old bridesmaid, although that might have been easier to stomach.

Her own stomach reminded her she'd worked through lunch and that dinner better be on its way fast or she'd be of no use to Lisbeth tonight, or pleasant to be with. Jenny didn't do well when she was hungry. Five minutes of rummaging in the pantry and fridge resulted in a wilting potato, shredded cheese, and a carton of sour cream that didn't smell too far gone, despite the expired date on the bottom of the carton. She stabbed the potato a few times with the tines of a fork, popped it into the microwave, and went back to searching for something else to compliment her faked-potato bar. A jar of stale bacon bits didn't seem appetizing, so she tossed them into the trash, counting it as her effort to start decluttering the kitchen. A start was a start.

Another two minutes and Jenny sat in front of the television to consume her make-shift meal. Not that tonight's dinner was different than any other meal she prepared for herself. *Get used to it*, she thought. *A life staying single means delicious meals like this every night—for the rest of your life!* The idea of the clean-up required after actually cooking something that was more nutritious, more well-balanced was

171

enough to stop her from making the effort. Besides, thinking about preparing a full course meal would require preplanning—and shopping. If there was one thing Jenny hated, it was shopping.

Dinner finished and her plate rinsed and placed in the nearly empty dishwasher, Jenny checked the clock. A few minutes before seven. No time for a nap if she was going to help Lisbeth with anything this evening. She retrieved her cell phone from the bottom of her purse—vowing once again that she really should keep it in one of the little inside pockets where she could find it more easily, but knowing she wouldn't—Jenny called up Lisbeth's number in her favorite contacts, and hit the button.

"Hi, Jenny." Lisbeth's voice was as bubbly as ever, almost effervescent and breathy, just like it had been since the engagement.

Where is that shy woman I used to know? "Hey Lisbeth. This is the first chance I've had to call since I got your text," Jenny said. "Since I'm your maid-of-honor, I'd probably better start doing something that shows I deserve the title."

A childish giggle greeted her from the other end of the phone. "Oh Jenny, you are *sooooo* funny. My mom and I were going to City Creek Center tonight and start the registration process at Macy's, but she can't make it after all, and Phil is tied up with work. It would be much more fun for me if you were to come along. Can you come right over?"

Before Jenny could answer, the cell phone gave off a ding that said she had another caller. *Maybe I can beg off from*

172

going with Lisbeth. "Hang on, I just got another call." She pulled the phone away from her ear and looked at the number. Long distance and none that she recognized. *Probably some telemarketer.* Jenny couldn't disappoint Lisbeth with such a lame excuse as a telemarketer. What if her best friend found out? She chose *ignore* on the phone's options.

"Okay, I'm back, and I'll be right over," Jenny said, once again holding the phone to her ear. She hated herself for almost lying to get out of the trip, almost as much as she hated shopping.

"Oooh, Jenny, I can hardly wait to talk with you about the new colors I've chosen."

"And I can hardly wait to hear all about them," Jenny said. She hoped they wouldn't be anything outrageous. She's sort of gotten used to the idea of the blue that Lisbeth had mentioned a few days ago. If it were shimmering anything, Jenny feared she'd look like a blimp.

Another bridesmaid dress. Just what she needed—another unusable bridesmaid's dress to hang in her closet. Someday she really was going to have to take a serious look at purging her closet. "Clutter sucks all the breath out of you," she'd heard on a recent TV show. Just like some people sucked all the energy from you. As she headed for the car, Jenny began to wonder if there was anyone in her life that fell into the category of human clutter. Of course, the name that popped into her mind immediately was her new team boss—James Cox.

173

19

The number rang twice then the phone went dead. Stephie pulled the handset away from her ear and looked at it for a minute, as though that would explain the problem. She rattled the silver tab between the receiver like she'd seen people do on various movies and television shows, hoping somehow that doing so would reconnect her to Jenny's number which she had dialed. It didn't.

Luckily the ancient pay phone didn't keep her change either. A clattering of coins fell into the change bin at the same time she stopped attacking the tab. She was surprised she hadn't needed to use the coin return handle to get that to happen, but returned change in hand, Stephie decided to try another number. She was disappointed that Jenny hadn't answered the phone. Just talking with her would have helped Stephie know the next steps she should take. In the last half hour, she'd been fighting down an urge to run home to Utah. But the thought of completely giving up on her marriage seemed almost as horrible as when her dad left home and found himself a new wife. Did she want to raise this baby alone, like her mother had been forced to do?

Since Jenny wasn't available, then Tamlyn was the next best choice.

Actually, it was possible that Tamlyn was the better choice anyway. *She's a newlywed*, Stephie thought. *She'll be able to tell me what I'm doing wrong.*

Stephie was glad she remembered Tamlyn's cell number. It was an easy combination of twos and threes. She punched them into the pay phone and waited for the phone to ring. This time the phone was picked up almost immediately.

"Randy? Is that yooooou?" The final word came out in almost a moan.

Stephie recognized Tamlyn immediately. "No, Tam, it's me, Stephie. Are you okay?"

"No. No, I don't think so. Can you come over right away?"

Something *was* wrong, and Stephie was worried, but she had no idea what she could do. "I can't. I'm in Boston. In Massachusetts."

A loud groan came through the receiver. "I . . . I need help," Tamlyn said. "I think it's the ba—baby."

Oh my gosh, Stephie thought. She knew Tamlyn was pregnant, but she couldn't be very far along, not yet. "What's happening?"

"I hurt. It hurts so bad," Tamlyn said. "Wait, I have to sit down."

The connection was silent for a few moments. Stephie strained to hear anything that would give her a clue either what was happening on the other end of the phone, or some sign as to what she should do.

175

"Please deposit another two dollars for an additional two minutes."

The operator's voice was automated, and Stephie looked at the small stack of change she had lined up along the tray of the public telephone. She dropped in eight quarters and heard the machine accept them just as Tamlyn came back on the line.

"I think . . . I think I'm bleeding. What if I'm losing the baby?"

"You're not going to lose the baby." Stephie prayed that were true, but who was she to know anything about these situations? "You're going to be fine." She couldn't bring herself to say anything else. She wouldn't want to make Tamlyn worry any more than she was already.

"Stephie, I don't know what to do. It hurts so bad. Tell me what to do."

If only she had some idea what to tell her. If only Phil hadn't taken the two of them so far away. If she were still in Utah she would have been in the car and on her way to Tamlyn's apartment. Maybe she still wouldn't know what to do to help the situation, but at least she would be there to hold her friend's hand, to put her in the car and take her to someone who *would* know, to get her to the hospital. But she wasn't there, and now she had to tell her something, something that would be difficult.

"Do you know where Randy is right now?" Stephie tried to keep her voice calm, the tone soothing.

176

"He's on his way home from work, but his cell isn't ringing through." It sounded like Tamlyn was sobbing.

"Okay, then here's what you need to do," Stephie said, not wanting to break the connection, but knowing it was the only thing she could do that would help Tamlyn. "I'm going to hang up now . . ."

"No!" Tamlyn wailed, either at the suggestion or in pain, Stephie wasn't sure which.

"Yes, it's the best thing for you," she continued. "As soon as I'm gone, you need to call 9-1-1. They can come to you. I'm too far away to do you any good. Will you promise to do that for me?"

"Y-y-yes," Tamlyn said, her voice cracking between the sobs. "I'll call 9-1-1. They will know what to do."

"Okay, Tamlyn. I'm hanging up now. You'll be okay, and remember how much we all love you." Stephie wasn't sure why she said that last part, but she knew it to be true. She had already touched the pad to end the call when she realized she hadn't given her friend one last assurance about the safety of the baby.

"Dear Lord," she prayed aloud. "Please let this baby, and its mother, pull through."

The message was meant for Tamlyn and the tiny life she carried, but somehow the words seemed to Stephie that she meant them for herself too. But what would it take for her marriage to also pull through? And did she still want that now that she'd seen the real Phil?

Temporary Bridesmaid

***

Jenny almost wished she *had* answered the long distance number that had come through on her cell phone. At least she could have pretended she knew who was calling and used them as an excuse for avoiding this shopping trip with Lisbeth. Registering at Macy's had been a breeze, but that had been an hour ago. If there was anything she hated more than shopping, it was shopping for clothes, and yet here she was in the third formalwear and dress shop of the evening, being dragged around by the ever-enthusiastic Lisbeth from one design to another as she tried to match her chosen color-scheme palette to the dresses already available.

It was Jenny's job to ooh and aah over each one, shake her head when Lisbeth decided a certain color would never do, and patiently hold the stack of sample dresses Lisbeth draped over her arm before pushing Jenny toward a dressing room door and stating, "Go try them on!"

"I thought you'd already decided on the kind of dresses you wanted?" Jenny couldn't stop herself from asking.

"My mother thought maybe I should let you have some say, you know, as the maid-of-honor." Lisbeth held another dress against the color swatch booklet she had brought along with her.

Jenny hated trying clothes on almost as much as she hated shopping in general. And trying on a dozen or more dresses was doing nothing to help her mood. What would she gain out of this anyway? Yet another bridesmaid dress

178

that she wouldn't ever put on again after the wedding, a hole in her wallet—grr! Just the word made her upset again about the theft, and James Cox—and worst of all no one she wanted to impress would even see her in the darn thing at the wedding because none of the men she had ever been interested in would be coming.

Somehow she found herself blaming James for that problem as well. As silly as her false accusation might seem, she still didn't know for *sure* that it wasn't James who had taken her wallet, just like she was sure it *was* James who had nearly crashed into her car, and why had he been following her home anyway?

Obeying Lisbeth's orders, Jenny stepped into the spacious dressing room with the identification tag "Bridal Salon" hung in the center of the door. It was by far the most impressive dressing room she had ever entered, and Jenny told herself that it was the only time she'd ever again use a room by that title. If she thought she could get away with it, she'd blame that on James as well.

A tapping on the door told Jenny she'd been lost too long in her thoughts. "Just a minute," she called as she stripped off her slacks and shirt and pulled the first gown over her head, allowing the ruffles to settle down over her body. *Yuck!* she thought, hoping Lisbeth would see immediately that all that chiffon and those *ruffles*—everywhere—would be too much, too overwhelming for not only Jenny to wear, but for everyone else in the wedding

179

party. She reached behind herself and attempted to move the zipper up just enough to give the dress its shape, then she fluffed the ruffles one more time to add their full effect before opening the door.

"Oh, Jenny, you look . . ." Lisbeth's hand flew to her mouth to stifle the laugher.

"Stunning?" Jenny said, moving from the room and into the light where she could spin, the ruffles flapping in the breeze like the feathers on a frizzle chicken.

"Actually, silly is more the word I was thinking."

"So glad you see it my way," Jenny said, letting her relief come through in her first bit of laughter since she accepted the invitation to be a part of this whole thing.

"Maybe I'd better look at the others I gave you to try on a little more carefully," Lisbeth said, stepping into the dressing room and moving each dress from one side to the other on the rack.

By the time she was done, she had pulled an additional four gowns from the selection. The first to go was one with an empire waist—the kind Lisbeth had at first wanted them all to wear—that might have made Jenny and Kira look as pregnant as poor Grace, who didn't dare accept an invitation to be a bridesmaid for fear she'd never make it to the wedding with her baby being due soon. Next was a dress with a lacey bolero jacket, fancy enough, but the whole thing almost looked like it would compete with any wedding gown for attention, competition that Lisbeth didn't really need.

Dress number three was covered with lace and likely expensive, so it was a relief for Jenny to see her remove that one. A second of holding the final dress up against Jenny's torso proved why it needed to go away.

"Just an inch or two too short, I'd say," Lisbeth said.

"More like six you mean," Jenny said. The hem came closer to mid-thigh than mid-calf in length. "I'm afraid I'm way too old to wear something like that." *Ouch!* She had let the words slip without thinking beforehand how bad they would sound, even though she was saying them herself. *I sound like my mother.* And that was certainly no one Jenny wanted to sound like when it came to the subject of her age—or getting married.

"I'm sorry, Jenny," Lisbeth said, as though she were responsible for the thing Jenny had just said.

"Nothing to be sorry about. The truth is, I *am* too old to wear a dress as short as this, and you know what, I'm okay with it," she said, trying to reassure her friend that nothing was wrong. That nothing about this wedding had been upsetting to her. Nothing.

Now if only she could convince herself.

Three dresses later, Jenny and Lisbeth discovered the perfect dress. The pale green organza—Lettuce Sparkle by the official description—complimented the shades on her color palette without being too overwhelming. The design was flattering and modest, something that made Jenny feel better about both her age and her weight. She was sure the other

181

bridesmaids would love it as much as she did, if it was possible for her to love a bridesmaid dress that is.

Less than an hour later, the initial order was placed, Jenny's measurements done, and the wedding date verified by the saleswoman against both Lisbeth and Jenny's calendars. Jenny would be in charge of calling the other bridesmaids to come to the shop within the week to have their measurements taken, then getting everyone back in time for their final fittings before she picked up the dresses and got them to the location for the wedding. One thing she could do that would take the pressure off the stress that would soon be entering Lisbeth's life, as happened to every bride, it seemed, the closer it got to her wedding.

"You're going to look like a princess, Jenny," Lisbeth said as they headed to the car.

Yeah, she thought, *one who is* eternally *going to be without her Prince Charming.*

***

James spent the evening at home, working on his ideas for the project. Or at least that's what he tried to tell himself he was doing. It seemed he was spending more time thinking about Jenny than anything. He actually thought she was rather cute when she was mad, although he hoped he didn't have to see her that way again anytime soon.

Of course, he probably would deserve her being mad at him again after this evening. What on earth was he thinking, following her home from work, then almost crashing into

182

her car because he wasn't paying attention to the fact her car had stopped in the turn lane. If there hadn't been rain . . . *Am I being some sort of stalker, or something?* No, a stalker would have been more secretive in his approach, at least at first, to the girl of his dreams. *Whoa! Where did* that *come from?* His mind had gone from daydreaming about the near crash with Jenny, to seeing her as the girl of his dreams?

He reined his suddenly-crazy idea back in. Sure she was cute, and her ideas in the team meeting had proven she was smart, but James didn't know her well enough for *this*. No use getting sidetracked with a woman now that he had a reason for coming to Utah. It was all about work, and taking this opportunity at Tech Aide to expand the software and microchips ideas he had had before he sold his company.

He enjoyed the rush of being the first to develop a concept and make it big. He wondered if Steve Jobs or even Mark Zuckerberg ever felt this way. The thrill of the kill, in a business sort of setting, had to be more exciting than any conquest he'd ever made in the dating arena. But that could be because he hadn't really made any conquests there.

Girls in high school had seemed silly, as though nothing else but being cute mattered to them. By the time James had gotten into college, he was too focused on his class work and computing ideas to concentrate on much of anything else. Sure, he'd gone out with a couple of girls that were nice to look at, but none of them had impressed him when it came to brains. He had decided a long time ago, if he were ever going to settle down and get married he wanted a woman who could take care of herself. One who understood what it meant to work hard, and maybe even saw herself someday at the top of the corporate ladder. He wanted someone who could run an office, as well as she could run a home.

He wanted someone smart, driven, self-sustaining. He wanted someone like Jenny.

But with the way he was making nothing but bad impressions on her, James figured that was never meant to be. He settled back into his work, telling himself there would be no more thinking about Jenny Grant.

Not tonight, not forever.

***

Despite the fact Jenny was exhausted from her bridesmaid shopping trip with Lisbeth, her mind simply would not give up the fight and let her drift off to sleep. A bridesmaid, no it was worse. A maid-of-honor.

Always the bridesmaid. Always the bridesmaid. Always the bridesmaid.

The stupid refrain simply would not give up. It was worse than trying to count sheep, Jenny decided. She sat up in bed and checked the time on her phone. Two-thirty and she hadn't been to sleep yet. Tomorrow would be a horrible day, if only because of the lack of sleep she would be getting tonight. *If* she ever got to sleep, and that possibility was looking more unlikely as the minutes marched by.

"Arg!" she couldn't hold her frustration in any longer.

Jenny slammed a pillow onto the opposite side of the bed, as though she were attacking someone who wasn't there, and never would be. A bump from the other side of the too-thin apartment walls reminded her she'd better at least stay quiet in her effort to burn off the concerns of her life. She wouldn't want an irate neighbor storming over to bang on her door in the middle of the night.

Darn you Lisbeth Connor, anyway. Why did you have to ask me to be your maid-of-honor? I'm a total wreck. Jenny could just imagine how she would look in the morning. Her hair a mess from tugging on it in frustration, dark circles outlining her eyes like a raccoon caught in the headlights, and she knew she'd be more than grumpy. Her mother always complained that she was unbearable to be around when she hadn't had enough sleep. It was all Lisbeth's fault.

Leaving *me* to be the last one married.

Jenny had learned long ago that staying in bed when she couldn't get to sleep would never solve the problem, so finally accepting defeat she reached over to turn on the light, then climbed out of bed and padded into the kitchen. When she was little, her mother used to give her a cup of warm milk with a pat of butter in it to help her sleep, but Jenny wished she could have something a little stronger. Like a shot of whiskey—she knew she'd never do it. She had promised herself years ago that no alcohol would ever pass her lips, and no matter how depressed she was at losing the last of her single friends to the institution of marriage, now was not the time to break her promise.

Her mom had never had the luxury of using the microwave to warm the milk when Jenny was a child, but that's the way she made it for herself. She thought about adding chocolate flavoring, but she knew any hint of caffeine and she'd definitely be awake the rest of the night. There was no real butter in the fridge, so a dollop of margarine would have to do. She sat at the kitchen table and flipped on the television. An infomercial about losing weight did not seem appropriate with her warm milk and butter sitting on the table before her. The next two channels featured celebrities hawking the latest in exercise and dietary plans meant to save the masses who needed to also lose weight. *What's up tonight with weight loss products?* One look down at herself made Jenny realize she too could probably stand to lose a few pounds. *But not tonight.*

She clicked through a half dozen more channels, those filled with classic sporting events and fishing shows. The stations about people who hoard were interesting, but also depressing and she didn't need a downer like that.

"One-hundred and sixty-two channels and I can't find a thing to watch," Jenny muttered.

The station landed in the middle of an old black-and-white film, one she didn't recognize. After only a minute or two, a loud chirping noise came from the movie and a giant ant crawled onto the screen. *Eeep!* Jenny started to scream then she caught herself. How embarrassing! The giant ant was part of the movie, one she suddenly recognized from her

186

own childhood filled with the Saturday matinees at the local retro theater. *Them!*—a classic film, but not for her in the middle of the night. Not without a guy to hold her hand or put his arm around her shoulders to let her know it was going to be alright.

Who was she trying to kid? Jenny had never had a guy to do either of those things her entire life. Boys and men only treated girls like that in the movies. No one ever really acted like that.

She pushed the remote another three or four times before she stopped again. *Somewhere in Time* was on. Christopher Reeve had just entered the scene, his bowler hat too small upon his *Superman*-head. He was following Jane Seymour—still as stunning today as she was back then—as she walked along the beach of Mackinaw Island. It was one of the most romantic scenes in the entire movie, and Jenny found herself immediately caught up in it. The pulse at the base of her neck quickened as Christopher moved closer to Jane with every step. Jenny knew she was holding her breath, but she couldn't help it. She had memorized the words that were coming, and she wanted to hear them once again.

"Is it you?"

Jenny moved her lips in perfect synch with Jane—Elise McKenna—as she said them, the pounding of Jenny's heart noticeable deep within her chest.

The camera panned to Chris—Richard—as he waited a brief moment to respond, but it wasn't the actor she

187

imagined she saw. It was James Cox—Mister Tall-Dark-and-Handsome—who waited only a beat before nodding his head. Jenny sucked in her breath, then that terrible man—the one played by Christopher Plummer—stepped in and took Elise away, breaking the moment inside Jenny's head in the same way.

She had always hoped that meeting between Richard and Elise would end in a kiss, but no matter how much she yearned for it to happen, it never did. Not even the end of the movie worked out the way Jenny had hoped, not really, with the two of them only walking through the clouds into eternity and no time spent together while they were both still young enough to enjoy it. What a gyp!

"And they call that romance," she said, clicking the off-button and silencing the rest. If only she could mute her mind the way she just had the TV. *There will never be a man like that for me.*

Not even James Cox?

No, not even James Cox. She wasn't sure where that little voice had come from inside of her head, but she wasn't going to let it get the better of her. She turned out the lights as she climbed back into bed, determined to remember, *I've sworn off all men.*

188

20

James was not in a good mood on his way to work the next morning. He'd tossed and turned most of the night, unable to get his near-encounter with Jenny Grant out of his head. There were only so many ways to berate oneself for being stupid when it came to women, and he thought he'd covered most of them last night. Number four hundred and ten came in at almost smashing into the back of her car while accidently following her home from work. He hoped he didn't add another hundred items to the list at work today.

But mostly, he wondered why he cared.

He managed to find an open place in the parking lot, glancing around to make sure he wouldn't be walking across the street to Tech Aide at the same time as Jenny. No, she wasn't here yet. He could make it into the building and bury himself in his cubicle to work on the project without having to look her in the face. *What an idiot to follow her home! How am I ever going to work with her today—or any day!* The messages from last night didn't seem to be done running through his head.

A quick "Hello" to Gretchen at the front desk, and James was sure he could make it to his space, until he saw

Tiara Brinkerhoff heading toward him. It was true that she'd been quieter and less enthusiastic about her matchmaking, but he was still wary, especially since she seemed perkier today than she did yesterday.

"Good morning, Mr. Cox," Tiara said, as she stopped in front of him.

"My name is James," he said, trying to keep his sleepiness and frustration at himself out of his voice. "How are things with you this morning?"

"Oh, much better," Tiara said. "I got some good news. Vickie, over in accounting, took my advice and decided to go out with Mitch, down at the packing room, and they had, to quote her 'a wonderful time.' With any luck, I'll be adding number twenty-nine to my list of matches, setting an all-time record among all my matchmaking friends."

He could hardly believe she had said such a thing, especially to him, who he knew she saw as yet another single to add to her list of matchmaking conquests. "Um, how nice for you."

"*And* for them!" Tiara's smile was so broad it made her head shake and her ringlet curls bounce against the side of her face. "I also have some good news for you."

Oh, no. Here it comes. James tried to push past her and get into his cubical, now determined to not only miss running into Jenny, but also to get away from Tiara before she brought Jenny up again.

"I had a great idea," Tiara said, as she continued to follow him down the hall toward his office. "It's about . . ."

190

He made it to the entrance of his cubicle at the same time Jenny popped her head out of her own cubicle across the aisle. "Hey, has anyone else had trouble this morning with the . . ."

"Project," Tiara said, as Jenny finished her sentence with, "Internet," and James came to a halt, nearly crashing into Jenny, while almost being crashed into by Tiara from behind.

"Not again," he said, forgetting for a second that he meant to think the words, not say them aloud.

Jenny's head disappeared back into her cubicle like one of those little Whack-a-Mole creatures in an amusement park game. Apparently she wanted to avoid him as much as he wanted to avoid her. James broke his concentration from the spot where he'd last seen her face, and turned toward Tiara.

"That's great, Tiara," James said. "I look forward to hearing all about it, later, once I've had time to get settled in for the day." He stepped into his space, pretended to close a door that didn't exist there, effectively telling Tiara he was through with her for now, and sat down at his desk. One final glance toward the cubicle opening and he saw Tiara again wore the look of shock she had spent most of her time with since Friday. This time it was his fault, not Jenny Grant's.

He turned on the power to his computer and waited for it to boot, figuring the rest of the day could only improve.

***

191

Jenny had not wanted to run into James first thing this morning, not when her thoughts of last night were still so fresh in her mind. She hated to admit it, but he did look a little like Christopher Reeve, and now she'd never be able to watch another movie one of her favorite actors was in. *Darn you James Cox anyway!*

She sat at her desk, unsure what she'd be able to do since the internet didn't seem to be working, and she needed to research the ideas she'd had for the project—the one she was being forced to work on with James—*Darn you Rick Myers!*—and without the web as a resource she was now stuck in her office with nothing to do.

She'd already tried everything she knew to solve the internet problem, closing and reloading her browser, trying a different browser, rebooting the entire computer. Heck, she'd even banged her hand against the side of the unit, hoping that would somehow shake the thing into submission, even though all her years in computing had taught her that was only something an idiot would try. Well, this morning she *felt* like an idiot. Who else would spend the night mooning over a guy she didn't want who looked like a guy she couldn't have and who didn't want anything more to do with her than what she did with him anyway?

It was all too exhausting to even think about. All these years of searching for the perfect man, a guy she could look up to, someone who would fall in love with her the same way she'd fall in love with him. Then finally getting her act

192

together and deciding to give up on that fairytale dream since it would never happen, and in walks someone as perfect as James Cox directly into the cubicle right across from her. And still she couldn't have him.

Life wasn't fair; love wasn't fair, and she wished she'd never met the man.

What could he ever do for her anyway? She still wasn't positive it hadn't been him who had stolen her wallet, although she remembered how indignant he had been when she accused him. And then there was the incident after work last night, where he'd almost totaled the rear end of her car— *and possibly me along with it.* And now, he'd seen her this morning, looking like a frazzled wreck after a night of sleeplessness, all because she was thinking of him.

What she needed to be thinking was how she could get rid of him. She wanted that promotion and the raise for this project, but her ideas weren't nearly as good as the ones he'd presented in the team meeting yesterday, and now she couldn't even research her own solutions because the internet was down. Somehow she wanted to blame it all on him, but she knew she couldn't.

I hate you James Cox!

But she didn't. As much as she was trying not to allow herself to think about him, James was the only thing on her mind. And it was driving her crazy.

After a few more minutes of tapping the reload, hoping the browser would somehow suddenly take her to the website she wanted, Jenny called the front desk. "Gretchen, what's going on with the internet this morning?"

"What do you mean, Jenny?" She could hear Gretchen pop her gum too near the headset. "Mine's working fine here at the front desk."

"Mine's not," Jenny said, more frustrated than ever.

"Ummm, wonder what's wrong?" Gretchen said.

"If I knew, I guess I wouldn't have to call you to check," Jenny said. She heard the irritation in her voice, but couldn't stop herself. "Can you send in someone from tech?"

Gretchen laughed. "That's funny. Send in someone from tech to help you fix your computer problem at Tech Aide." She laughed again.

"Okay, okay, I get the joke," Jenny said, but the smile on her face was really a smirk of sarcasm. She was glad Gretchen couldn't see it. "Just send someone in to help me fix it."

"Why don't you ask James?" Gretchen said. "He's in his cubicle across the aisle and I'm sure he will know . . ."

"I don't *want* to ask James," Jenny said, angry that Gretchen would make the suggestion, but more so at her own reaction to it. She hoped she hadn't spoken loud enough that he had heard her. That would be just one more reason for him to hate her. "Just get someone over here, and get them now." She slammed the phone into the cradle and again smacked the side of her computer, not because she

194

thought it would fix the problem—she'd already proven that theory wrong—but because she needed something to do to relieve the tension of her morning.

It didn't work. Her tension wasn't gone.

***

When his phone rang, James hesitated before deciding to answer it. He didn't think it would be Tiara, who had finally taken the hint and moved away from his cubicle. He *knew* it wouldn't be Jenny, who ran into her own office space the second she'd seen him. His parents or family would call his cell, and his friends were all back in California. The only people left would be either Marie or Gretchen, and both of them were safe.

"This is James Cox," he said, just in case Gretchen had put someone through from the outside.

"Hi, it's me," Gretchen said.

James could hear the girl's gum chomping through the phone line. An annoying habit, and somehow he thought if Marie Davis ever caught her doing it on a business call she'd be reprimanded for it.

"Jenny Grant doesn't seem to be able to connect to the internet," Gretchen continued. "It's working fine up here for me. Since you're right across the aisle and everything, I thought maybe you could go check on it for her."

James certainly did not want to go over and help Jenny. If Jenny had wanted his help, she could have asked for it herself. No telling what her reaction to his uninvited appearance might be.

195

"What do you think?" Gretchen asked. "I could call over to the tech guys." She interrupted herself with a giggle then finished what she had started to say. "But you're so much closer and if you can fix the problem, I know Jenny won't be mad at me."

Now what does that *mean?* "And if I can't?" James said, hoping his hesitation came through loud and clear in his voice.

"Oh, you'll be able to. You're a computer whiz. You can fix anything."

Except the messes I manage to get myself into. "Okay, I'll see if she'll let me in," James said. "She didn't seem like she wanted to see me when I arrived earlier."

"Jenny's okay," Gretchen said. "She just has a thing when it comes to men—she doesn't like them."

"In general or just me?"

"Oh, she likes men okay, I guess," Gretchen corrected herself. "She just has a complex. She thinks that no man will ever like her, not the way she'd want them to anyway. It's the reason she yelled at Tiara the other day. Poor Tiara. She really thought that you . . . Oh, gotta run. The other line is ringing."

James didn't need to hear the rest of what she would have had to say anyway. He knew exactly what Tiara had been thinking, and he was sure that Jenny did too. But Jenny had been living with the woman and her conquest list of matchmaking for who knew how long. He'd only had to

196

put up with her for a few days, and it was already too much for him.

He placed the phone back in its cradle and allowed himself a long minute to look across the aisle toward Jenny's cubicle. Was is possible that Jenny could ever like someone—fall in love with a man, a man like him? That was nothing but ridiculous, a foolish thought running around in his head. If the Lord wanted him to find a woman, He could have had that happen anywhere. You didn't have to move thousands of miles away from home to meet someone, not anymore, not in the age of the internet.

And it was the internet he was called upon to fix. Jenny didn't have access, for whatever reason, and he had been fixing glitches like this almost since he had been introduced to his first computer at the age of six. He let out a deep sigh then walked across the hall and tapped on the partition that designated her office from the aisle. She didn't answer, and he wondered if somehow she had sensed it was him and refused to acknowledge him.

No, just as James raised his hand to knock again, Jenny stood to the right of the opening, her face turned away and only a wisp of her hair visible to him from the angles they both were standing. "Are you here to fix my internet connection?" she said.

There was no way she could see it was him. It was like she was playing some sort of game, like hide-and-seek. *What was up with this woman, anyway?*

197

"Yeah. Gretchen called from the front desk," James said. No lying there at least, even if he was sure she didn't recognize his voice yet.

He stepped into her cubicle, and the look on Jenny's face when she saw him was curious, to say the least. A little shock and a great deal of anger eventually mixed with a look of relief and lastly, embarrassment.

"I *told* her . . ." Jenny stopped midsentence, and shook her head, as though she were trying to clear her thoughts before she proceeded.

Not to call you, James allowed his thought to finish hers before she proceeded.

"Umm . . . thank you . . . thank you for coming over to help. I've tried the usual, but there's still nothing, no connection."

"Let me take a look at it for you," James said, moving behind the desk and dropping into the chair she had likely just vacated. The seat was still warm and an acknowledgement that the warmth had come from Jenny flashed through his head.

Forcing himself to focus on the task at hand, James touched a few keys, closing the browser and opening the control panel instead. He was pretty sure what he was looking for, the same problem that had stopped Marie's computer from working on the day he was hired. *Yep,* there it was, the code for the virus he suspected. With all the shared files in a place like this the fact that the virus existed

198

on more than one computer wasn't all that unusual, more annoying than anything, but if a tech aide hadn't known what to look for like James did, it could have taken him days to find the problem and fix it.

Gretchen's joke suddenly hit him. *A tech aide at Tech Aide.* No wonder she had giggled when she said it to him. Not very sophisticated, but then, neither was Gretchen. She didn't have the class that Jenny displayed, despite the fact she always seemed to be either mad at him, or avoiding him. And who blamed her? He could have totaled her car, or even hurt her last night with his stupid behavior at following her home. *Maybe I owe her an apology.* Maybe they could just start over and actually become friends.

Before he could say something to her about it though, her phone rang. She picked it up and said, "This is Jenny."

James let the computer finish its scan and purge of all the files associated with the virus, but he had trouble not letting his eyes stray to watch Jenny, her back turned toward him as she spoke on the phone.

"Yes, Mother. I'm at work. No, it's the middle of the day. They don't keep me here all night."

James thought her tone sounded like she was worried, but it could be frustration at the way the conversation seemed to be going nowhere.

"Do you need help with something? I can stop by over lunch . . . Oh, okay. If you're sure? Well, okay then. I forgot to tell you, I spoke with the nice man down at The Rose

Shop. The Rose Shop, Mother. The place where you always order your flowers. Here, in Salt Lake. What do you mean you've never ordered flowers? Mom, are you sure you're okay?"

The initial scan and purge was finished, but James didn't know how to exit the room graciously, and he could tell Jenny was getting upset on the phone with her mother. If he left now, drawing her attention back to him, would it make the situation better or worse? He wasn't sure what to do, but decided to at least look like his work at her computer was intense. He leaned forward and set the computer to rescan, hoping the problem really would be fixed so he could get out of here once she was through on the phone.

Maybe right now wouldn't be a great time to tell her he was sorry for last night, sorry for looking like the guy who had taken her wallet, sorry for coming to work at Tech Aide if that's what it would take for her to forgive him. The idea had hit him that he wanted Jenny to like him. He wanted her to consider going out with him. Was that the reason he had followed her home last night? Was he acting like a boy with a school yard crush?

No! It couldn't be, but right now he wanted to fix more than just her connection on the internet. As he listened to her end of the conversation with her mom, he wanted to fix whatever was going on there as well. He wanted to fix everything that was wrong in her life, but especially he wanted to fix the concern Gretchen had told him about. He wanted Jenny to know that there was a guy in the world who would like her, and that guy was *him*.

"I'll call you later then," Jenny was saying as the second scan came to a halt. "Bye."

She replaced the receiver and turned back to look at him. "Oh, I'm sorry. My mother . . ."

"Not a problem," James said. "The computer's all fixed. Just a little virus. I ran a double scan. Everything should work fine now."

He knew he was staring at her, but he couldn't help himself. How had he missed that she was so beautiful? Even with that little strand of hair that was out of place? He stood abruptly, and nearly tripped into her as he walked past the corner of the desk. His hand reached out involuntarily to steady her in case she started to fall, and his eyes seemed tolock on hers, as hers were now on his.

"Jenny, I . . ." but James wouldn't allow the words to come. Instead he bolted for the exit and across the hall, into the sanctuary of his own office.

Even if it didn't have a door he could slam.

***

Once James was gone, Jenny felt drained. *What was that all about?* How was she ever going to work on a team with him, especially now that she couldn't get the romantic notions that had started swirling out of control again out of her head? And why had he looked at her that way? He'd

201

given her a look that she'd only seen between her closest friends, the ones who had recently married. It was the look she associated with romance, the kind that led to marriage. The only other place she'd ever seen it was in the movies, and she was savvy enough to know the look wasn't real, at least not in that place. Maybe it was real between her friends and their new husbands, and maybe it was real between a mother and her baby, but that didn't mean it was real anyplace else.

Unless it could be real . . .

She shoved the idea away from her mind, then brought it back out again, touching upon it gently the way one touched the tip of their tongue against a sore tooth, testing it out to make sure it was still there, hurting.

No, not hurting. She wouldn't let this hurt. Not this time. She was through. No men, ever. Not even one as good looking and convenient and available as James seemed to be. She'd given them all up. She was going to live a life that was free. One where she didn't have to answer to anybody, and she certainly didn't have to worry about James sticking around to be a part of her life.

Even though Marie Davis had hired him, in Jenny's mind he was still a temporary. He'd already left one computer tech company. Who could say when he'd pack up and leave another one? It could be today. It could be this minute.

When her cell phone rang, Jenny considered not answering. It could be James.

No that was just silly. Her own crazy mind taking her places where it didn't belong. It could be anybody. If it was Lisbeth, she'd never be able to stand the bubbly. If it was her mother again—then it was her *mother*, the very person who would not only guess something was wrong, but who would also immediately jump to the conclusion it had something to do with a man. And that's the last conclusion Jenny wanted anyone to jump to right now, especially herself. Besides, she'd just gotten off a very strange call with her mother. Surely she wouldn't call back again.

And James had just dashed out of her office. She wasn't sure what she had done that was wrong, but there was no way the phone—her cell phone at that—would be him.

I've got to stop thinking about him. I've got to stop thinking about James.

One look at the number said it wasn't anyone that she recognized. It had already rung three times, and if she didn't answer before five it would drop into her voicemail. It was the third call she'd had from numbers she didn't know since her wallet had been stolen. It could be the police, or maybe someone had found her wallet and was calling to find out how to return it.

She punched the answer button. "Hello?"

"Jenny?" A man's voice, one Jenny didn't think she recognized. His voice was husky, sounding almost as though he had been crying, and recently. "Jenny? Is that you?"

"Yesssss," she drew out the word as though hoping it would illustrate her uncertainty.

"This is Randy."

Randy—Tamlyn's husband. Jenny's mind raced through all the possible reasons Randy would be calling her, settling almost immediately on the one reason she most hoped couldn't be happening. "Is there something wrong with Tamlyn? Did she . . ."

"Tamlyn lost the baby."

The words hung in the air between them. *How could that be?* Jenny tried to piece the words into the confusion her mind had made, as though everything that had happened was part of a puzzle. A thousand piece puzzle with nothing but raw edges that made no sense when you first looked at them. Tamlyn, the baby, Randy.

It took her forever, she feared, but finally the words she needed came to her mind, allowing her to speak like the sort of supportive friend she needed to be. "Oh Randy, I'm so sorry. What can I do, and where do you need me to be?"

Randy burst into sobs, but Jenny was sure she heard him say, "I'll be taking her to the apartment. Can you come to the hospital?"

"I'll meet you there," Jenny said then she hung up the phone, not sure she could even stand for the moment, let alone be strong enough to leave.

"Jenny?" James spoke softly. He was standing once again in her doorway. "Is it . . . is it your mother?"

21

Stephie had tossed and turned all night, worrying about Tamlyn and the baby, and her own baby too. Phil hadn't come home all night, again. *Still paying me back?* She never would have thought that before their move to Boston, but lately it seemed that everything Phil did was like he was out to get her, or at least to upset her. He was always mad, and nothing she did made it right.

Where had the gentle man gone who she had dated? Was their romance all a game to him? Stephie didn't want to believe it, but what had happened to change him so quickly after the honeymoon? They'd been home less than twenty-four hours before he was begging off to go be with his friends.

"We've been together every minute for a week," he complained. "A man needs some time with other men."

Sure, she'd missed her friends as well, but she thought she could go longer than a week without them. She'd been much longer than that without them now. Phil had met new people in his classes, and until Rachel had knocked on her door, Stephie had been alone, cut off from everyone else.

Rachel was a lifesaver, and she was glad the young couple had let her see even a tiny glimpse into their life, a

205

doting husband, a loving wife, and an adorable new baby. Stephie sighed. *If only my life could be so perfect.* Looking at it in comparison to theirs, she was becoming more doubtful that it would ever be.

Stephie tried to find something to do around the apartment, but she didn't dare touch any of Phil's gaming equipment, and the rest of the place had already been cleaned every day for a week. There wasn't much else she could do. She thought about going back to the coffee shop and calling to see if Tamlyn was alright, but she had used all of the money she had found last night, and since Phil hadn't been home, there wasn't a chance of anything lying around that she hadn't already found.

I wonder if I could borrow a few dollars from . . . but she didn't finish the thought, knowing it would sound ridiculous for her to ask to borrow money from Rachel to make a phone call.

Besides, a young couple like Rachel and David, with a brand new baby, wouldn't have even a few extra dollars to spare. No, she was stuck, unless Phil came home.

Unless I call my mom collect and ask her for the money to come home.

The idea shocked Stephie. Where had it even come from? But now that she'd thought it she started to mull it around in her head. Would her mother accept the collect charges? It was expensive to accept a collect call and her mom never had the proverbial two nickels to rub together,

206

to hear her tell the sad story when Stephie was a kid. And if her mom did accept the call, how would she ever have enough money to buy her a plane ticket home? Would she even consider it? She had almost seemed glad when Stephie and Phil married, as though at last she could stop worrying about her only daughter, the one that she'd raised alone after her husband had abandoned them.

Abandoned. Would her child ever feel like that—lonely and abandoned, like she had—if Stephie left Phil and ran away back home, back to her mother, back to Utah, and back to her friends? Would she be justified if she did?

Stephie shook her head, trying to clear the ideas that were swirling around her mind. Even now she felt abandoned, and not just by her dad. Phil had abandoned her too. He'd only been gone physically since Saturday with a brief moment at home yesterday morning, but how long ago had he abandoned her emotionally? Since before they moved to Boston, since the night after their honeymoon ended? Or had he ever been truly attached to her at any time since they had met?

That seemed crazy, but Phil had always found excuses to go out with his friends before they were married, for ridiculous amounts of time, sometimes on camping or boating trips. He didn't want to have long conversations with her. As a matter of fact, if he could say it in a text, that was good enough. The fewer words he had to actually speak, the less angry he seemed. Phil regularly bounded from the

207

table after meals, heading off to do whatever he wanted to do, without her. Even if he just planted himself in front of the television, he didn't seem to care if she was there.

Stephie had watched the other couples she knew—Grace and Isaac, Tamylyn and Randy, Kira and Ben—and none of those men, certainly not since they had married, had gone off for hours and hours to spend time with their friends, not while they were engaged, or as newlyweds as far as she knew. And none of those women complained that their husbands found TV more entertaining than spending time with them.

Of course, it was possible they didn't share their concerns, but the stories she heard were filled with fun activities these couples had done together. Hiking, movies, dinner dates, overnight trips—a list of things that sounded like their husbands continued to spend time with them, just like while they were dating.

Has there always been something wrong with my marriage?

She tried to convince herself that was nonsense, but the niggling worry was still there. "I've got to stop thinking like this," Stephie said aloud, as though hearing herself say the words would stop the conversation going on in her head.

But every place she looked reminded her of how Phil had already abandoned her. The gaming system, the television she didn't dare touch, and his undisturbed side of the bed. When was the last time he had touched her—held her tenderly? Even when they had last made love he had been the one in control, the one who fulfilled his need, then

208

turned away from her as though her feelings didn't matter at all to him.

And now, as a result, she was carrying his baby, and he didn't know.

Stephie wasn't sure if she ever wanted him to know. But how could she hide the pregnancy from him? She had to get out of here. She needed time to think, to weigh her options, and she knew she couldn't stand another minute alone in the apartment, not with only the crazy thoughts that were getting further and further out of control.

She picked up her key and pulled the apartment door shut, but as she stood in the hallway, she realized she still had no place to go. Glancing toward Rachel's door, she worried that she might already be becoming a pest, but what other choice did she have? She took the few steps to her neighbor's apartment, hesitating a moment before raising her hand and knocking three times on the center of the door.

***

Jenny didn't want James to ask about her mother. She didn't want anyone at work or among her friends to know how bad things had been going when it came to her mother's health. She'd been trying to deal with it all by herself, although keeping her brothers informed as well. The doctor said there were no clinical signs of Alzheimer's, despite the confusion her mother seemed to be experiencing. She didn't want to think about her mother, not while Tamlyn needed her, but James had asked.

209

"No, it's not my mother," she said, her tone almost a reprimand.

She saw him flinch, but she couldn't care. It wasn't James or his feelings, or even her mother that mattered this minute. It was Tamlyn and her baby, and she had to get to her now. James had pulled away from the cubicle opening and stood in the middle of the hall, his face a study in confusion.

"I have to go," Jenny said, as she breezed past him, headed toward the receptionist desk. "I'll be out of the office the rest of the day," she said to Gretchen on her way.

"Is everything okay?" Gretchen asked then popped a big bubble with her chewing gum.

Jenny stopped short, turning back for only a moment. "Actually, no. If I hear you snap that gum one more time, under any circumstances, I'm taking a complaint to Marie, and you'll be properly reprimanded. Act like a grown-up if you want to work in a place like Tech Aide."

Jenny gave another yank on the door which had started to close, and was on her way to meet Randy and see Tamlyn. She could only hope that something comforting would come to her mind by the time she got there.

She knew she had lots of explaining and apologizing to do when she returned.

***

"Well, talk about someone needing to act professional," Gretchen said.

"How does anyone work with that woman?" James had followed Jenny to the front of the building, although he wasn't sure why he bothered. All he had done was try to be nice, and once again Jenny Grant had nearly snapped his head off.

"This is really unlike her. She's usually one of the nicest people who work at Tech Aide. One's thing's for sure," Gretchen said, looking up at James as she did so, "she's been a lot more moody since *you* came to work."

"What's that supposed to mean?" he asked. Was this girl blaming him for Jenny's constant bad mood?

"If you want to know the truth," Gretchen said, "I think she likes you a little too much."

"That is ridiculous," James said. He leaned against the receptionist's counter, as though he suddenly needed propping up. *Isn't it!* "She can't stand me. You heard her blame me for the wallet missing from her purse."

"Yeah, and I also saw her accept her placement on your team for the big project. If she had wanted to, trust me, she would have put up a big stink." Gretchen waved her index finger in the air to emphasize her point. "She's not afraid to stand up to Rick, I've seen her do it too many times before, and when it comes to product development, she knows what to do. She wanted to be on your team, and not just because of what you know. She likes you, even if she doesn't yet know it."

"Right." James made no effort to keep the sarcasm out of his voice.

Jenny Grant liked him. He'd have a hard time believing that. And if Jenny knew the rumors Gretchen had been passing on to him, the man she said was the source of Jenny's bad mood, he was sure there would be hell to pay. He didn't plan on finding himself in the middle of it when Jenny's temper blew.

Although she was cute, even when she accused me of being a thief.

Even though she was *still* wrong. He wondered what had happened that caused her to rush away. And would she ever be in a good enough mood for him to get to know more about her? Something about her determination had impressed him enough to want to try.

***

Jenny didn't know why she had done it. Sure, she was upset about Tamlyn, and she had been taken off guard when James poked his head back in her office to see if there was something wrong with her mother, but that didn't justify the fact she'd snapped at Gretchen. Or the way she had spoken to James either. He'd been nothing but helpful, and as soon as he tried to show her a little common courtesy she jumped right at him like a bulldog.

He must hate me by now.

The thought really bothered her. She wasn't sure *exactly* when it had happened, but Jenny had lowered her guard, the one she had decided on just a few days before to protect herself. *No men.* No more men to ruin my life. Yet here she was, thinking about James Cox when she should be worried about Tamlyn, and Lisbeth's wedding, and her mother, but mostly Tamlyn and her lost baby.

She tried to concentrate on traffic as she headed through the center of town on her way to University Hospital. By some stroke of luck, the traffic wasn't heavy, at least not yet. Not like it had been yesterday afternoon when James almost rear-ended her car. She glanced at her watch. It felt like it had been hours since Randy had called, but in reality it was only fifteen minutes.

She had already crossed State Street and started the slow climb up the east bench of the Wasatch Mountains. Jenny had always loved the mountains. She didn't think she could live anywhere without them. Oh sure, she'd enjoyed the few vacation trips she had taken to Southern California, and there were mountains there, but nothing like the ones that surrounded her in Utah. The changing colors as the seasons passed—the brilliance of fall, the snow of winter, and the green of a new spring, a new beginning. Of course, the dull brown of a too-dry summer wasn't a color palette she dwelled on, but even the mountains were entitled to a time to not be at their best.

And that's exactly how she had been since James Cox spent his first day at the place she worked—not at her best. She wondered if she needed a new beginning, a fresh start if she was going to work with him. She could convince herself to be nice. He had been nice enough to help her, and he

213

asked about her mother, even though she didn't want anyone to ask. Jenny didn't need to go down that path though. Her mother was getting older. She was just forgetful, the doctor said. *Nothing to worry about.* But she worried anyway. All she'd ever wanted to do was make her mother proud, but all her mom wanted was to see that wedding ring on Jenny's hand.

Well, it wasn't going to work out that way, and being nice to James wouldn't change that one little bit. Still, work might be less stressful if she was nicer to him. And to Gretchen. And, of course, to Tiara.

But right this minute, the thing that counted was being there for Tamlyn. She pulled her car into the parking structure at the hospital and focused her thoughts back on the issue at hand.

Inside the hospital, she went to the front desk. An elderly woman was seated there. A loose pink jacket covered her white blouse. The jacket signaled to Jenny that this woman was a volunteer, who probably could not provide much information about Tamlyn, of even her whereabouts. Unsure where else to go though, Jenny approached her.

"Excuse me." Jenny said. "Can you tell me where I need to go? My friend, Tamlyn Robison has been here at the hospital. Her husband called me. Randy . . . Randy Robison. She . . . she lost her baby today."

The woman immediately jumped from her seat and came around the desk to wrap Jenny in her arms. "Oh, my dear. I'm so sorry."

Definitely a volunteer. But the woman's hug was so warm and comforting Jenny could not bring herself to break away from it. How she had missed these kinds of moments with her mother since the forgetfulness had grown worse. And right now, Jenny needed someone to hold her and give her strength.

When at last the older woman broke away, Jenny repeated the reason she was here. "I'm trying to find Tamlyn. Randy called to tell me he was taking her back—" The realization of what Randy had really said during his call suddenly hit her. "—to their apartment. I'll bet they've already gone."

"Let me just double check," the woman said as she settled back into her chair, tapping a few strokes against the computer keyboard in front of her and concentrating on the monitor. It only took her a moment to discover what she was looking for. "Robison, Tamlyn. Released at ten-fifteen, a.m." She glanced at her wristwatch. "Almost thirty minutes ago, so I'd imagine she's already gone."

Jenny nodded. "I'm sure she is. Thank you anyway."

"Sorry I couldn't be of more help," the volunteer said.

"You've been more help that you'll ever know," Jenny said. That hug had meant everything to her, and it was what she had needed today, if not for a long time.

As she returned to her car, she found herself once again thinking about her mother, and the changes that had come over her personality, along with the moments where she lacked clarity. The doctors had to be wrong. There was something going on with her mother's mind; Jenny just didn't know what. She wished she had someone she could talk to, someone who could help her think things through. The last time she talked with her older brothers they were no use. They were hundreds of miles away and believed the doctors knew what they were doing, so if the doctors weren't worried, they wouldn't be either. Jenny didn't think she'd be able to convince them of anything different, so why even try?

She'd love to talk over her mother's situation with her best friends. But Lisbeth was soon getting married, so that was the only thing on her mind. Grace had a baby ready to pop at any moment. Kira was off still being a newlywed, and Stephie had moved across the country. She'd put a huge damper on ever being able to talk with Tiara again, at least until she offered a major apology. And there was no one at Tech Aide who knew that something was going on with her mother.

Except for James.

But as far as sharing her feelings about her mother, or about anything, Jenny would never admit that James even counted.

216

22

James was mystified by Jenny. He thought he'd forgiven her pretty quickly about the wallet. He hoped she'd do the same thing about the near-accident. She'd accepted his help when it came to the computer, but as soon as he tried to act concerned about her second phone call and the health of her mother, she refused to tell him what was going on, and then went all ballistic on Gretchen, making her the second woman at their shared office who had gotten the wrath of Jenny laid down upon them.

Quite the temper on that one. But Gretchen said Jenny's behavior lately was unusual. James shook his head as he walked away from Gretchen's receptionist desk toward his own cubicle. He couldn't let himself think about Jenny anymore today. There was work to do, and as the team leader he needed to lead the way.

Opening a new file on his computer desktop, James typed up the notes he had made during the initial meeting with Rick and did the same for the notes he had taken during their team discussion that followed. Val hadn't been much of an asset, making him wonder if she really had what it took to be a program developer. From his own experience as a boss, he knew that occasionally non-productive workers

217

were kept on the payroll because they hadn't proven themselves to be completely worthless yet. Was that what had happened with Val, or was she really talented, just too distracted by her flirtatiousness to get herself down to business?

An instant message from Tech Aide's internal mail server popped onto his screen. *Val*, as though she knew he was thinking about her.

"How about a break for a cup of coffee?"

James looked at his watch. They'd only been in the office for a couple of hours, but he hadn't gotten anything done as of yet. Between fixing Jenny's internet virus and watching her rush from the building, he was getting ready to settle in, and here was Val already looking for a way to get away from working. Had she just answered his question? She would have to do a lot to prove she was an active member of a team like his.

"No thanks." He typed the words quickly and hit send. How would she read them at the other end? He didn't want to offend her, so he added, "Just getting started on my day's agenda, so I'll have to pass. Talk with you later about how my end of the project is going."

That should do it. A nicer refusal and a little nudge about the project and working, tying the two ideas together. Hopefully Val would take the hint.

The next few hours flew by as James pulled apart a competitor's program, data-bit by data-bit, searching for

218

places where it overlapped with the programs he had developed with Info-Systems. Starting with his own designs as the working model gave him the insight he needed to understand how the other developer's thought process worked when it came to building a program. The exercise in comparison would help him when he tackled the programs from Tech Aide as well.

He hadn't wanted to work on Tech Aide designs just yet, hoping to get to know a little bit more about the developers on his own team, their strengths and weaknesses as they brought him pieces and asked questions about the work they were doing. Parsing the programs they had already developed and tested as parts of another team would eventually be useful, but not yet. Finding places where he could improve upon their past work might make for a better product, but it would tell him what he needed to know about his colleagues, and at this stage and with these high stakes, that might be more important than anything.

He only decided to take a break when his stomach told him it was time for lunch. He'd never been much of a cook, so the toaster pop-up he'd had for breakfast was convenient, but not nourishing. One of his neighbors had mentioned a place to eat that sounded good—Biaggi's Ristorante. He'd be willing to bet a place with a name like that made wonderful fettuccini, one of his favorite Italian meals. He looked up the location online and saw that it was within walking distance. He'd take a break, work out the kinks in his back and neck by walking, and enjoy the fresh air in the process.

James set his computer for sleep mode, figuring he could get back to work more quickly when he returned if he didn't have to reboot and reopen everything, and headed out the front door and down the street. One thing he'd noticed about his co-workers at Tech Aide was that they weren't on any kind of unified schedule. Oh sure, they all seemed to arrive about the same time in the morning, and thanks to Marie's rules they all left the building around the same time at the end of the day, but breaks and lunch time were up to each of them as individuals. He only hoped he didn't run into anyone he knew at the restaurant, or at least not anyone like Tiara or Val. Especially not Val.

A quick glance told him he was in luck. Biaggi's wasn't very busy on this Tuesday afternoon, probably because the official lunch hour was long over. A young waiter named Paul seated him right away at a single table next to a window. Picking up the menu, James scanned over the listings and found what he wanted—Farfalle Alfredo. With grilled chicken and Italian cured bacon, the pasta dish sounded like the balanced meal his body needed if he hoped to think clearly the rest of the day. A good meal like this at lunch would also take him off the hook for coming up with something elaborate when it came to dinner.

He'd learned to live simply during his time spent in France, and those habits had carried him through at home as well. People always asked him how he'd ever been able to stand American-made food again after living abroad, but

220

honestly he hadn't found anything he ate—even in Paris—as satisfying as the food he was enjoying now. Sure, the French pastries had been good, but you couldn't live on sugar alone, and the other things he had eaten there had never satisfied his hunger.

Just like none of the French women had satisfied his soul.

He topped off his meal with a Crème Brulee, something he had learned to love on his mission. If he was going to splurge, he might as well make it good.

After all that food, and since he'd never before been to The Gateway, James decided to walk through the plaza and check out the stores, just in case a mood to shop ever hit him. He doubted it ever would, but it was best to be prepared.

He found most of the men's apparel stores too trendy for his liking. At his age—mid-thirties—he had long outgrown the need to look like a celebrity fashion designer had fitted him for a magazine shoot. The sporting goods shops and specialty stores—*Called to Surf?* Catchy, but no—didn't appeal to the computer-geek within him, and the sunglasses on display didn't seem worth the money the shop was asking.

James made a mental note that he might come back and spend an entire lunchtime checking out the displays at the Clark Planetarium, but he hurried past the bridal store and Victoria's Secret like they would suddenly reach out to strike him.

He didn't know why, but something near the entrance to Bath & Body Works caught his eye. A dark brown piece of fat leather peeked from beneath the wire legs of a garbage receptacle. Normally he wouldn't have stopped for such a trivial thing, but a strange feeling hit him that this was important. He used the toe of his shoe to dislodge the thing, moving it a little father out into the open. A wallet. He stooped and picked it up. A plain brown woman's wallet.

Could it be?

Jenny had lost her wallet days ago. And it had been stolen. There was no reason for it to be lying here, out in the open. Except, it really hadn't been out in the open. This wallet had been shoved under a trash bin, and he had been prompted to find it. *No*, James told himself. This wasn't a prompting. It wasn't anything. But wouldn't it be something if he knew the owner of this wallet, and it was Jenny?

He was reluctant to actually open the wallet at first. What if it was hers? What if it wasn't? She had been so upset today when she left the office, and if he'd been lucky enough to locate her missing wallet, maybe she would start to feel good again about something. It was obvious she'd not been happy in the days since he'd come to Tech Aide, and even though he didn't know if something he had done had been part of the cause, he hated to see her unhappy.

He didn't know why, but her unhappiness bothered him.

Well, there was only one way to find out. James opened

222

the wallet and rifled through the papers inside. A couple of receipts. No cash and a definite emptiness of credit cards. Those were probably the two things a thief would be looking for. A driver's license was tucked inside an almost hidden pocket. He took a deep breath and turned the card over where he could read the name on the other side. It was just as he'd hoped—her smiling photo was there to prove the wallet again had an owner.

And the owner was someone he wanted to find and return it to at this very moment.

James dropped the wallet into his pocket, and whistled a chorus of "It's a Small World" as he returned to his office. He didn't know if she'd make it back into Tech Aide today, but he would be there ready and waiting with his surprise if she did. And if she didn't, there was always tomorrow.

***

Jenny arrived at Tamlyn and Randy's apartment in record time. She couldn't believe how much time she had wasted by heading first to the hospital. She had heard Randy tell her they would meet at the apartment, but that information just hadn't registered. She tried to blame it on the problem with her computer, the upsetting phone conversations with her mother, but neither of them was the problem. She even tried to blame it on James Cox, but he had been too helpful today for her to honestly lay the blame on him.

But what about last night?

223

It was true. The near accident had been upsetting and the sleeplessness all were reasons to blame James, but not her mistake about where she was supposed to be going. *Maybe I'm getting as forgetful as my mother.* Jenny hoped not. Her mom's forgetfulness had been upsetting enough, and she certainly didn't want to go there in her life, not ever.

Jenny parked her car in front of the complex where Tamlyn and Randy had lived since they had married. The place was filled with young couples, and the sounds of happy children or crying babies always seemed to permeate the air when Jenny stopped by to visit. She was sure those sounds today would be upsetting to Tamlyn after losing a baby of her own.

Would Tamlyn ever be able to get pregnant again? Although she wasn't quite Jenny's age, it was still harder for women to carry a full term pregnancy as they themselves got older. *I hope she will be willing to try again someday,* Jenny thought as she tapped on the correct apartment door.

It only took a minute for the door to open. Randy stood inside, his hair disheveled, and from the look of his face, he had been crying. "Jenny, thanks for coming. I didn't know who to call, and Tamlyn asked for you since her mom is too far away. It's been a really tough day for her."

"For you both," Jenny said. She stepped forward and gave Randy a little hug. "Is there something you need, or should I go to Tamlyn?"

Randy scrubbed a hand across the rough stubbles on his

chin. "I could use a few minutes to shower and shave." He looked at the wrinkled clothes he wore. "And a change of clothes. Can you go in with her while I take care of those things?"

"Of course," Jenny said. "Take whatever time you need."

Randy nodded and headed toward the bathroom down the hall. Jenny knew where their bedroom was because Tamlyn had given her the grand tour when the couple had moved in. She hesitated at the doorway only long enough to take a deep breath and let the whisper of a prayer pass though her mind.

"Tamlyn?" Jenny leaned into the room, not sure if her friend was awake or asleep.

A matching sigh came from the bed, where Tamlyn lay on her side, facing away from the doorway, and Jenny. "I lost the baby." Her words were a statement of fact, making them sound empty, hollow. "It was a little girl. We named her Heather."

"Heather is a beautiful name," Jenny said, moving closer to the bed so she could rest her hand on Tamlyn's arm for a minute. "I am so, so sorry."

A sob broke from Tamlyn's throat, her body shaking as she began to cry. "She was perfect," she said, as she rolled onto her other side, allowing Jenny to see her face for the first time. "She was perfect on the outside, but the doctors said there were problems on the inside, problems we

225

couldn't possibly have known about before she was born. And it's all my fault!"

Tamlyn's comment caught Jenny off-guard for a half second. *Why would she feel responsible for the miscarriage?* But before Jenny could say anything, Tamlyn continued.

"I was her mother. I gave her that body. If there was something wrong with it, then it's my fault." Her crying grew worse.

"You know that's not true," Jenny said, stroking her hand now against the top of Tamlyn's head, the same way her mother used to stroke hers when she was upset. "These things just happen. It's not your fault, and it's not her fault. It just happened."

"Things don't *just* happen," Tamlyn said. She started to sit up, and if to make her point stronger, more believable. "Do you think God did this to punish me for something I did?"

"No," Jenny said. "God wouldn't do this to punish you. And you can't let Heather's passing punish you either." She took a minute to think about her words before she continued. She didn't want to make Tamlyn's sorrow worse by anything she said. "She was perfect. You told me so yourself. And you'll always be able to remember her like that."

Tamlyn's sobs had reduced to a series of catches in her breath, and her eyes followed Jenny's as she continued to stroke her hair. "Do you think so?"

"I know so. You're her mother. You'll never forget this darling baby, no matter what."

"Oh, Jenny." The tears came again, but this time they were gentle, quieter, and they flowed from Tamlyn's eyes and onto her cheeks. "I will love her forever."

"I know." Jenny had a hard time keeping her own brimming tears from spilling. Of course she was sad for her friend, and the loss of her baby, but the tears Jenny had suddenly experienced were not for them, not really.

Thoughts of her own mother had filled her heart when she spoke of never forgetting. Her mother who was always forgetting. Her mother who she feared losing. *My mother who has always loved me.* Jenny promised that she would stop by her mother's on her way home from Tamlyn's, and that she would spend a little more time being there for her. When she was a child, her mother would have sacrificed everything to make Jenny happy. Maybe it was time she did the same thing in reverse for her mother.

I love you, Mom. Jenny couldn't believe how much she suddenly felt the true depth of that love. She supposed it had been too easy to forget as she grew up and tackled her own life, but now was the time. She hoped her mother could forgive her short-comings as a daughter. She had meant to take better care of her after her father passed, and as her mother's health deteriorated.

Yes, she needed to spend more time with her mother, so she wouldn't forget again.

And she needed to do it now, before it was too late.

227

***

In the short time that had passed since Stephie had taken the pregnancy test, she'd already begun to notice things were different about her body. A little snugness in the waistband of her pants, tenderness where she hadn't noticed any before, and she cried over everything. A romance novel she'd brought with her from Utah and had never read before made her cry—of course that could be because her own romance wasn't working out so well. Powdered sugar spilled on the counter, and she cried. That was just plain silly in her opinion. One look at Rachel's baby, and she cried, thinking about her own baby that so far only she and Rachel knew about.

Stephie knew she needed to tell Phil about the pregnancy. She would need new clothes, and she wasn't sure if their insurance would cover the necessary doctor visits and the hospital. That alone could break her budget for years to come. She wasn't sure how she would pay for anything, especially since Phil kept tight control over all of their money.

Tonight, she thought. *I'll tell him tonight*. But she'd been making that same promise to herself for too many nights already, and most of them he'd not come home. What if Phil came in grouchy, or he told her to leave him alone because he had a test to study for, or he was only there long enough to change his clothes and he was out the door again, leaving her one more night of spending the time alone?

228

The worst nights of their marriage though were when he came right into the house and flipped on the switch and his gaming started. He wouldn't even say hello to her on those nights, and she had learned quickly not to try. If he was playing his games, he expected a supply of soda, maybe a sandwich and some chips, then the rest of the time she'd better stay out of his way. And for the next several hours it was just Phil and whoever he was playing against as he screamed at the system and fought against scantily clad avatar-women and anger-raged men as they rushed across the screen into rooms and out of them again, from one battlement to another. She had tried at first to make sense of it all, but there wasn't anything sensible about it.

She hadn't gone all out with a meal since the fiasco of trying one of his favorite Mom-recipes. It didn't matter. Stephie felt like she was going to throw up everything anyway, and since Phil's appearances had stopped she didn't want to spend the time, or the money, fixing him something he likely wouldn't be there to eat.

When the door opened at six, she could hardly believe it. Phil was actually home, and at a decent time for dinner. She mentally did an inventory of what was in the house, something quick and easy that she could fix, if the gaming system didn't immediately come on.

"Stephie? You home?"

She moved to the door of the bedroom, poking her head out just far enough that Phil could see. "Hi, honey."

229

She thought it was always a little better to try for the honey, avoiding the vinegar, and see if her pleasant mood could take him there as well.

"What's for dinner?" Phil flopped onto the couch, but he didn't reach for the remote, at least not yet.

Generic. Keep it generic. "Umm, I didn't know what time you'd be coming home," she said as she crossed the room and headed for the kitchen. "I can put together something for you though. Just give me a sec." So far his mood seemed to be okay, and she didn't want to upset him by asking where he had been for the past few days.

"No hurry. I already had a bite to eat with the guys after the test." He rolled his head around on his neck, like he was trying to work out the kinks he often got when he sat in one place too long.

She hesitated, halfway in the kitchen yet still in the living room. The apartment was so small that moving from one room to another was only a few steps. It was a good thing because of the pain in her swollen ankles. She knew she needed to get in to see the doctor, but not yet. The baby would wait a few more days.

"So, you had a test?" She hoped trying to make small talk would at least head the two of them toward actually communicating again. If things were starting to be right between them then she could tell him about the baby.

But what would he think? Would he be mad because she hadn't told him before now? She could always pretend

230

she hadn't known. Honestly, she hadn't until the day before he'd left. Men didn't know much about these things. He'd believe her. She could convince him.

She hesitated a moment before moving farther into the living room. Did she dare sit down on the couch next to him? She needed to get off her feet, and the couch was the only piece of furniture in the room where she could sit.

As though he sensed her hesitation, Phil scooted over and patted the now-open spot beside him. "Come sit a minute. I really don't need to eat anything. Unless you're hungry?"

"No, I'm fine," Stephie said. She hadn't been planning to eat anything anyway, and this was the most friendly Phil had been in weeks. She didn't want to ruin the moment, or spoil the possible opportunity to share her news. She battled herself for a minute about how she could tell him, but finally decided to start slowly. "I haven't been feeling too well lately."

"Um, sorry I hadn't noticed," he said. He closed his eyes and yawned.

Stephie fought back the sarcastic remark that first came to mind. *You haven't noticed because you haven't been around,* forcing herself to accept what he said as a form of apology, though she doubted that's the way he meant it.

"I guess you've been busy, studying," she said, giving him the out he needed for her reasoning, even if he didn't know it was important.

231

"Yeah, finals week has already begun."

She calculated the number of weeks since the term had started, almost identical to the number of weeks she had been pregnant. Another term and she'd nearly be a mother. It hardly seemed possible. She had to tell him, and she had to tell him now.

"Phil."

He opened his eyes and looked right at her, but Stephie couldn't read his eyes well enough to guess how he'd take her news. "I have something to tell you."

"Okay," he said. "Spit it out."

"I'm . . . I'm . . ." She fought the sudden overwhelming sense of nervousness that washed through her, telling her to let it go, to move, to get out of there, but she couldn't. Phil was her husband, the father of their baby. She had to let him know. *He's been so pleasant tonight. Everything will work out.* She thought it odd that she was having this instant battle with herself, and she wasn't sure where it had come from, but she knew the feeling was wrong. It *had* to be. "I'm pregnant."

Instantly Phil leapt from the couch beside her. The feeling had been right! The anger clouded over his face and deep into his eyes. Stephie tried to get up, terrified he was going to hit her. *Where had this man come from?*

"What do you mean you're pregnant?"

"I'm . . . I'm expecting a baby, our baby, your baby!" At last she stood, using the arm of the couch to support her, the water building up around her ankles making her shins hurt like they were expanding much farther than her skin could hold.

"I don't believe you. Don't you mean it belongs to that guy you spent the night with?"

"David? No, no! He had a baby with Rachel," Stephie said, trying to make sense of his accusation. Why would Phil think she'd be having a baby with their next door neighbor? Especially when he was obviously so in love with his own wife and their sweet little son. "I don't know where you came up with that crazy idea . . ."

"*Crazy?*"

She realized the second he slapped her that she had called him crazy, and why he reacted so sharply. His own mother had suffered from depression, but most people thought she was crazy. Phil had always been reactive when anyone said it, and now the same word was being used about him. Stephie wished she could take it back, but Phil had truly *gone* crazy. He was storming through the house, yelling and swearing, calling her every name she had ever imagined.

He'd moved into their bedroom and she heard glass breaking—the picture frame with their wedding photo?—and things crashing. *What will he do to me when he comes back?* She had to get out of the apartment, and there was only one place to go.

She hated to bring Rachel and David into the middle of this, but it was her only option. She shut the door softly, hoping Phil didn't realize she was gone, at least until she was inside again and safe. She tapped lightly on the door to the Leeds' apartment. Almost immediately David opened the door.

"Can I come in?" Stephie asked, nearly pushing past him before he could respond. "Phil is mad, and I'm not safe in our apartment."

David shut the door and locked it behind her.

The minute she saw Rachel, her new baby cradled in her arms, Stephie burst into tears.

"Stephie! What's wrong?" Rachel took hold of her arm and drew her to the couch and its matching chair.

She sat on the couch and Rachel took the chair, where she set into a natural rocking motion to comfort the baby in her arms. David slipped out of the room and into the bedroom, but close enough in case Phil did something that could bring them harm.

"Are you okay?" Rachel asked.

The young mother's voice sounded so much like she remembered her own mother when she was a child in need of some comfort. Was the tone a natural part of motherhood? Was it something she too would discover once her own baby was born? Just the thought of her baby made the tears pour from her eyes.

Rachel leaned forward, touched her free hand against Stephie's knee. "Did he . . . did he hurt you?"

Had Phil's slap left a mark? She remembered an earlier

234

conversation where Rachel had thought Phil had been hitting her all along, abusing her physically instead of mentally like she had been describing.

"No, he hasn't touched me." It was a lie, and she knew it, but she didn't want to bring David rushing out from the bedroom, ready to defend her. He needed to watch out for Rachel and their baby, not the next door neighbor whose husband had suddenly gone crazy.

"But there's something terribly wrong. Please tell me. I'm your friend, and maybe I can help," Rachel said. The look on her face said she wasn't sure Stephie was telling her everything.

Stephie didn't know how a girl so young—was she even yet twenty?—could be of much help, but keeping her worries all bottled inside was not going to help her a single bit. "I told him. I told Phil I'm expecting his baby. And he . . . he's been horrible to me since we moved to Boston." She shook her head, knowing that wasn't quite true. "Actually, he's been horrible almost since our marriage began. I can't bring a baby into the middle of the mess I've gotten myself into."

The look of horror that crossed Rachel's face told Stephie that once again she had said something that this innocent girl didn't understand.

"You wouldn't . . . you wouldn't . . ." Rachel cradled her baby closer to her chest. "You wouldn't, you know, go to a doctor and . . . you wouldn't get rid of the baby, would you?"

"No, no, no," she hurried to assure Rachel that wasn't at all what she meant. Her tears were gone now as she tried to explain. "For days I couldn't bring myself to tell him. I didn't want him to know. He has shown me time and again that he doesn't really love me. I'm not sure why he decided to marry me. He might as well be married to his gaming system for all the attention he pays me compared to it. And it's only gotten worse since we came to Boston. And then when I came home the morning after you gave birth to Jeffrey . . ." Stephie reached out her finger to rub against the tiny bootie and toes that poked from the blanket Rachel had wrapped around him. "Phil tried to accuse me of spending the night with David, and not as a friend. And he brought it up again tonight."

"Oh! That would never happen," Rachel said. "How could he think such a terrible thing about someone like David, who he has never met? Or how could he think it about his wife?"

Stephie sat back against the couch again. "That's my question. How could the man I fell in love with turn into the man I'm now married to? They don't seem to have anything in common. Phil has removed a mask I didn't know he was wearing."

"What do you think you're going to do?" Rachel asked, her voice soft enough not to wake the baby, yet intense, as though she were really concerned about what Stephie might do.

"I'm not sure, but I was thinking about calling my mother."

Rachel giggled. "I'm *so* sorry. I don't mean to seem rude, but that's the last thing I thought you might say, and it seems sort of out of place for someone as experienced in life as you to want to call her mother, don't you think?"

It took Stephie a moment to consider, but she agreed. "I guess it does sound sort of silly, and a little out of place." She allowed herself a giggle, relieving a little of the tension she had been feeling as she had poured out her worries, even if it didn't change the situation or the anger she had just been facing from her husband. "But, I still think it's what I want to do. Phil has taken all of our money. I don't have a credit card or a dime to my name. I don't think I can stay here, not with him, not with the man he's become, and I want to go home. I want to go back to Utah, and my mother, and the women who are my best friends." Suddenly concerned she might have hurt Rachel's feelings when she mentioned her friends, she added, "Not that you aren't one of my friends, because you are, but these are the women who have known me since I was just a kid. We have a special bonding, you know?"

"I understand," Rachel said. "I have friends of my own who will always be my best friends, no matter how far away we live from each other. And as for my mom, I'd give anything if she could be here with me right now." A wave of sorrow passed over Rachel's face. "It's been two years that she's been gone."

237

"I'm so sorry, Rachel," Stephie said. "I didn't know." She suddenly realized she didn't know much of anything, not about Rachel, not about marriage and babies, and certainly not about taking care of herself and the husband she thought she had married. "I wish there were something I could do."

"You've already done so much to help me," Rachel assured her. "Now it's time for me to do something for you." She got up from the chair, and walked into the bedroom. When she returned, the baby was gone from her arms, but she held out a cell phone to Stephie. "Call her."

Stephie stared at the phone for a moment, fighting back the tears that had once again come into her eyes. She couldn't believe how kind and loving this girl was to a near-stranger like her.

"She will want to hear from you," Rachel added. "I'll step into the other room so you can have privacy while you talk. Take as long as you need. Phil and I are here for you."

"Thank you," she choked out before Rachel left the room. It felt good to know that someone cared. But she also knew there was someone else who cared about her even more.

She looked at the keypad for a minute, rehearsing her mom's number twice in her mind before she had the strength to make her fingers duplicate the numbers against the keypad for real. The phone rang once-twice-three times.

"Hello?"

She'd know that voice anywhere, even if it had been a long time. "Mom? It's Stephie."

"Stephie, my baby." The warmth in her voice flew across the miles between them.

"Mom, I need to come home."

23

Jenny was true to the promise she made herself at Tamlyn's. It was important that she spend more time with her mother, and now was as good a time as any. She knew she'd be of no use to anyone at the office, and the way she had snapped at everyone on her way out, they would likely be relived not to see her again for the rest of the day. She had managed to offend just about everyone anyway. *Why have I suddenly become so mean?*

The pressures of work had only grown worse with the new project and the organization of the new team, but Jenny was used to that. Rick liked to move them around from project to project, thinking that new blood and new combinations would get their ideas flowing more rapidly. She wasn't sure she agreed even under normal circumstances, but with the addition of James Cox as her team leader, this time was even more disturbing than ever before. *What on earth is a guy like that doing working in a cubicle, for heaven's sakes!* Something had definitely gone wrong in her part of the technological world.

But having someone like James there could do Jenny some good as well. She loved competition almost as much as she loved being the best. Maybe she'd let herself get a little complacent, not really offering a challenge to herself to improve her position at Tech Aide. Well, now was as good a time as any—actually, now was the *best* time to show just what she was made of when it came to the development of new technology. She'd show James, and she'd show Rick and Marie as well. Jenny wanted that promotion, and starting first thing in the morning, she'd make sure that happened.

She pulled into the familiar driveway of the home her mom had been living in the past several years. An oversized garbage bin sat at the end of the driveway. *I wonder if Mom can even move that thing?* She parked the car, thinking she'd help her mom out by putting the can next to the garage door, but then thought better of it. What if her mom hurt herself trying to move the can back down the drive on collection day? *Better ask her how she's been handling it before I make things harder for her.*

Jenny rang the bell at the front door, chastising herself for not ever asking her mom for a key. A wave of fears—coming to the house and finding her mother had fallen and was stuck on the floor for days with nothing to eat and no water to drink—rushed through her mind. Another thing she needed to take care of right away. *I have been a crummy daughter!*

Several minutes passed, with Jenny pushing the tab a second time to make sure she heard the sound of the doorbell ringing inside the house, but at last the lace curtain at the window beside the door moved almost imperceptibly and Jenny knew her mother was checking to see who was standing at the door outside.

"It's me, Mom. Jenny," she called, hoping her cheery voice would allay her mother's fears of opening the door when it was starting to get dark. Jenny hadn't really thought about how late it was when she left Tamlyn and Randy's apartment, but now that she stood in the deepening shadows of the early evening that stretched across her mother's porch, she could see why her mother was being so cautious.

"Jenny?" Her mom's voice sounded feeble through the heavy glass next to the door.

"Yes, Mom. It's Jenny. Can I come it?"

She tried not to be impatient as her mom unlocked the series of deadbolts and the chain that kept her safely in. *Even if I had a key to the house, I'm not sure I could get in past all those locks.* At last the door cracked open just far enough for her mother to peek through, making certain it was really her daughter before opening the door the rest of the way.

"Oh, Jenny. It is you."

"Hi, Mom." She decided that keeping her voice cheery would be more assuring than letting the worry about her mom that suddenly hit her full force creep into her voice. "Can I come in?"

Mrs. Grant stepped away from the door, giving room for Jenny to pass through and into the perfectly-kept living room. Her mom had always been a perfectionist for details, something Jenny had not picked up in her own housekeeping skills, although she did expect perfection from herself when it came to her work. The end tables and coffee table looked freshly polished, the carpet had a pattern that indicated it had either been recently vacuumed or that no one had walked on it for days, and the air carried a faint whiff of Lysol, despite the automatic air freshener that spat out a shot of vanilla right as Jenny walked past. *Hope that stuff doesn't ruin my clothes.*

"What brings you by?" Mrs. Grant asked. She had sat down in her favorite chair, a rocker, the same one Jenny's parents had kept in the living room of their former house, the place where Jenny had been born.

"Nothing in particular," Jenny said, although that wasn't exactly true. Concern for her mom's safety and welfare, needing to touch base with her memories, even a healthy dose of guilt for not spending more time with her mother, who had to be as lonely as she was—all of those things mixed in together with the emptiness she had felt being with Tamlyn and discussing the loss of her baby. For her mom, the loneliness had to be worse. At least Jenny was in her office all day, surrounded by people who were friendly to her even though none of them were her best friends.

"Didn't you tell me that one of your friends is getting married?"

Her mother didn't always remember everything, but

243

Jenny wasn't surprised her mom jumped right to the question of marriage. "Yes, Mom. Lisbeth is getting married, and I'm her maid-of-honor."

"Oh, that's right. *Maid*-of-honor. Not *matron*."

Now what was that supposed to mean? Jenny wondered then the answer came to her own question. A matron-of-honor had to be married, and of course, she wasn't. *Thanks, Mom, for once again reminding me.* At least she hadn't said anything about Lisbeth being the last of her single friends.

"So what are you going to do now, since you don't have any other single girlfriends to spend time with?"

Zing! Mom always hit her mark. A weak smile seemed to satisfy her long enough for Jenny to change the subject. "How are you feeling?"

A great sigh came from her mother, but her voice sounded happy and cheerful. "I'm feeling just wonderful. I went to see Dr. Stevens the other day, and he said I'm in perfect shape. He asked about you."

"Dr. Stevens?" Jenny was confused. The only Dr. Stevens she knew was the one who had delivered her, the one she had gone to through most of her youth. But that Dr. Stevens had retired by the time she was in high school, and she thought he had passed away a year or so ago.

"Yes, you remember him, don't you dear? His office is a block off Main Street, right across from Dr. Myers, your dentist."

Dr. Myers hadn't been her dentist since she had moved

to Salt Lake. "Do you mean in Tooele?" If she thought that was Jenny's dentist then maybe her mother *was* talking about the doctor who had delivered her.

The look of shock on her mother's face showed her own confusion. "Of course I mean Tooele. Where else would I mean? Are you alright, Jenny? You've seemed confused lately."

Talk about the pot calling the kettle black, Jenny thought, using the words her mom had drilled into her head so many times in her childhood. If anyone was confused, it was her mother. And if she was so confused that she thought they were still living in Tooele, Jenny worried that something more serious than confusion could happen to her mom.

Does she still shop for herself? What if she gets lost downtown? Another raft of questions and concerns rushed through Jenny's mind. Perhaps leaving her mother alone simply wasn't safe, not anymore. She could wander off. She could accidently burn the house down. She could forget she had taken any kind of medicine and take too many pills.

Suddenly, being single was the least of Jenny's worries. She could live her entire life without the company of a man, but she would always feel guilty if she didn't take better care of the woman who had given her life. "Mom, I think we need to talk about what's happening with you."

"Me? Oh, nothing's happening with me," Mrs. Grant said. "I live a pretty simple life. I have my friends to help if I need anything, and I have nice people like you." Her mother reached out to pat Jenny's hand. "Now what did you say your name was again, dear?"

"What?" Jenny could not believe the question she had just heard. Was her mother serious? Had she forgotten who she was talking to? "Mom, it's me, your daughter, Jenny."

"Yes, I do have a daughter named Jenny. I don't see her very often though, I'm afraid." Mrs. Grant gave another great sigh.

Jenny wasn't sure what she should do first. Calling her brothers seemed important, but they lived too far away to be much good. It was obvious her mother didn't remember Dr. Evans, the man she was currently going to. Jenny had his number programmed into her cell, but it was after seven, and she was certain no one would be in that she could talk to. She'd do that first thing in the morning and see if she could bring her mother in for a check-up appointment. She didn't think the hospital could do anything about her mother's apparent confusion, so she ruled that out of the question for the time being.

"Have you had anything to eat, Mom?" Her mother had always been notorious for solving all of Jenny's childhood problems by serving a good meal or a treat. "Let's go into the kitchen and see what we can find." Jenny stood and her mother did the same.

Several minutes later, Mrs. Grant sat at the table, finishing the last bite of a sandwich Jenny had made. "That was good. Where did you learn to cook?"

"No cooking there, Mom, but I learned it from you."

Her mother furrowed her brow for a second, as though she was trying to piece together the information she had just heard. "Well, in any case, thank you."

"Should we see about getting you ready for bed?" Jenny knew her mother often went to bed early, probably for lack of anything better to do, and she needed to call her brothers and possibly a neighbor or two since she didn't want to leave her mother alone.

"That sounds nice," her mom said. She pulled a napkin from the rack in the center of the table, wiped her mouth, and carried her plate and glass to the sink.

It only took a few minutes before Mrs. Grant was changed, tucked into bed, and nodding off to sleep. Jenny placed a kiss on her mother's forehead—just like her mom did when Jenny was a child. "Night, Mom. See you in the morning."

Jenny had already decided she would spend the night, but she hoped she could find a neighbor or someone who could take over for her while she went to work, if that was necessary. She picked up the cell and dialed the number for her oldest brother, wondering what suggestions he would have for her.

***

Jenny hadn't returned to the office the rest of the day, but that was okay with James. He patted the leg of his trousers where her wallet was awaiting its safe return to her

247

purse. Just knowing he had it in his possession had given him a reason to smile every time he thought of it. Jenny Grant was a beautiful woman, and even if marriage was not a top priority for him anytime soon, he certainly didn't mind giving a beautiful woman a reason to smile. A smile on her face might change the snippy mood she'd been in most of the time since they'd met. But the moments when she was not mad—that afternoon in the rain and when he fixed her internet connection—she actually knew how to be quite pleasant, and it kept him intrigued.

He could hardly wait to get to work the next morning and give the wallet to her. He knew she'd be ecstatic to have it returned. Even if she'd already taken care of all the replacements and having her accounts transferred, he imagined the peace of mind of knowing the actual wallet had been found and returned would do much to make her happy, and she seemed to have reasons why she needed to be happy.

He wondered if something serious was happening that upset her. Something had made her rush from the office earlier. She'd been abrupt with both him and with Gretchen as she left through the front door, but he guessed that wasn't any different from the way she had treated Tiara. *Is she always rude to people?* James dismissed the thought as soon as he had it. He already knew that wasn't true. Most of the people he'd met so far in the office seemed to like her, and several had told him that something was going on with

248

Jenny lately that had her upset. Whatever it was, that was probably affecting her mood. He hoped it didn't also affect her work.

James needed Jenny to think clearly, to come up with ideas outside of the box, and to have the programming skills to carry them through. He knew what he wanted to see happen in this project, but he also knew that strong team members could take an idea and improve upon it, removing many of the potential bugs before they became huge problems, and he had the stinking suspicion that Jenny was just the one to sort out any problem she might be faced with, even the ones that were setting her mood.

A ding from his cell phone caught his attention away from the notepad lying before him. *Val.* Not someone he really wanted to talk to, but maybe she had come up with an idea that would help further the project.

"Interested in meeting somewhere for a drink?"

Persistent, James thought. "Sorry. I'm busy," he keyed into the phone.

He reached into his pocket and pulled out Jenny's wallet. *But I wouldn't be too busy for you.* Another text message and once again he picked up the phone.

"Another time then." It was Val, and as far as James was concerned, there would never be another time. He hoped the woman didn't become too annoying. He hated to consider what Rick would think of him if he asked to have her removed from his team. *Yeah, I just can't work with her. All she wants to do is chase me home.*

249

He hoped that wasn't what it appeared he'd tried to do when he found himself following Jenny home. *Stalker dude,* James chastised himself, then got back to work on the project, the same thing he'd do any other night. Or at least any other night before he'd met Jenny.

24

By the next morning, Jenny felt better about her mother. Her brothers had agreed that things were changing with their mother's health and that Jenny should not be forced to handle it alone. Richard promised to drive up on Friday and assess the situation with her, considering that they might need to help their mom make a move into a care facility, if that was necessary.

Jenny had called her mother's doctor's office as soon as she woke up and had an appointment set for 8:30, lucky to get a spot opened by a last-minute cancellation of another patient. And now they were on their way to see him.

Her mother seemed a little better this morning, less confused, and at least she recognized her as her daughter. Jenny had been spooked last night when her mom didn't seem to know her, but today her mom remembered not only her name, but everything about her and her situation.

"How are things coming along for Lisbeth's wedding?"

"All is going well," Jenny said. "I helped her pick out the gowns for the bridesmaids, and they are actually not awful."

"That's nice, dear," her mother said. "You already own too many of the ugly ones, and what do you do with them afterwards? I mean, you don't have a reason to wear them on a date or anything, right?"

Jenny inwardly groaned. "Right, Mom. Not the kind of dress you'd wear on a date." *If I had a date . . .*

Once this wedding was over, Jenny promised herself she'd work on decluttering her apartment, and the set of bridesmaid dresses that just hung there, taking up space, would be the first things to go. Would anyone buy something like that in a yard sale? Not that she had a yard to sell anything in, but it was the principle of the thing. She had paid good money for those dresses, and a few dollars back into her savings account would be wonderful. But even if she couldn't sell them, those awful reminders that she was always the bridesmaid needed to go!

"What kind of flowers is she having?" Mrs. Grant sat with her hands folded in her lap, as though already waiting in the doctor's office for her turn.

"Hawaiian orchids," Jenny said. "The man at The Rose Shop has them on order. I think I told you he said to tell you hello."

"Hmm. That's nice," her mother said, but Jenny had the feeling her mom still didn't remember him.

They pulled into a parking spot right outside the clinic door, the first time she'd ever been able to get a spot that was close when she came to these visits with her mother. Luck was on her side. "We're here, Mom."

Mrs. Grant again wore an expression that said she was

252

confused, and Jenny almost hoped that were true. Maybe this visit would let the doctor see why she and her brothers were more worried about their mom's condition than the doctor seemed to be on previous check-ups. Jenny ran around to the other side of the car and helped her mother out, not wanting her to feel unsteady on her feet. Who knew what other symptoms her mom could be having, or what the confusion might cause?

"Thank you," Mrs. Grant said, as she took a second to adjust her skirt and top before the two of them stepped inside.

Jenny signed the register to let the office staff know her mom was here, verified that the contact and insurance information was all still correct, and sat to wait until the two of them were called. Because it was so early in the day, the doctor shouldn't be too far behind, and apparently he wasn't, because less than three minutes later, they were called into the door that led to an examination room.

"How are you feeling today, Mrs. Grant?" the nursing technician asked as she read the numbers on the scale, popped a thermometer probe in and out of the patient's ear, and started to walk toward the room at the end of the hall.

"Oh, I'm fine, just fine," Jenny's mom said. "Except, that I'm not sure why I am here."

"We want to make sure that you stay fine," the technician said. She opened a door and indicated that Mrs. Grant and Jenny should go inside. "Let's see how your blood pressure is today."

Jenny mentally kicked herself for never taking the time to figure out what the numbers meant when the test was done and the technician repeated them back to her. She'd ask the doctor once he came in, Jenny promised herself.

"The doctor will be here in a few minutes," the technician assured them. "Let me know if you need anything." And she was gone.

Jenny's mother sat almost stoically as she waited, and Jenny couldn't think of much to say. She had a million questions running through her mind, prepared to ask the doctor, but she knew she wouldn't have much time, and she didn't want to upset her mother. She might have to call and schedule an appointment to talk with him when her mother was safely back at home. *Whatever it takes to care for my mom.*

"How are you doing, Mrs. Grant?" The doctor swooped into the room and immediately went to the sink to wash his hands, then turned around toward Jenny and her mother once the drying was done. "I hear you've been keeping your daughter up at nights, worried that you might not be doing so great."

"Me? Oh, I'm fine, doctor," Jenny's mother said. "Fit as a fiddle as my mother used to say."

Jenny couldn't help smiling. She knew all those same sayings because it was exactly what her mother would say, and now she was blaming it all on Jenny's grandma.

The doctor continued with his examination, tossing a few questions out to her mother and to Jenny along the way. "Having any trouble sleeping?"

254

"Mom called me at lunch the other day, asking me why it was so bright out at midnight."

"I did no such thing," her mother said, almost indignant that Jenny would say it.

"And last evening she didn't know my name," Jenny added.

"Umm . . ." the doctor said as he used the ophthalmoscope to look into the pupils of her mother's eyes.

"Any headaches?"

Jenny didn't know the answer to this one, so she assumed her mother was telling the truth when she said, "Nothing too bad. Not like those migraines I used to have when I was younger."

"How often?" He was running his fingers along the sides of her mother's neck, letting the tips probe into the sagging skin like he was searching for something buried within.

"Every other day or so, I'd guess."

"Okay . . . other episodes of forgetfulness?"

Jenny jumped in before her mother could deny this symptom was happening all the time. "She doesn't remember a lot of the people and things I try to talk to her about, but sometimes she knows exactly what she's talking about, remembering situations and events I wish she'd forget."

The doctor laughed. "Sounds like a lot of moms I meet."

255

Jenny felt like she'd been chastised, but the feeling soon passed when the doctor said, "I'd like to run some tests. Is it possible to take her over to the hospital this morning? I'd like some blood drawn and maybe an EKG, to see what's going on inside that pretty head of yours, Mrs. Grant." He pressed his finger briefly against her mother's forehead in several places.

"Any idea how long it will take?" Jenny asked. "I do need to go to work today."

"It's early," the doctor said. "They should be able to get her right in. Maybe an hour and a half? Maybe less."

"Okay," Jenny said. "I can do that." The doctor tapped a few notes into the keyboard of his computer before turning back to the two of them. "Okay, the order will be waiting for you at the front desk. I'll give you a call, Miss Grant, when I see the results."

"Do you think it's safe to leave her home alone?" Jenny asked. She hated to say it in front of her mother, but there was no other option and Jenny needed to know.

"I'd see if someone can stay with her, at least until I get the results and we decide on a line of defense," Dr. Evans said.

"I'm not a baby," Mrs. Grant said, indignant.

"Of course not, Mrs. Grant, and there's really nothing too great to worry about, but I figure we want to be safe rather than sorry." He turned and spoke directly to Jenny, his voice hushed as though he didn't want her mother to

256

hear. "If she's often confused, it's hard to say what kind of scrapes she might get herself into. Having someone with her will at least keep her from straying away, or doing anything that could alter her safety." He stood and walked toward the door. "You'll hear back from me soon."

"Thanks, doctor," Jenny said, as she and her mother stepped from the room and down the hallway. A trip to the hospital for some tests, and hopefully they would all know soon what was really going on.

***

Stephie felt better after her talk with her mother, but she still worried about what she would say to Phil if she saw him before she was packed and ready to go to the airport. She had spent the night on the couch at Rachel's apartment, and having David so close made her feel safer, but every noise she heard in the hall the entire night through had made her jump. As far as she could guess, Phil had no idea where she had gone. *Does he care?*

At least he hadn't come knocking on the Leeds' apartment door. If Stephie understood her husband–the new and unimproved version of him, at least–he had probably calmed down, and spent the rest of the evening with his gaming paddle in hand. *At least he has the internet and his online gaming buddies to keep him company.* Stephie allowed a little snort to come from her nose, a mild commentary on the man she once thought she had known.

Phil had two more days of finals yet before he'd be done

257

with this semester's courses, at least he'd mentioned them to her last night, so she had anticipated he would leave by eight to either study or take another exam. At 7:30 she heard their apartment door slam. She was right, Phil was gone and the apartment had been silent when she carefully opened the door.

She was worried that she might find the place in a complete mess. His anger had been great, and it was possible he'd want to take it out on her somehow, even if that meant destroying her things, since he couldn't do anything to actually touch her because she wasn't around. Relief washed over her though when she found the place exactly like she had left it the night before. A couple of extra dishes were in the sink, an opened loaf of bread lay on the counter, and, of course, the bed hadn't been made.

Since she didn't know exactly how long Phil would be gone—did he have work today, or just a test?—she wanted to pack quickly. Her suitcases were stored under the bed, so she pulled them out and laid them open on the bed. She didn't have many clothes. There hadn't been room for all of her things when they moved from Utah, and Phil certainly hadn't given her any money to buy new. A quick search through the drawers and the bathroom counter allowed her to collect her personal items. She didn't care about anything in the rest of the apartment. There was nothing that couldn't be replaced.

In less than a half an hour, she was back at Rachel's

place. "I'm ready whenever you can take me," she said to David as he carried her luggage inside the door. "My plane leaves at two, but I don't mind waiting at the airport." She stopped talking long enough to chew her bottom lip for a second. "Besides, I don't want to be anywhere around when Phil comes home. He could cause trouble for you."

"I can handle . . ." David started before Stephie cut him off.

"No, I mean it. He's not the man I used to know," she said. "He never would have hit me, and now. . ." She held her hand against the place where Phil had slapped her the night before. "Now I just don't know."

Rachel moved toward her, arms outstretched, ready to pull Stephie into a hug. "I'll miss you, you know."

"And I'll miss you, too, but I've got to go." She touched her own abdomen. "It's better for both of us." She knew that Rachel understood, but she doubted that David knew anything about the baby of her own that Stephie was now carrying.

Rachel gave her one more hug, and Stephie squeezed her back. "Thanks for everything you've done."

"I only wish it could have been more," Rachel said.

She noticed tears forming in the younger woman's eyes. "I've gotta go." She picked up one of her suitcases, while David took the other. "Take care of that sweet baby."

"And you take care of yours," Rachel said. She gave a little wave as Stephie pulled the door closed between them

259

and hurried to follow David into the elevator and down into the parking garage.

She gave a sigh of relief when she made it into the car, the luggage actually fitting the trunk better than she had fit into the back seat on their way to the hospital, and they left the structure without her seeing Phil or their car anywhere. The drive to the airport was quiet—she couldn't think of anything to say to David, and the whole thing felt like an escape scene from a movie anyway. She was surprised that it didn't seem to take too long either.

David pulled up to the drop-off site and jumped from the car. He had opened the trunk and removed both suitcases by the time she had gotten to the back of the car to help him. "Here, Stephie," he said, shoving a wad of bills toward her. "You'll need this for tips, and you might get hungry. Rachel told me how Phil has been treating you, and how he controlled all the money."

Now it was Stephie's turn to have tears well up in her eyes. "You don't have to. You just had a new baby. I know you both need the money."

"Rachel would kill me if I didn't give this to you," David said, "and I'd be pretty disappointed in myself as well. I think it's horrible the way he's been treating you."

"I can't say how much your help has me-meant to me," Stephie said, a catch in her throat.

"Do you need me to stick around, stay with you until your plane leaves?"

"No, I'll be fine. My mother said the ticket would be waiting at the gate, and she will meet me in Salt Lake. Everything is taken care of."

"Leave it to mothers," David said. He reached forward and gave her an unexpected hug.

"Yeah, leave it to mothers," Stephie said as he jumped into the car, checked the line of oncoming traffic, and slowly pulled into the lane and drove away.

***

Jenny and her mother had already been at the hospital for half an hour and there was no sign of progress from the check-in desk at the lab where her mother was waiting to have her blood drawn. Another day Jenny would be late for work, but this time the reason was crucial. She had to know why her mother was having so much trouble remembering things lately. Jenny hadn't heard about the headaches before their visit to the doctor, so that too became a worry. Was it possible her mom had had a stroke? Was her brain bleeding at this very moment?

"Ooh, I'm feeling a little dizzy." Mrs. Grant covered both eyes with her hands, and shook her head slightly.

"Mom? Mom, are you alright?" Jenny heard the panic in her own voice. Maybe her mother really *was* having a stroke.

"I'll be fine," her mother said, trying to be reassuring. "Just a little headache, and I'm kind of dizzy."

"What do you need me to do for you?" *Me? I'm in a hospital for heaven's sake!* "Let me see if I can find a nurse."

261

Jenny started to move away from where her mother was seated then she thought better of it. What if her mom couldn't hold herself up and fell? If she hit the linoleum, she could do some serious harm to her head, or any part of her fragile body.

Not sure what else to do, Jenny called out, "Could I get some help out here? Hello?"

A nurse—or maybe a technician—poked his head from the deep recesses of the lab room.

"My mother, she's suddenly gotten dizzy, and she's complaining of a headache. Can you come out and help me find out what's wrong with her?"

In response, the man disappeared.

Great! Jenny started to call out a little louder, but a woman, probably about her own age, ploughed toward the two of them from inside the lab's back room. "Let's see what we have here."

She motioned for Jenny to move out of her way, and Jenny was glad to do so if it meant someone was paying attention to helping her mom.

"I know this seat is a little short, but let's see if we can get you lying down." The woman helped Jenny's mother swivel in the chair and lowered her head onto the arm rest before lifting her feet onto the other end of the couch.

"Oh, I feel better already," Mrs. Grant said.

"When's the last time you had something to eat, young lady?"

262

Jenny thought at first the nurse was talking to her then she realized the question had been directed toward her mother. Suddenly she realized how much time had passed since they had grabbed a piece of toast together this morning. It had been hours, and neither one of them had eaten anything since then. No wonder she was hungry, and she'd bet her mother was feeling the same thing, and her mother didn't have as much body fat to live off of as Jenny did herself.

"You stay right here for just a minute, and I'll get something for you," the woman said.

True to her word, she was back in a flash with a container of orange juice. "Just what the doctor ordered." She helped Jenny's mom sit up enough to use the straw that poked from the container. "Not too fast, now."

Jenny guessed the woman was worried that her mother might choke if she drank too quickly, especially since she was only halfway sitting up.

"Can you drink just a little more?" the woman asked when Mrs. Grant seemed to be finished. "We need to get your blood sugar stabilized and orange juice is the quickest way to do that."

"Maybe a sip," Mrs. Grant said, taking another tiny pull of juice into the straw.

"Is there anything I can do?" Jenny asked, suddenly feeling useless and uncertain how she could do more in so many aspects of her mother's life to make things better.

In response, she held out her hand toward her daughter. "I'd like to sit up now. Can you help me?"

"Of course," Jenny said. She stepped forward, taking her mother's hand. *When did Mom's skin become so pale?* "Don't move too quickly. We don't want you dizzy again." *Why is she suddenly looking so old?*

"Are you doing okay?" the lab technician asked.

"I think so," Mrs. Grant said. "I guess I needed something to eat." She looked toward Jenny with that teasing look Jenny recognized so well. "*You* need to take better care of me."

But the words struck Jenny a little too close to home. They echoed the exact feelings she'd been having herself, and the guilt that washed through her was palpable. She *did* need to take better care of her mom, before her mother wasn't able to take care of herself. *Unless that time has already come.* Jenny felt worse than ever.

"That's why we're here at the hospital, Mom." Jenny wondered if this was something they should have done a long time ago, but the doctor hadn't really seen any signs of trouble before now. A simple case of old-age forgetfulness setting on.

"Let's see if we can find a vein and get those tests started," the technician said, offering her hand to support Mrs. Grant as she stood and walked into the lab. Jenny's mother took a seat in the chair specially designed for ease in taking the blood samples for the lab work.

Jenny followed along behind, wishing she could be with her mother all the time, but knowing her job, the project, and a possible promotion would make that dream impossible. Maybe it was a good thing Jenny didn't have a husband and a family. She was already stressed how to balance the obligations she currently had, and now she needed to add more time to spend with her mom. Jenny didn't see how there could ever be time enough to do it all.

25

Once again, Jenny was late for work, but this time had an excellent reason. After dropping her mom off at the house, and making sure she had lunch prepared, a book in case she felt like reading, and knew where the TV remote was located, Jenny had talked on the phone with Mrs. Trumble, her mom's neighbor and good friend, and the woman promised to be over within the hour to stay with her mom.

Jenny had rushed home to shower and change before heading to the office. Just because she'd gotten into the habit of casually dressing for work—probably because that's the way the younger employees came—didn't mean that she didn't understand the value of dressing to look like a professional. Jenny needed to look like she was headed to the top of the corporate ladder.

Gretchen noticed the first thing. "Wow! Are you headed to a party on Wall Street?"

The tailored skirt and blouse, along with the suit jacket and spiked heels helped distribute her weight so she looked slimmer than when she came to work in a pair of slacks and a stretchy top. Those things had brought her comfort, but this suit was intended to bring her power. If she was going to pull off a promotion for herself, despite the fact her team leader had programmed one of the most successful pieces of software by any competitor in her field, Jenny needed her clothes to scream *Winner!*

And the low whistle she got from Nathan Greenly on her way toward her cubicle showed her that her plan was already working. *Slime!* She sauntered past him, letting her hips sway just a touch. Nothing like the blatant way Val did when she wanted to capture someone's attention, but just enough.

Jenny already felt like she was on top of the world, and headed toward the top of Tech Aide. So many times she had heard from self-help gurus to "Act as if . . ." Well, she was going to use that advice now. She would act as if she had already been promoted, had been given a substantial bonus, and had a new office with a real door, one she could use when she needed to shut the world out—or at least to keep James Cox from coming around to ask about her mother.

Today, however, that door wasn't attached to her office space, and Jenny didn't want to waste the efforts she had made to look like a professional businesswoman, so she took her time as she neared the opening to the cubicle right across the aisle, hoping James would at least see her before she stepped into her own space and got to work.

She was in luck. Jenny let her eyes drift toward James and his computer at the same moment he decided to look up. She could almost feel his eyes drink her in as the moment in time seemed to stop, the same way the one between Christopher and Jane had during *Somewhere in Time*. A beat, then two. Jenny lowered her lashes then raised them again, but the whole process felt like she was standing in a pool of water that was somehow deeper than her entire body, covering her from head to foot.

Locked in his gaze, she slowly shook her head, her hair moving like the mane on an L'Oreal commercial model. It was silly, she knew, but she wanted the moment to go on and on.

"Jenny!"

The spell was broken. Tiara had come running up the aisle toward her, almost failing to stop in time from crashing into her.

"Jenny! You look beautiful! What's happened to you?" Tiara was fanning herself, as though the exertion, or perhaps excitement, of the moment had been too much.

One more glance toward James, and Jenny knew the connection had passed. He had put his head down, one hand covering the eye nearest her, as he seemed once again absorbed in the depths of his computer screen and the work he was doing.

"Nothing, Tiara," Jenny said, as she stepped into her cubicle. "Nothing at all."

She gave a half smile toward the older woman, a wiggle of her fingers that said "Catch you later," and settled into her desk, ready to do some work of her own.

***

Jeez! What was that all about? James didn't know what had hit him, but Jenny Grant had suddenly become more than attractive. She was *hot!* Her choice of clothes today was enough to make a woman look beautiful, but with Jenny it was much more than that. The change in her demeanor brought a softness to her face that James hadn't really seen before, and she was gorgeous, no, *stunning* was a better word. Jenny suddenly looked confident, self-assured. She was the cougar on the prowl, the lioness ready to take on the predators of her world. And James couldn't help but think that Jenny Grant was ready to take him down.

Somehow he was convinced that he wouldn't mind.

He hadn't been able to pull his eyes from her, and only Tiara Brinkerhoff had saved him from making a total fool of himself. He wondered how Jenny would feel about going out today for lunch with him? *Or dinner tonight? Or a movie?* Or spend the rest of his life with him? He shook his head, hoping to clear the crazy thoughts that were swirling around inside it, but the motion didn't seem to be working.

He simply had to get control of himself. He had work to do, and a team meeting was already planned for just prior to lunch. Jenny would find the memo as soon as she logged onto her computer. He could make it; he could stay focused for another hour—that's all he needed, one more hour until the meeting would start. One more hour and he could see her again.

This is stupid! But James didn't believe it. He really was looking forward to seeing Jenny again. No matter how rude she had been to him, and to others in the office, he didn't believe that the woman he had just seen was anything like the shrew he had seen in the office. Jenny simply had too many things on her mind. She was worried about her mother and whatever else had upset her on the phone yesterday. And the project. Maybe she really needed the bonus, or the promotion. Maybe he would make sure she got it. James knew *he* certainly didn't need it.

He had always been a careful planner when it came to money. The same when it came to developing software. He used to think he was the same way when it came to meeting women and occasionally dating, but right now he felt like all that planning had flown right out the window, and his heart was heading in the opposite direction—right across the hall and into Jenny's office.

***

Jenny knew she had put things off long enough. It was time to make her apologies, all around the office. She'd start with Gretchen. The receptionist should be the easiest, and getting that one out of the way would help Jenny warm up to making the others. She debated for only a moment before deciding in person was better than making a phone call, so she set her computer screen to sleep mode, and walked the short distance to Gretchen's desk.

"Hi." Jenny stood a couple of feet away from the desk,

not wanting to seem too intrusive into Gretchen's workspace. She wasn't sure how the younger woman was feeling about her right now, although she had been friendly when Jenny entered the office a little while before.

"Hi," Gretchen said, her gum popping once before her face turned bright red. She reached a slender finger into her mouth and snagged the offending item, pulling it out and dropping it into the wastebasket beside her. "Sorry."

"No, I'm sorry," Jenny said. "I came over to apologize . . ."

"You don't need to apologize," Gretchen said. "I'm the one who's at fault. Marie has told me a hundred times there was to be no gum chewing while I was on the phone, and I couldn't make myself listen to her. I don't know why; I just couldn't make myself remember. And I guess I still can't remember, but I'm trying. I know it's an annoying habit, and I've really got to stop it, but you were right. If Marie hears about me popping my gum while I'm talking to a client, it's all over. No more job for me, and it will be all my fault."

Jenny felt sorry for the young woman. She really was a good receptionist. She made sure everyone got their messages, took care of lots of little things around the place, and was always friendly. "No, Gretchen, don't be so hard on yourself. We all have habits we wish we could break." *And I have about a million of them, including spouting my mouth off at people without stopping to think.*

271

"I promise I'll try to do better," Gretchen said.

Jenny held out her hand to shake. "And if you'll forgive me, I'll try to be nicer."

Gretchen chuckled then held out her own hand. "Deal."

"Deal," Jenny said. "Now do you know where I can find Tiara? I owe her an apology as well, a really big one."

***

It wasn't hard to find Tiara. She loved to hang out in the break room and could often be found there, stale donut in hand and either a cup of strong coffee or a carton of chocolate milk from the vending machine to wash it down. *It's no wonder she carries a few extra pounds. No, I'm the one with a few extra pounds.* Tiara was just plain overweight.

Jenny made herself stop right there. She had come to find Tiara so she could apologize, not to find reasons to tear her down, even if it were only in her own mind and her opinion of the woman. Tiara had always been nice to Jenny—too nice perhaps as she tried to find Jenny a husband—but too often her meaning well was not enough to cover the hurt she had inadvertently caused. Jenny wanted a husband, but not at the cost of having Tiara try to run her love life. *What love life?*

Taking a deep breath in an effort to steel herself against the deluge of mean thoughts that were running through her mind, Jenny stepped into the break room where Tiara was having what some might think was a meaningful

272

conversation with Val, but was really just another talk about finding a match with the perfect man. It seemed to Jenny that was all the two of them ever talked about, so she had no reason to expect anything different now.

"Hey girls," Jenny said, hoping to break the ice and possibly end their conversation.

"Look at *you*," Val said the minute she looked at Jenny. "Trying to impress somebody?"

Jenny offered a smile that could easily have been mistaken for a smirk. She'd have to work on that. "Not in the way you're thinking." *That's for sure.*

"Good," Val said, "because James is mine."

Jenny wondered what has possessed Val to think such a thing. First of all, she *wasn't* interested—*or am I?* And secondly, James wasn't interested in Val, so she would be no competition. The way he had tried to avoid Val every time she scooted closer to him, batting her eyes and flipping her hair, proved he wasn't interested. But Jenny didn't care, or at least that's what she was trying to tell herself. Yet a part of her wondered if that was just not true. "Well, you can have him." Her heart gave a funny beat when she said it, but Jenny refused to let on to Val the thoughts she'd been having about him.

Val gave a satisfied nod of her head before returning to her bottled water, and seemed to forget her earlier conversation with Tiara. It was obvious Val wanted to get to know James better, and she was definitely dressed the part of

273

the flirt today. Tight skirt, a couple of buttons too low opened against her full-sized chest, stiletto heels to challenge Jenny's own—yes, Val was on the prowl. Jenny had seen her there before—Rick, Isaac, and even Nathan had all found a spot in the middle of her radar for a time, with only Nathan taking the bait and dating Val for a couple of months. But he saw through her eventually and let the relationship cool. Now he hardly spoke to Val, choosing instead to give his compliments and attention to Jenny, despite the fact she'd told him too many times that she wasn't interested. *I wonder what Val did to make him drop her? I'd love to give it a try.* Actually, she knew she wouldn't. There was no time she ever wanted to be like Val Paterson.

Jenny had dropped a few coins into the vending machine and selected the button for a carton of orange juice. *Time to drop a few pounds.* The carton came crashing through the hole at the bottom of the delivery mechanism and she picked it up, carefully opening the top so the juice didn't splash all over her. "So, Tiara . . ." Jenny began then immediately stopped. She didn't want to offer her apology in front of Val, not when there were so many ways that woman could possibly use her words against her. She'd seen Val do it before, drop a bit of information into another conversation at the time it could be the most damaging. "Can you stop by my desk when you're done with your break?"

Safe. That's what Jenny hoped her request would come off.

274

"Sure. I'd be glad to," Tiara said, but Jenny suspected from the sudden flush on the woman's face she felt anything but glad to do so.

"See you in a few then," Jenny said. She tipped her carton of juice at the two women, took a final drink and dropped the empty carton into the trash on her way out of the break room.

***

James caught a glimpse of Jenny as she returned to her office. He couldn't get over how different she looked today. He had always thought she was attractive, but the business suit added a level of class she hadn't displayed before in her more casual attire. And the glint of determination he had noticed in her eyes made her all the more attractive to him. He liked a woman who knew where she was going in life and who wasn't afraid to take the necessary steps to get there. This was a Jenny Grant that he was happy to be working with.

But her new demeanor also meant he had better be ready for their team meeting. James was sure she was going to give him a challenge when it came to developing the new software, and although he was happy to take suggestions from a talented woman, he also didn't want to look like a fool by not having fresh ideas and suggestions of his own, especially when Rick had appointed him as the team chair.

James looked at the stacks of scattered notes and hand-sketched diagrams he had spread across his desk. He chuckled a little at himself. *You'd think a computer geek like me would use a program to keep track of his notes.* He found the specific sheets he was looking for, opened the browser on his desktop, and waited for the Info-Systems program to load. It only took a few seconds, but James knew even loading would be faster once the new systems they were developing were in place. He typed in his password—*butter churn*, an idea he'd stolen from former Silicon Valley bigwig, Jeff Savage—and found the spot where he had coded the day before. Glancing once again at his notes, he nodded approval for his own work, then set the papers down and started typing. He knew exactly what he needed to do to make this program work.

If only life were so simple. He'd love to understand people in the same way he understood computer language. And the more he thought about her, the more he wished he understood Jenny.

***

Jenny hated the way she had snapped at Tiara last week, but the thing she hated even more was having to apologize. Ever since she was a little girl she had found it hard to look someone in the eye and say she was sorry for some wrong she had done. There had been way too many of those times. Jenny knew what her problem was—she had a terrible habit of opening her mouth and inserting her foot. Her mom had always said she was too blunt, and her dad had silently agreed, even though she was more like him than he'd probably like to admit.

276

She'd gotten though the apology with Gretchen, and Tiara should stop by her office any minute. Jenny was ready. She'd practiced all the way from her apartment to the Tech Aide offices. Saying the words to Gretchen had actually felt kind of good, and although she still didn't want Tiara trying to poke her nose into Jenny's version of a love-life—non-existent—she hoped she could at least put the woman's smile back on her face.

Jenny knew there really was a third apology she owed as well. James Cox had to be innocent. There was no other way he could face her each day at work. If he'd really been the one to steal her wallet, Jenny was certain she would somehow know, some action or comment from him would let her know. The look he had given her when she came into the building did not even hint at guilt—well, maybe for looking at her the way he did. Jenny had felt a rush of warmth across her cheeks and into her very soul when he had given her a second look and a slow smile formed on his lips. He'd been impressed by the way she looked, and she couldn't wait to blow him away with the ideas she had come up with for their joint project.

She might not ever have a romantic relationship with the man, but she was ready to challenge him all the same, even if it was just with her brain.

A soft knock on the door told Jenny that Tiara had arrived, and the second apology was ready to begin.

***

277

Tiara and Jenny entered the meeting room, chatting like old friends. James was pleased to see them getting along. Women could be difficult enough to work with at times, especially since he found more often than not that he didn't understand them. But to have to work with a group of three women—one who hated him, one who was afraid to speak for fear of getting her head snapped off, and one who threw herself at him every time he was in the room—made for miserable working conditions. At least Tiara looked like she was no longer afraid of Jenny, and he could handle someone like Val if he really needed to. He hoped she would eventually take the hint on her own though. Confrontation in the middle of a project would not be a good thing.

"Good morning, ladies," James said as all three of them gathered in the room he had claimed as their official meeting room.

"Good morning," Tiara said, as she took a seat across the table from where James stood. She carried a notepad and ballpoint, both of which she placed on the table before her, lining them up into what she considered the most optimal position for her to use. The top sheet was clean. Not a good sign in James's opinion as he was hoping that all members of the team would come filled with ideas.

Val didn't hesitate and joined him on the same side of the table, slipping into the seat to his right, and patting the chair right next to her. "Have a seat, James. No need to stand and be uncomfortable while meeting with a group as small as ours.

James didn't have much choice in the matter. Val was right, and he couldn't very well move away from the chair he had chosen before she had entered the room. He tried not to sigh as he sat, pulling the chair just slightly to his left as he did so, hoping to give himself a little breathing room away from the woman. Her perfume this morning was heavy, and her skirt too short, both distractions James hoped he could overlook entirely.

Jenny took a seat at the table as well, but hers was in a much more neutral location, as far away from James as was physically possible. She sat straight, as though her suit jacket concealed a brace against her spine. Her posture didn't make her look uncomfortable, but determined, and James knew she wanted this project to work more than anything. He supposed he did too, but he wished the sparkle in her eyes had something to do with being there with him, instead of the promotion and raise they had each been offered if their team developed the best ideas.

"Let's see what everyone has come up with since yesterday's meeting," James said, hoping each of them had something new to bring to the table, so to speak. "Just a quick overview. Val, can we start with you?"

Val suddenly seemed unsure of herself. James had never seen her fidget in the short time he had known her, at least not in the way she was now. Her eyes trained on the empty desk in front of her, and her crossed leg bouncing until her high heel looked as though it would fall off at any moment.

"Umm," she started." I uh . . . I'm not sure I have anything new. I've been working with the frame you gave us, but the platform is entirely new to me, and I . . . um."

Entirely new? James hadn't expected the frame to be a problem for anybody. He had started with Tech Aide's own platform in an effort to keep the programming language simple, at least at the start. How did Val not understand the platform which was so closely linked to the framework? He'd better check to see if that had caused any problems for the other two women, but before he could say anything, Jenny chimed in.

"It's *our* platform, Val, the one we've been using now for over a year. What do you mean it's entirely new to you?"

"Well . . . uh . . . I guess . . ." Val stammered, unable to come up with any reasoning that supported either her claim, or contradicted what Jenny had said.

"I'll tell you what her problem is," Tiara said, jumping in. "Val hasn't done any programming for the past year. Isn't that right?" She looked straight at Val, but the smile she wore was not friendly. "I told you there would come a day when you were caught in that game."

Oh, no! This was *not* what James wanted to be hearing. Val wasn't familiar at all with the programming platform, and Tiara seemed to have known about it for some time. Had she been covering for Val's ineptitude?

"I . . . I wanted to learn it," Val said, her voice breaking for a minute. "Nathan promised he would help me, but we

280

just never . . . never got around to it." She suddenly stood and pushed her chair away from the table. "I need to go. I'm sorry."

Tiara rocked back into a more comfortable position in her seat. "I warned her that hanging out with Nathan Greenly would never bring her any good, but she knew better. I wanted her to date that guy from marketing, but she insisted she needed to spend her extra time with Nathan, learning the new programs. Well, as you both can see, that didn't work out quite the way she promised. Sorry for the interruption," Tiara said. "Go on. Time to get back to the purpose of the meeting."

James was dumbfounded, and one look toward Jenny told him he was not the only one who felt that way. Jenny's mouth was hanging open, and the calm resolve she had shown since her arrival seemed more than shaken. Tiara, on the other hand, seemed stronger than she had been since the first day when she had approached him, claiming that she had found for him the perfect woman—Jenny. What a relief that it wasn't Val that she had intended to introduce him to. A woman like her had no place in the life of a guy like him. Maybe he was glad she was gone. There was a possibility that some actual work could be done.

"Okay, Tiara," James began. "How about if you share with us what you have come up with."

He totally wasn't expecting the presentation she delivered over the next fifteen minutes. Without a note on her pad,

Tiara delivered answers to questions James had but had not yet shared, explanations for the inner working relationships of a variety of platforms, and improvements they needed to make on the one used by Tech Aide. She also anticipated the questions that both he and Jenny were sure to have as to the feasibility of her concept of the new program.

"Wow!" James said when she was finished. "That's amazing. How did you come up with all of that, and so fast?"

Tiara looked pleased with herself. "It's just what a great programmer knows how to do."

"Then let me congratulate you," he said. "You had an amazing presentation there, don't you agree, Jenny?"

Once again, Jenny looked thunderstruck. "Um, yeah." She looked at the notes she had on the table before her. The ideas she had formulated between all the chaos in her life didn't seem so great compared to Tiara's. "I'm not sure what else I can add, at least at this point. I might need another few hours to think it all through."

James felt exactly the same way, but he still wanted to appear to be in charge of this project, despite Tiara's display of knowledge and ambition. "How about if we call another meeting for later this afternoon? Take an early lunch break, mull over the suggestions Tiara has given us, and meet back here at . . ." He glanced at his watch for a moment. "Let's say around three."

"Sounds good," Tiara said. "I'm game for an early lunch."

James couldn't stop himself from thinking, *I'd bet you are*. She stood, gave a nod of her head to each of the people still sitting at the table then waddled from the room. Jenny sat, still looking a little shell-shocked, but James had already formulated his plan before he came to work that morning.

"Care to go out together for a light lunch?" He kept his voice even, not allowing the fear she would lash into him to creep into his tone.

"Lunch?" Jenny shook her head, but he was certain it was only to clear her thoughts, not to refuse his offer.

"I'm buying," James said. He touched the pocket of his pants to make sure not only that his wallet was still there, but that Jenny's was too. "Biaggi's Ristorante sound good?"

"Wonderful," Jenny said.

The sparkle was back in her eyes, and James was sure that was good.

26

Jenny wasn't sure what had just happened, but she was now walking toward The Gateway and lunch at Biaggi's Ristorante with James Cox. Although she tried to convince herself it was nothing more than a business luncheon, she knew that wasn't true. James could have asked Tiara to come along, but he didn't, although her sudden change in behavior had likely thrown him too. *What had come over her?*

Tiara had never taken the lead in a presentation like that before, and Jenny couldn't remember the woman ever attacking another worker before either. Val had all but confirmed Tiara's accusations, but to put a co-worker on the spot was not in tune with Tiara's usual desire to help everyone, even if that was mostly in the field of getting married whether the person was interested in her matchmaking targets or not.

The thought of Tiara as matchmaker drew Jenny's attention back to James. He had been fairly quiet on their walk from Tech Aide. *Maybe he has regrets about inviting me.* But he'd been polite, walking on the street side of the sidewalk, touching her elbow to guide her across the street when the light had changed, and now that they had reached the restaurant, he held the door open so that she could enter first. *Such a gentleman.*

It was nearly lunchtime so the place was packed, but a party of two was easier to place than many of the groups that were clustered around the entryway. Several clusters of people stood outside in the plaza, window shopping or talking, their purpose evidenced by the reservations indicators they held, waiting for the red light to go off signaling their table was ready.

"Right this way," the waiter said to James, indicating that he and Jenny should follow.

"Smells wonderful," James said, looking right at Jenny and giving her a big smile.

Her heart did a little flip, and Jenny wondered only for a moment if her body was trying to tell her something. She passed it off as nerves. After all, it had been ages since she'd been on a date, and business lunch or not, she was being seated at a favorite restaurant with a man she couldn't help but find attractive. And one she still needed to apologize to for treating so rudely when she thought he'd been the one to steal her wallet at this very location.

"Thank you again for inviting me," Jenny said. "This is one of my favorite places."

"I can *smell* why," James said. He chuckled at his own joke, and Jenny smiled to let him know she approved.

"Will this do?" the waiter said as he stopped in front of a table for two.

"Jenny?" James said, as though asking for her approval. The seat was in a cozy spot, close to a window that looked

285

onto the center plaza of the mall, yet not too far into the depths of the restaurant.

"This will be great," she said. The waiter pulled out her chair, but James stepped into his place to scoot it in as Jenny took a seat. *Mom would certainly like his manners.*

James hurried to his seat and took the menus from the waiter. "Give us a few minutes, if you please," he said.

The waiter nodded, but said, "I'll be right back with water for you."

"Thanks," Jenny said, as he walked away. "I already know what I want. Farfalle Alfredo." As soon as the selection was out of her mouth, she started to worry. *What if James thinks it's too expensive?* She had almost not ordered it for herself the other day because she always considered it too spendy, and he had mentioned a *light* lunch.

"I love that myself," James said. "I think we'll make it two." He set his menu down and offered to place hers on the table as well. "Now if the waiter comes back soon . . ."

She noticed he had let the sentence fade off. *Is he hoping to get this lunch over with?* Jenny hoped that he wasn't having second thoughts about inviting her, but James still wore a smile on his face, although maybe he was a little nervous. For some reason, he kept touching his hand to the right pocket on his slacks, like he was checking for something. *Maybe he's worried about his wallet.* He knew this was where Jenny had lost hers, so maybe he didn't want the same thing to happen again.

286

"Everything okay?" she asked.

"Oh, um, yeah everything is fine," James said.

Before the conversation could precede any farther, the waiter—Paul, the same one who had waited on her the previous time she came—stepped to the edge of the table. "Terry asked me to take this table for him while he went on his break. What can I get for you?"

Jenny wondered if he recognized her, hoping maybe her wallet had turned up and he would make the connection long enough to return it to her. But Paul didn't seem to really look at either of them as they placed their orders, and he was gone before she could ask him if there had been any luck in having it show up. *Why fool myself? The guy who took the wallet was not the man sitting across from me now.* She was certain there was no way it could be James. He was too kind, despite her outbursts. Besides, she had cancelled everything and hoped she'd been in time to keep anyone from ruining her credit by charging up her cards.

A tap on the window next to their table startled her. Lisbeth had her nose pressed against the pane and her hands cupped the sides of her cheeks as she peered in directly at Jenny. Her mouth was moving, but Jenny couldn't understand a word that was being said.

"Friends of yours?" James asked.

"Yes, it's my friend Lisbeth and her fiancé, Gary." Jenny touched her ear, shook her head, and lifted her shoulders, hoping Lisbeth got the message that she couldn't understand

287

her. She must have, because suddenly the peeking form of Lisbeth grabbed hold of Gary's arm and was pulling him toward the entrance of the restaurant.

"Looks like we might have company," Jenny said. "Sorry."

"Not a problem," James said, although the look on his face didn't prove to her that he meant it. "I think I recognize Gary. Does he live in your apartment complex?"

"Yeah, he does." Jenny wasn't sure how that information would provide a connection for James, but she didn't have time to ask him because Lisbeth and Gary came to the table at that very moment.

"Jenny, I'm so glad I ran into you," Lisbeth said, a little out of breath from rushing from one side of the window to the other. "The dresses. The fittings. Did you call everyone and remind them to get scheduled?"

Crap! Jenny knew she had forgotten something in the chaos of Tamlyn losing the baby, and taking care of her mother. She wasn't being much of a help to Lisbeth. "I'm planning to take care of it this evening." *I'm a horrible maid-of-honor. How could I forget?*

Lisbeth's already pale face had blanched even more white than usual, if that were possible. "Did I wait too long to decide? Will there be enough time?"

I certainly hope so. "I'm sure we'll be fine," Jenny tried to assure her.

As though James could tell Jenny was in trouble, he

jumped into the conversation, standing to offer his hand to Gary. "I think we met a few days ago, in the parking lot of an apartment complex."

Jenny's heart leapt inside her breast. *My apartment complex. What was he doing there?* Was he really stalking her? She still hadn't asked James why he was following her home after work, but now she wasn't sure she wanted to know. Forget the lunch. Maybe she should just get out of here.

"That's right," Gary said. "You were looking for Jenny."

She thought even Gary's voice sounded like he had his suspicions as to James's intentions. *Am I being paranoid?*

"And I found her. Tech Aide had sent me over to pick her up when her car wasn't working," James said, "but I guess she got it running before I arrived, because she was long gone."

Relief passed through Jenny. There was a reason for him to be at her complex. He was sent to give her a ride. "The automobile service sent someone over," she started to explain then caught herself. That was why Gary had seen James on that morning, but what about when James almost crashed into her after work? There had been no problem with her car that day.

"Well, nice to meet you, formally," Gary said. "If you're a friend of Jenny's, then you're a friend of Lisbeth's and mine. Consider yourself invited to the wedding."

"Wedding?" Jenny caught the raised eyebrow James shot her way as he spoke.

289

"Yeah, we're getting married soon," Lisbeth said, the bubbly-voice the way it had been ever since Gary had given her the engagement ring. She gave a loving smile and lifted her eyes to look at him. "We'd love to have you come, wouldn't we, Jenny?"

"Huh?" Jenny couldn't stop the sound of surprise from her mouth. "To the wedding? To *your* wedding?" *Why had she phrased her question like that?* As if Jenny felt she was the one to decide. "I . . . I guess so, if he wants to come. James?"

***

If there was one thing James didn't like, it was going to a wedding, and this one was for a set of strangers at best. But he'd already decided he wanted to spend more time with Jenny, and if going to this wedding gave him the chance to do that then he was game.

"Sure. Why not?"

Jenny immediately looked like someone had just doused her with a bucket of ice cubes. *Guess that was the wrong answer.* James hoped he could convince her that everything would be alright, that he didn't have to go if she didn't want him to, but he'd wait until her friends left to have that conversation. No use getting everyone into an argument over whether the stranger came to the wedding or not.

"Then it's all settled," Lisbeth said. "Jenny maybe James can give you a ride."

James jumped in before Jenny had to. "We'll get the details all worked out. Don't worry." But she still looked

290

worried. Luckily, their meals arrived and the waiter busily started arranging their plates around the extra couple standing in the aisle.

"Guess we'd better go so the two of you can eat in peace," Gary said. "We've got lots of errands to run anyway." He offered his hand toward James. "Nice to see you again."

"Thanks. Same to you, and congratulations." James stifled the groan he felt inside at just saying the word. It always seemed so disingenuous.

Lisbeth sidled over to Jenny and gave her a hug. "Thanks for taking care of those dresses. Talk with you soon." She gave a little wave, and the two of them were on their way out the door.

"No problem," Jenny said to empty air, and James noticed she typed a note into her cell phone as soon as Lisbeth had turned away. Probably a note to herself to call the other bridesmaids.

"Shall we?" James said, and immediately dug into his food. He didn't look up at Jenny but sensed when she started to eat. He slowed down his pace, certain now that she wasn't planning to bolt from her seat and exit the place. He hadn't been too certain she wouldn't when he accepted the invitation to attend Lisbeth and Gary's wedding. A smile played at his lips as he thought about seeing Jenny in a gown perfect for a wedding attendant. If she looked hot today in her power-suit, he imagined she would be stunning in satin and lace.

After a few minutes of eating in silence, James knew he would have to do something to break the ice again and get their conversation restarted. Once more he touched the spot where Jenny's wallet lay. Satisfied, he decided a compliment was always a good way to make someone feel comfortable. "I meant to tell you earlier, that I really like your suit. It's very flattering."

"Th-thank you." Jenny pulled away from her half-finished meal and set her fork down.

He wasn't sure if he'd said the right thing, but he decided to plow forward, hoping something would bring her back to wearing that smile on her face he'd caught glimpses of since their earlier team meeting. "When you came into the office this morning, I thought 'Wow! There's a woman ready to take charge.'"

"I-I see." Jenny pushed her chair away from the table and tapped the screen of her phone.

The cell face lit up and James could see the time. 12:35. He'd have to act fast so they could have time to prepare before the second meeting—the one where they could recoup their thoughts—the one he had called for 3:00 p.m. He reached into his pocket and withdrew Jenny's wallet, just as he noticed she pulled even farther away from him, her face paling even more, if that were possible. *What's going on with her?*

***

Jenny felt a swirl of emotions raging through her. How had this happened? James was now coming to the wedding,

292

and with her? Why had Lisbeth assumed she wanted to have him there, let alone take her to the wedding? Did she think Jenny was desperate for a husband of her own and that lunch with a guy would lead to a quick engagement? She was embarrassed to look at him. Did James feel the same way? Why was he reaching his hand into his pocket? Why had he been touching that same pocket repeatedly ever since they had left Tech Aide? What did he have hidden inside? The crazy thoughts that came next terrified her. *Is he pulling a gun?*

The fear washed through her even as Jenny tried to calm herself. *Don't be stupid. This is James. He is safe. He's not here to hurt you.* Then she remembered her earlier thoughts. *Then why did he follow you to your apartment?* She tried to read what he was thinking by looking into his eyes. The smile on his face proved he was innocent. James was just a guy who worked with her in the office. She was in a public restaurant with him. She was safe.

He placed his hand on top of the table then slowly lifted it off, his smile growing even wider as he did so. The whole moment felt like it was moving in slow motion. She looked away from his face and down at his hand. Lying there in the spot where his hand had just lifted was her wallet.

Her response was unfiltered, like her mother had always warned her. "You *are* a thief!" she whispered. "*You* stole my wallet!" She grabbed the wallet from the table, and jumped out of her seat, heading for the exit and out the door before James could attempt to respond.

How could he have taken my wallet and pretended all this time? Why had I started to trust him? She swiped at the tears that formed in her eyes as she hurried across the mall and back toward her office.

***

What did I do now? James couldn't believe it. Once again Jenny Grant had accused him of being a thief. She had to know he didn't steal her wallet. Why else would he be the one to return it? "See if I ever do *you* another favor," he muttered under his breath. He wanted to shout it at her, but all he wanted to do now was get out of there. And never come back again.

He stormed toward the front of the restaurant, ready to leave when he realized that the waiter—Paul—was calling out after him. "Hey, what about your check?"

The check. Of course it had to be paid. James slowed down enough for Paul to catch up with him. He took the order form from Paul's hand, and tried to smile. "Thanks."

"She sure can be a hothead," Paul said. "She was furious the day that wallet went missing."

"Really?" James said, giving Paul a once-over, trying to decide if he had anything to do with the original disappearance.

"Yeah, she wasn't happy, even though I did something nice by returning the phone she left at the table," Paul said. "Seems to me she's got a nasty habit of losing things."

James relaxed a little. "I agree." *And the most recent thing*

294

she might have lost is me. He glanced around and realized no one was staring at him anymore then wondered if they ever really had been. He had been humiliated by Jenny's accusation, but it suddenly was obvious that no one else seemed to know anything about what she had said.

He wished he could say the same thing. *Damn her!* He'd done the right thing. He'd kept his eyes open for her lost wallet, a gesture of kindness, and by a stroke of fate he'd found it. And what did he get when he tried to return it? James headed back toward Tech Aide, not entirely certain he wanted to even step foot inside the place. But he was in the middle of an exciting project, and he was the head of the team. How would he be able to face Jenny?

The bigger question was would she be able to face him? Was it always going to be a battle between them? And could he continue to work with her when she seemed to always be accusing him? Just thinking about it was wearing James out. This was the reason he hated women.

That was a lie. He knew he didn't hate them, but he sure didn't understand them, and Jenny Grant was harder to understand than most of them he'd ever come by, but he still felt like there was a reason she had become a part of his life. He'd always been quick to forgive people, and Jenny had so much stress that he felt she was someone he needed to forgive. He only hoped she was willing to forget.

***

The walk through the terminal had physically tired

295

Stephie. The fight with Phil had already left her emotionally exhausted. She found the assigned gate for her flight to Salt Lake City and wedged herself into a seat. Although she wasn't that far along, Stephie had certainly noticed a gain in weight, especially in her own seat. The plane ride was going to be uncomfortable, but even more so, if she couldn't keep her mind focused on something other than her failed marriage. Despite the fact there was a baby involved, Stephie knew it was over. Phil's accusation had been too cutting, his selfishness too evident for her to imagine there would ever again be any room for her to put her trust in him.

Fool me once and all of that. Her mother had gone that route with her father and look where it had left them. No, Stephie was certain she would never turn back. As hard as life had been at home with just her mom, she knew it was better to raise her baby alone than to be with a man who cared more about his friends and gaming than he did about the two of them.

Time passed quickly and the two airline attendants who stood at the counter split up, one going to the gate and the other entering the walkway toward the plane. Stephie reached down and touched the handle of her carry-on, assuring herself it hadn't gone anywhere while she'd occupied herself thinking.

"Now boarding for Flight 262 to Salt Lake City," the attendant said into the handset. "We're ready to board First Class passengers."

Stephie's ticket would put her in the back of the plane, so she figured she'd be seated next. Back to front seemed to be the way most flights were loaded. She stood and pulled the long handle from her luggage, allowing her to walk while the suitcase rolled toward the line forming at the gate. The less weight she had to carry, the better.

From the number of people gathered in the waiting area, it seemed to Stephie the flight was going to be full. She wished it weren't. She would have loved to move to a set of seats where she could stretch out, getting her feet up once the plane was in flight, but it didn't look like there was going to be a chance for that to happen.

"We are now ready to board all passengers with boarding passes for rows thirty to forty-four," the attendant announced.

Several people moved along in the line with her as they slowly progressed forward. Stephie showed her ticket to the flight attendant, nodded at the woman's, "Have a nice flight," and entered the narrow hallway that led to the plane. She checked around to see if she knew anyone, although she thought herself silly for doing so. Just because the plane was flying her home to Salt Lake didn't mean she *should* know anybody.

The people who had boarded earlier seemed to be settled into their plush seats in first class. Many of them were already sipping on a drink and reading a book or a magazine. She was forced to close the handle on her bag and

297

carry it toward the back of the plane, trying not to bang into the seats along the way. Once she was into the empty seats, she didn't worry so much about hitting them, but carrying the bag was tiring all the same.

A man and a woman, who had four young children, arrived before her so Stephie had to wait to work her way past them, into the row behind where the six of them were getting situated. They had already used up all the overhead storage bins in their row on both sides of the aisle, and in Stephie's row as well it seemed. She hated to put her bag too far away. What if she needed something during the long flight? Deciding to wedge her carry-on into the space under the seat in front of her, she bent over just far enough to guide the bag between the metal runners, hoping she didn't do too much damage to the canvas sides of the bag. She smashed her shoulder bag and wedged it under the seat as well. When she righted herself, she was startled to see a man standing beside her, patiently waiting.

"Oh, excuse me," Stephie said. "I was just putting my bag . . ."

"Not a problem," the man said.

She thought he appeared to be about her age. Probably a businessman on his way home to a family, she decided.

"I have the seat beside you," he said, a warm smile lit up his face.

"Oh," Stephie said, knowing that wasn't much of an answer, but she suddenly didn't think she could find any

298

words to say. His bright blue eyes looked right at her, and that smile stayed on his face as she sat down with a thump in the too narrow seat.

True to his word, he slipped in beside her, leaning over just long enough to wedge his own bag into the storage space in front of him. There were only two seats on each side of the aisle in their row at the back of the plane.

Two of the kids in the three seats in front of them had already started to fight over who got to sit next to the window during the flight, and their mother didn't seem interested in doing anything to settle the problem.

Stephie gave a heavy sigh and rolled her eyes. *Guess I'd better get used to the behaviors of children.*

It was almost like the man seated beside her had read her mind, but not quite. "Good thing I like children."

"I was trying to remind myself I felt the same way," Stephie said, letting a chuckle add to her comment. "Do you have any?" She couldn't believe she let herself ask the question. It was almost like she was flirting. And here she was pregnant, and still married. Flirting was out of the question.

"I'm not married," the man said.

A surprising revelation. Stephie had been almost certain he would have been. He was the right age and everything. *Maybe for Jenny, but not for me.* After the past year with Phil, Stephie wasn't sure she ever wanted another man for herself, especially not a guy she happened to meet on a plane.

"My name is Gary," he said, holding out his hand for a businessman's shake. "Do you live in Utah?"

Stephie found herself a little flustered, but she reached for his hand. "Yes, yes I live in Salt Lake." She wasn't certain what was happening, but something told her that this plane ride wasn't going to be as terrible as she thought it would be. She wouldn't have to think about leaving Phil, and the way he had treated her. There were still nice men in the world, despite what he had turned out to be. Having a conversation with another guy as they traveled across the country might not be such a bad thing, letting her emotions rest before she started to worry about what Phil would do once he figured out she'd run away.

A few hours of peace was all she wanted then she would worry about getting out of her bad marriage, something she had to do if she wanted to have any kind of a life for herself and the coming baby.

27

Jenny was mortified. She had once again accused James of being a thief, when all he had done was return her wallet. She knew it was hers by the scratch next to the pocket, but still she checked inside, and there was her driver's license. Nothing else of value, but this was her wallet. The wallet that she was certain had been stolen, by a man who looked just like him. Just like James Cox.

But it wasn't him. She'd mentally fought that battle over a hundred times. She had to admit that with as nice as he'd been to her at work, and then inviting her to lunch, she didn't want it to be him. Weren't thieves supposed to be grimy and shady-looking characters? James didn't fit any stereotype she'd allowed herself to believe, but he had been sort of creepy when he followed her home from work. She'd never asked him about that, although she was curious as to what he'd been doing.

And now she was supposed to sit with him in a second team meeting. She could feel the embarrassment wash over her face. There was no way she was going to that meeting. Not now. Maybe not ever. *Except.* Jenny wanted that promotion. She wanted the raise. And she needed to prove herself if she wanted to even be in the running for either.

301

She had reached her cubicle and paced around the tiny square, wishing once again that she had an office with a door, a place she could hide from the reality of what she had said and from the person she had said it to, but like it or not, she saw him anyway. He only stopped briefly outside in the hall, but long enough for her to feel his eyes staring at her. She couldn't help it. She was drawn to return his gaze. His eyes were cold, but his face somehow questioning. She had to fight back the tears that threatened to overflow. In a second, he had turned away, and she did the same.

It couldn't have been him, Jenny thought. *If he were the thief, I wouldn't feel this way.* Jenny had suddenly known she was falling in love with him. There was no reason why, or maybe every reason in the world. It wasn't anything in particular that he'd done, but James Cox had somehow worked his way into her heart. He'd been kind and was fine about her being on his team. And what had she done? Accused him of terrible things. Embarrassed him not once, but twice. There was no way he would ever forgive her, and she knew he'd be right not to. Who had she become? She didn't used to be so mean. Did she? Was her attitude the reason why she didn't get asked on dates? Did guys avoid her because she might go off on them for no particular reason?

I have a reason, she tried to convince herself. But she knew she didn't. She was angry and frightened when her wallet had gone missing. She didn't even know if the dark-haired guy had taken it, or if she'd simply dropped it along the way. And just because she'd seen a dark-haired man and James happened to have dark hair didn't mean that he or anyone else was responsible for her misfortune. Yet she'd blamed him. And now he blamed her. Only *he* had the right to. She deserved it if James never forgave her, never spoke to her.

She still had to work with him on this project. More than another failed romance was at stake. This was her job, her fortune. And the problem was entirely her mistake. She flopped down in her chair, the seat leaning back too far and the wheels nearly propelling her across the room and onto the floor, but she caught herself in time. Whether he hated her or not, James seemed too much of the gentleman to ignore the commotion if she landed on the floor again.

The blank screen of her computer reflected her image back at her. *Who are you?* Jenny wasn't sure she liked the woman she was seeing. In the last few days she had yelled at Tiara, yelled at Gretchen, and yelled at James, accusing him of a crime *twice*. She had experienced bad feelings about her best friend getting married, been frustrated with her mother's forgetfulness, and stormed around like a bull in the proverbial china shop if anyone or anything got in her way.

For the first time in almost as long as she could remember, she had a date. Sure, it was only a lunch date and somewhat spur of the moment, but James had asked her out to lunch at her favorite place, and he had offered to pay for her meal. *Crap!* She banged the palm of her hand against her forehead a half dozen times. And even though she had walked out on him, she knew he was the kind of guy who would pay the bill and cover his promise anyway.

She needed to get out of her chair, walk across the hall that separated the two of them, and apologize, apologize for everything, for every mean word she had said, for her rudeness and her behavior. She owed him that much. But maybe she owed him the real reason too, but how could she ever tell him, 'I'm a jerk because the last of my single friends is getting married and I'm not even dating anyone, and it makes me mad and sad all at the same time, so I took it out on you'? There was no way she could tell him that. First he'd think she was crazy, and second none of it would make a difference. He'd still hate her for the embarrassment she had put him through.

Jenny knew she deserved it; she deserved to have him hate her. But she still wished he didn't have to. If only he could forgive her. If only they could make up.

If only he would kiss me.

There she went again, thinking thoughts that had no attachment to reality. *I'm getting as confused as my mother!* At least her mother didn't know what Jenny had been thinking about James. She'd never let that one go, hoping beyond hope to see her daughter married at long last, as though Jenny's wedding would make her own life complete.

Wedding. Lisbeth's wedding, and James was invited to

attend. With *her*. Jenny tried to brush the thought aside. There was no way he'd be going now, and especially not with her. There was no reason for him to attend a wedding for two complete strangers, and if he'd felt uncomfortable about it before, he certainly would feel uncomfortable now, after her repeated accusation. No, she'd have to face Lisbeth's wedding and reception alone, and that was okay.

What had happened to her resolve? *Or lame idea?* She'd made the decision to stay single the rest of her life. *Did she really mean it?* To stop thinking about men. *Right.* Yet here she was hoping and dreaming and wishing that she could have a relationship with James Cox, the man who would likely never speak with her again.

***

James didn't know how he felt about Jenny Grant anymore, as if he ever had. *Ignore her, maybe!* When he moved to Utah he'd had no intentions of looking for a woman to date, and the thought of finding a wife was so remote he had immediately dismissed it. Until he asked Jenny to go out to lunch with him. Their walk had been pleasant, and he was seeing a side to Jenny that he had expected was there all along, despite the false start they had had with her accusing him of stealing her wallet. *The same thing she accused me of today!*

Jenny was beautiful, but that was just the surface. She was smart too. James knew she was an asset to his development team, that she likely deserved a raise just for

305

putting up with their self-absorbed supervisor, and that when she was given a project she would stick with it until she had done the best she could do, then she would get to work and do some more. He couldn't understand why someone hadn't snatched her up and married her before now. Well, there was the problem with her snap judgments and controlling her anger, but James decided he would probably be pretty angry, too, if he'd been robbed like she had.

Plus, she seemed to be the sole caretaker for her mom, and if the indications he'd noticed were correct, her mom's health was deteriorating and that was likely another worry for Jenny. If James thought she could once and for all get over her notion that he was the one who took her wallet, then he was pretty sure he'd like to spend more time with her. Maybe he could even help lighten her load when it came to her mother. But the first hurdle would be to find a way to talk with her. Would she even come to the second team meeting they had scheduled at the top of the hour? Would she be too embarrassed? Or did she truly think he was the one responsible? He didn't see how she could, especially since she had all but apologized for thinking such things about him before. And now she had proof that he was innocent because he was the one to return the wallet.

James smacked himself in the forehead. *No wonder she thinks I stole it! I was the one to return it!* Only the thief knew where that wallet was hiding, at least from Jenny's

306

perspective. He hadn't had time to explain to her that he'd found the thing empty, but tucked under the trash can on the other side of the mall area, obviously emptied and thrown away on the day she lost it.

He reached into his pocket and pulled out his own wallet. He had been so angry when he left the table that he'd almost taken off without it. *Maybe that's how Jenny lost hers in the first place. Maybe there wasn't a thief at all, and she'd just thought there was. And then she thought it was me.*

Women! They could be so frustrating, yet so fragile. And for the oddest reasons, James felt like he needed to take care of this one, to protect her from the storm. *Is she why I was sent here? Has it been for Jenny all along?* He looked toward the ceiling panels in his office almost as though he expected one of them to slide open and an angel appear with an answer to his questions.

But no angel came. Instead he heard a tapping at his non-existent door.

"Mind if I come in?"

For a half-beat his heart leapt, hoping it was Jenny. But Marie Davis stood there, waiting for an invitation to step inside his cubicle. "Marie. Come in, have a seat." He stood up out of respect for the older woman.

"Thanks." She moved into the office space and took a seat across from his desk. "How's the project going?"

"Tiara had some brilliant data and information this morning," James said. "It sort of took the rest of us by surprise."

"I heard that wasn't the only thing that took you by surprise. Val Paterson turned in a letter of resignation a few minutes ago." Marie shook her head as though she didn't know what to think. "I knew she was struggling with her job. Actually, with lots of things. But I didn't know she was depending on someone else to carry out her work load. Especially someone like Nathan Greenly. Rick's not sure what he's going to do with him yet."

"If anything," James added, speculating. He couldn't see a reason for Nathan to be reprimanded, let alone let go. After all, he'd been doing the work of two people from what it sounded like, and so what if his morals weren't exactly squeaky clean? He was probably still a good programmer, and the other matter could be handled in a discrete manner, if Rick wanted it to.

"I guess you're right," Marie said. "You know, I actually used to be a lot like Val."

James never would have guessed that from this prim and proper woman sitting in front of him.

"It's true. I wanted to have someone like me, a man who would care about me and take care of me," she said. "I didn't go quite as far with the situation as she did. The flirting was more subtle in my day." She nodded her head at the memory.

"That wouldn't take much," James said, chuckling.

Marie laughed as well. "I guess you're right about that. She was pretty obvious as a flirt. Anyway, I can say this now

308

because I'm an old woman. I wanted to have someone care about me, I wanted to be a success at my work, and when the two didn't seem to come together, I had to choose."

James raised his eyebrow in enough of a question for Marie to continue.

"And I chose to succeed in my work." She leaned forward in her chair and gave him a hard look before continuing. "And that was *my* mistake. I missed out on life. I missed out on everything. I could have had a husband, and a family. I could have had grandkids by now to keep me company in my old age. But what do I have? Nothing but a lonely apartment to go home to at night."

"I'm sure . . ." James started to counter.

"No, you're sure of nothing," she continued. "I'm sure of everything. I'm sure of where my life has gone and hasn't gone, and I'm sure that yours is headed down the same lane, and I won't stand for it." She smacked her hand against the top of his desk to emphasize her point. "You have money, talent, and a future in this or any other company. What you don't have is a *wife*, and trust me, you need one."

James fought to find the words to respond to her bluntness, but nothing came. Deep in his heart, he knew she was right. And he knew who he wanted to be that wife—he wanted Jenny.

"You know she's falling in love with you, right?" Marie asked. "She might not know it, but she is. I've known her a long time, and I've been watching and listening to her since you came."

"Who?" James couldn't help asking, just in case Marie had someone else in mind. Someone like—it was too disturbing to think about—someone like Tiara.

"You know exactly who I mean. I've never seen Jenny so put out by anyone, and I've never known anyone to shake her to her very soul until the day you came." Marie sat back again in her chair, obviously more relaxed now that she'd said her peace. "She was embarrassed when she came back from lunch, so I don't know what she said or did, but I know that the two of you belong together, and that it's probably going to be up to you to make it work. So, if you want to stay employed at Tech Aide, you'd better get busy." Marie stood up and headed toward the door.

"Wait a minute!" James found his voice, but wasn't sure what he wanted to say. "You mean . . . you mean . . ."

"Yes, I mean." Marie smiled at him. "Work things out with Jenny Grant and you can stay. We can't afford to have one of our best programmers upset and angry every day, and as long as you're here that's the way it will be. Unless you can get her to stop being a bridesmaid and into the role of blushing bride."

"Maid-of-honor," James said, almost as though he were stunned.

"What?" Now it was Marie's turn to wonder where his answer had come from.

"She's the maid-of-honor, for her best friend's wedding. She told me about it as we walked to the restaurant for

310

lunch," James explained. "And the wedding is next weekend, and I'm supposed to take her. If she'll still go with me."

"Well, you'd better be sorting that out now, hadn't you? Because the next time I see Jenny helping plan a wedding, I expect it to be her own."

By the time James looked up to respond to her, Marie Davis was gone.

Her absence left James with two big problems. One, how could he get Jenny to ever want to talk to him again? And two, could he take her to Lisbeth's wedding after all? Then a third worry hit him. Her office was right across the hall, and neither one of them had a door. What if she'd heard everything that he and Marie had said? Would it help or hurt his cause?

The notification ping from his computer reminded him that he didn't have time to think about anything. He had a very important team meeting, and if Jenny didn't show, his team was left with him and Tiara. And he couldn't imagine a worse thing.

***

Stephie felt a lightness in her heart that she hadn't felt for months when the plane touched down in Salt Lake. She was home. The trip had been delightful. Gary had kept her entertained the entire way, telling her stories about his high school and college years, discovering they actually had shared a few friends along the way. And he'd managed to keep her mind off Phil, and his gaming, and the baby. Well, not entirely off the baby. She knew that would never happen, not now that she was going to be a mother. That would be a huge portion of her life, even without Phil. *Especially without Phil*, she allowed herself to think. Filing for divorce was going to be the first thing she did once she was home.

She almost hated to see the plane taxi to the end of the jetway in preparation for the passengers to depart. It would be the last she saw of Gary, and already she knew she'd miss him. He'd made her feel better about herself and the problems she would need to face as a single mother. The plane came to a halt and the "Fasten Seatbelts" sign dinged before its light went off.

"I guess we're here," she said.

"Yep, I guess we're here. You know, I feel like I've known you my whole life. Weird, huh?"

"Yeah, weird," Stephie said, not knowing what to think.

Gary stood and stretched, his long arms nearly smacking against the low lights in the ceiling. "Let me get your bag." He stepped a little father into the aisle and bent across the seat he had vacated, grabbing the handle of her stored carry-on and sliding the bag out easily, her shoulder bag still on top. She picked it up and draped the strap over her head, poking an arm through so the bag could settle into place on her hip.

Half the passengers had already crowded their way into the aisle in front of them in a hurry to get off the plane and

312

on with their lives. Although she was thrilled to be home in Utah, she wasn't in any hurry to get off the plane. It was nice to have someone take care of her, and who would actually talk to her. Gary handed her the carry-on bag. "Thanks."

"Is someone going to be here to meet you?" Gary wore a smile, and Stephie thought his eyes looked a little hopeful.

She wondered if he was ready to get rid of her. "I think so," she said, knowing she sounded disappointed. "My mom knew what time the flight was expected to arrive. She's probably waiting."

The hope she had noticed before in Gary's face suddenly dimmed. "Oh," he said. "Well, at least let me escort you to the baggage claim. She won't be able to come upstairs to meet you anyway. TSA rules and all that, you know."

"I'd appreciate your help," Stephie said, knowing that stating her true feelings—*I'd love it*—would be too much to share with someone she had barely met.

The smile was back on Gary's face as he let her enter the aisle in front of him. "Let me get that carry-on to the exit ramp, at least."

She laughed. "No, I'm not helpless, although I appreciate the offer. You'd just slow people down at getting off the plane, and I don't think that would make them too happy."

"I guess you're right," he said. "But when we get to the terminal, I can wheel the bag downstairs for you."

"Okay," Stephie said, happy to know Gary really did want to spend at least that much more time with her. She wondered what would have happened if her mom hadn't been meeting her, but that made her think about Phil, the husband she had left behind. She doubted he even had a clue why she had left, if he knew at all that she was gone. Would he have broken away from his gaming system long enough to realize it was late and he was in the apartment alone?

Once the two of them were off the plane and out of the jetway ramp, Gary was true to his word. "Give me the bag," he said as he helped her lift the shoulder bag strap over her head and placed it over his own. "And the handle," he said as he reached for the carry-on, latched the handle into its open position, and started to walk toward the baggage claim area, wheeling his small suitcase on one side of his body and hers on the other.

He looked like a clown from a circus ring, balancing four pieces of luggage around his body like Erich Brenn balanced a set of plates on those old Ed Sullivan Show clips on YouTube. "You look pretty silly, you know," she said.

"I don't care," Gary said. "No one here I need to impress." He stopped for a minute and looked at her. "Except maybe you." His smile burst into a wide grin as he turned and started trying to walk straight again, the wheels on both carts having something else in mind entirely.

What am I doing, letting this man take care of me? I'm

314

married, for heaven's sake. "Let me take mine," Stephie said as she hurried to stay beside him. *Even if it's not for long.*

"No way, and make me look like a guy who can't come to the rescue of a beautiful woman."

If he only knew how much I need rescuing. She couldn't remember the last time Phil had been helpful. And playful had never been a word she would use to describe him. Husband or not, and her heart knew it would be *or not* as soon as she got settled in and met with a lawyer, Phil was nothing like Gary, and really never had been.

"Stephie! Stephie!"

She heard her mom's voice before she saw her, but at last Stephie spotted her in the center of the crowded room. She lifted her arm to wave, and was happy to see her mom was doing the same. *Maybe she is happy to see me. Maybe it's okay that I've come back to Utah.* But how did her mom feel about her coming back without Phil, and being helped by someone new? Would she think Gary had been the problem that stepped between Stephie and her husband and the marriage? Would she blame everything on Stephie herself like her father used to do to her mom?

She had barely come to a stop when her mom was there giving her the biggest bear hug she could remember in a long time.

"Ooh! I've missed you!"

"I've missed you, too," Stephie said, and realized just how much she actually meant it. She *did* miss her mom, and

315

here they were hugging and jumping up and down together like two airheads from one of those 1980s high school reunion movies. What would people think? Worse yet, what would Gary think? Stephie was the first to break away, hoping her mom would understand everything.

"Mom, this is Gary . . ." It suddenly hit her she didn't know his last name. She'd been sitting beside him all this time, let him carry her bags, and even allowed her mind to wonder for a moment to what kind of a relationship she could have with a man like him once she was divorced from Phil, and she didn't even know his last name.

But Gary came to her rescue. "Gary Brimhall. Nice to meet you." He held out his hand to her mother, ready to shake if she offered her hand.

Do it, Mom, Stephie wished, uncertain how her mother would act toward the stranger her daughter had found on the plane.

She didn't have to worry though, because her mom stuck out her hand and said, "I know you. You're that little Brimhall boy who used to live on Cherry Lane."

"Yes, I am," Gary said, the smile Stephie had already grown to know was back on his face. "And you're Mrs. Payne."

How does he know my mom's last name? Stephie hated her maiden name. It reminded her constantly of the horrible things that had happened throughout her life. The way her dad had treated her mom, at least until he left the two of

316

them. How her mom had to work to support them, and now the things she felt about her marriage to Phil. She'd been so glad to change from Payne to Harris when she married him. Could she ever make herself go back to Payne? The thought flashed through her mind, but her memory was also working on what her mom had said. *You're the Brimhall boy who used to live on Cherry Lane.* She used to live on Cherry Lane. She and her mom lived there for nearly a year after her dad was gone. "You two know each other?"

A conversation had started between Gary and her mom, and they continued to talk while Stephie tried to wrack her brain. Did she know Gary from when she was a kid? Why didn't she remember him? She knew her life had been disrupted, and she spent most of the year on Cherry Lane upset with both her mom and her dad. But had she also blocked herself off from people who were her friends?

"I'm here for a wedding, and to visit my parents," Gary was saying.

"Anyone we know?" her mom asked.

"Maybe. Do you know Gary Page?"

"I do remember him," her mom said.

"Gary and Gary!" Stephie blurted out. "You're Gary and Gary! I *do* remember you!"

"And you're Stephanie Payne. Why didn't you tell me?"

"Because I guess I'm not anymore," she said, not knowing how to continue to tell him the rest of her story, not here, not now, and definitely not at the airport and in front of her mother.

317

"It doesn't matter," Gary said. "I'm so glad I found you, both of you." He opened his arms, ready to greet her mom with a great big hug. "I've missed you, Mrs. Payne, and I've missed Cherry Lane." He turned toward Stephie. "And I guess I've even missed little Stephanie."

"Thanks," she said, pleased at least that he wasn't ready to run away from her, like she just remembered that she once ran away from him. *Stupid move, Stephie.* She might have ended up married to him, instead of Phil who had turned out to be such a loser.

"Do you need a ride anywhere?" her mom was saying.

"I was going to rent a car," Gary said as he snagged a piece of luggage off the carousel.

"You don't have to. We've got plenty of room," her mom said. "Stephie, are you looking for your luggage?"

"Yeah, Mom." She hadn't been, and it was likely her mother knew it. Instead her heart was jumping up and down, the same way she had been jumping with her mother. Gary was riding in the car with them. She had known him when she was just a child. And he was here to attend the wedding of the other Gary, the one who was marrying Lisbeth, one of her best friends.

Suddenly she felt like she'd found another best friend, and things were looking up for once. Even if she did still need a divorce from Phil Harris.

28

James was nervous about their afternoon team meeting. Not only was he uncertain if Jenny would show—and if either one of them would be able to concentrate after their unfortunate lunch encounter—but Val Paterson was gone and Rick Myers had decided to pop in to see how their proposal was coming. Rick had taken a seat near James, as though he planned to take charge if the meeting didn't go well. At one minute before the agreed-upon time, Tiara was also seated, a yellow notepad and three sharpened pencils on the tabletop in front of her. James noticed a flash stick positioned on the top edge of her notepad.

At least Tiara is ready, he thought. Now if only Jenny would show up. He watched the door, willing it to open, which it did at the same time his phone alert said it was time to get the meeting started. He breathed a sigh of relief. It was Jenny.

She didn't look at him as she took her seat, but she still looked professional and ready to present her ideas. James didn't know when she would have come up with anything since their lunch and misunderstanding had used much of their time after the earlier meeting, but she also carried a yellow notepad and an iPad. He'd not seen her use anything before but the Tech Aide computer that was centered on her desk. He was hopeful this meant she had done *some* groundwork before today, maybe last night at home.

"I think we're ready to get started again," James said. "Tiara gave us a wonderful presentation prior to the lunch break, Rick. We're ready to hear now from Jenny, and since Val is no longer with us, I'll give mine next."

"I'd like to hear what Tiara has to say as well," Rick said.

"Oh, not a problem," James said, looking at Tiara for confirmation that she was willing to explain her ideas again.

"I'd be happy to," Tiara said, an almost smug smile on her face as she waited to listen to what Jenny had prepared.

"In that case, we should get started," James said. "I'd hate for us to go past Marie's hard and fast rule about leaving the building at six, but I'd also like time to discuss the ideas and see where the strongest points are leading us so we can work together if needs be. Jenny?"

She seemed a little flustered, as though she had forgotten why she was here, or that James had tagged her to go first, but when she glanced at him he put on his biggest smile, hoping it would encourage her and let her know he was over being upset. It worked. Jenny stood at the presentation table, her iPad stand turned so the others could see what came onto the screen, and began her presentation.

For the next forty-five minutes, James listened intently to what Jenny had to say. He thought her ideas were fresh, if not completely well developed, and he saw a lot of potential in them. She was as smart as he had felt she was all along and her ideas proved it. Of course, in his mind, the fact that she was confident and knowledgeable about the system added points in her favor, and that he thought she was sexy certainly didn't hurt either. He had to almost shake himself when she finished her presentation and sat back down.

It was his turn and it wouldn't do to be lost in the thoughts he was having about spending more time with Jenny, much more time. Rick was waiting, so James stood and presented his ideas and case, explaining how he could build upon concepts he had developed while CEO of Info Systems Technology, while keeping the line of ownership sacred that he had agreed not to cross when he sold the company. He tried to make connections to the presentation Jenny had just made, hoping Rick would see that the two of them worked well together. And because he was suddenly feeling generous, he also talked a little about the presentation concepts that Tiara had explained to their team early, not wanting to overstep his bounds, or take the spark out of what she would have to say, but being supportive toward her as a member of his team. It was something he had learned to do as CEO; always let the other guy appear to win, at least in some way.

"Thanks, James," Rick said when James sat back down. "I think the proposals both you and Jenny made would marry well, if we decide to go that way."

Marry? James thought that was a strange thing to say. *Proposals* and *marry* all in the same breath as a reference to himself and Jenny shook him up a little, and it took a second before he remembered to call on Tiara to give her presentation. Then it took him a little while more to realize that Tiara had gotten better at explaining her ideas this second time around. She had tweaked the concepts, added a slide show, and sounded like a lawyer delivering her closing argument to a jury that was hungry to convict. And James knew immediately her skills had paid off, and that he and Jenny might as well go back to square one.

Rick leaned forward against the table, his attention fully paid to Tiara and the diagrams she was displaying, the data she was quoting, and the applications she was describing. When she was through, he didn't have to ask questions. Rick seemed completely satisfied. "Well, then I think we know which plan has been more carefully thought through."

James knew he shouldn't feel so crushed, but he was used to winning. He was used to being the one who decided whose ideas made it through the initial stages of development, yet here was Rick, taking all those choices away from him, and it was obvious that Tiara's were the only ideas that would be approved.

He turned to look at Jenny. Her face wore the disappointment that he felt in his own mind. This project was now in Tiara's court. It was her baby to win or lose, and he and Jenny had nothing to say about it.

"Thanks for your ideas, guys," Rick was saying to the two of them. "Better luck next time." He stood to leave the conference room. "Tiara, I'd like to see you in my office right away." Rick nodded at James and Jenny and was though the door almost immediately. Tiara followed behind.

"Well, that certainly ends an interesting day," James said.

"I guess so. Sorry," Jenny said.

"I accept your apology."

"I meant about what happened at lunch," Jenny said, her eyes not quite reaching up to meet his.

"That too," James added. "I'd be willing to bet neither one of us gets that promotion."

"Or the raise," Jenny said, her voice almost a chuckle, in a sardonic way.

"At least we have each other," James said, then realized that Jenny might take his comment the wrong way. "I mean, to work with. We still have each other on the team." Jenny's brow wrinkled as though she were really confused. "Or . . . well, you know, I'm sure Tiara will need us to help her and everything."

"Right. And everything," Jenny repeated, and James heard just how stupid he suddenly sounded.

"Listen Jenny, I'm sorry that we didn't win Rick over. I take full responsibility. I should have shared my thoughts earlier, and maybe we could have worked closer together." James reached his hand across the table toward her. "Friends anyway?"

323

She paused only a half second before taking his hand. "Friends."

***

"Friends," Jenny had said, but she wasn't exactly sure what that would mean. And she wasn't sure that's what she really wanted anyway. Since James Cox came to work at Tech Aide, she had found herself all out of sorts. She'd tried to blame it on Tiara and her constant matchmaking. She thought she could blame it on Lisbeth and the fact her last single friend was getting married. She even hoped to blame it on the concern she had about her mother. But the fact was, Jenny knew why James drove her crazy. She had decided to forget all about men, and the first once she met had wormed his way into her mind and heart to the point she thought if she couldn't have him then her life wasn't worth living. Not that she'd do anything to herself, but she was tired of living alone, being without someone in a relationship. Yet, everything she said to him was aimed toward driving him away, and she couldn't force her mouth to stop.

James seemed like the perfect candidate, and as much as she tried to make herself hate him—blame him was more like it—the more she wanted to be with him. He was just plain *nice*, and it had been a long time since she'd known anyone like that, let alone dated him.

She'd gone back to her cubicle after their meeting, hoping for a little privacy, if privacy could be had around this place. *If I only had a door!* She kept her eyes trained just enough toward the imaginary door that she'd be sure to see James if he happened to walk by. *Now I'm acting like a teenager with a major crush!* She started to laugh, but soon decided if she didn't stop she'd be forced to cry, and there was enough drama in her life to give her reason for that.

Her cell phone started to chime, the signal that her mother was calling. Jenny picked up the phone and flipped it open. "Hi, Mom."

But the voice on the other end of the line wasn't her mother. "Jenny? I'm glad I found you, dear."

Mrs. Trumble had lived next to her mom for several years, and the woman had promised to stay with Jenny's mom while she was at this meeting. Jenny couldn't imagine why she was calling her, and on her mom's phone. "Is there something wrong?" She caught James stopping at her doorway at the exact moment she asked the question.

Mrs. Trumble explained that she had gone to the bathroom, and when she came back out the front door was open and the phone on the floor. "And your mother is gone! I can't imagine where she might be." The older woman sounded worried, which made Jenny worried too.

"I'll be right there, Mrs. Trumble," Jenny said as she grabbed her purse from her desk drawer. "Please keep my mom's phone with you, and call me the minute you find out anything. And thank you." She logged off her computer and headed toward the door where James now stood.

"I'm coming with you," James said.

"Wha . . .? Why would you do that?" She closed the phone and kept walking toward the front exit of the building. *Because he's nice, you idiot!*

"Because it's the right thing to do," he said. "I'll drive if you want me to."

Jenny nodded. "That way I can talk if Mrs. Trumble calls back. I can't imagine where Mom could have wandered off to. The doctor warned me . . ."

They reached James's car in the parking lot, and he unlocked the door then held hers open until she could get in. "Has she done this before?"

"Only once. Mrs. Trumble found her in the middle of the intersection, calling for someone to come and help her get home." Jenny tapped the palm of her right hand against her forehead. "And I don't think I mentioned it to her doctor."

"That doesn't sound good," James said as he put the key in the ignition and started the engine. "Is she suffering from Alzheimer's?"

"The doctor hasn't officially diagnosed that yet," she said, "but something is seriously wrong. She just doesn't act like my mom anymore, you know?"

"It'll be okay, Jenny," James said, his voice calming as he drove toward the parking lot exit. "We'll find her, but first, you'll need to tell me where she lives."

The bit of humor lightened Jenny's heart. *Maybe James is*

326

right. Maybe everything will be okay. She refused to let herself dwell on the response she knew she could make.

Or maybe not.

It only took them a few minutes from the time she shared her mom's address, until they pulled into the drive. That was one of the things she liked about both Tech Aide and where her mom lived. They were close to each other in case of an emergency, and her mother's disappearance was definitely an emergency. Jenny got out of the car as soon as it rolled to a stop. James was close behind her as she hurried toward the front porch where Mrs. Trumble stood.

"Any sign of her?" Jenny asked.

"No, I've checked all the rooms more than once and even went into the garage to make sure she hadn't fallen down somewhere and was lying there hurt. I was just on my way to walk around the yard to do the same thing when you two pulled into the drive." Mrs. Trumble gave James a once over, and raised her eyebrows and nodded as if to say she approved.

But James apparently didn't see. He was leaning slightly forward, concentrating on something down the street. "Jenny, is that your mom?" He pointed toward a house a few doors down and on the opposite side of the street. Someone—a woman wearing a bright orange Muumuu—was trying frantically to open the door, but despite all the pulling and kicking she was doing, she didn't seem to be making any progress.

"Mom!" Jenny yelled as she took off down the street. "Mom!" It was her. Jenny would know that crazy muumuu any day. Her dad had bought it as an anniversary present for her mom a few years before he died, and her mom loved the ugly thing. She would wear it everywhere, if Jenny would let her.

Stepping onto the porch, she laid her hand on her mom's shoulder. "Mom?"

Mrs. Grant was startled at first, but then a touch of reality crept in. "Jenny, I'm glad you're home. I can't get this door to open, and my key seems to be locked inside."

"It's okay, Mom," Jenny said. "Let's go for a little walk, and then we'll get you back inside."

"But I'm tired. I don't want to walk anywhere," Mrs. Grant said.

"If you'd like, I'll carry you," James said, letting Mrs. Grant focus on him for the first time. "You don't look like you weigh an ounce, so it'll not be a problem."

Jenny's mom looked at James then she looked at Jenny then she looked back at James again, studying his face for a minute like she thought she knew him. Then she turned to Jenny. "Well, it's about time. Don't know where you found him, but when's the wedding?"

Jenny could almost feel her cheeks turn beet red, but James laughed right out loud. "Let's get Lisbeth's wedding out of the way first this weekend, and then we'll see what Jenny has to say about an answer to that question."

Jenny had no idea what James was talking about, but for some reason it didn't matter. He was helping her mother walk back toward her own house, and the two of them were chatting and laughing like they were old, old friends. One more thing about James for Jenny to fall in love with, and she had the funny feeling even this moment of discovery would not be the last. *Maybe I should give up that crazy idea of staying single after all.*

***

Stephie hadn't been so happy in months, it seemed. She placed her hand against her growing belly, and once again thanked the universe for the changes that were being made in her life. Her mom had never been kinder or more supportive than she'd been in the nine days since Stephie had stepped off that plane. Her mom had never liked Phil very well anyway. Maybe she'd seen him for the person he would turn out to be. After all, Mom had married at least one of the same types of guys on her own, and was glad to be rid of him.

She was glad to be rid of Phil as well. She'd gone to see a divorce lawyer on the day after she'd gotten home, explaining the reasons why she was done with the marriage in such a way that the lawyer thought he could take care of everything without too much grief on her part. The two of them didn't own anything, well, except for the baby, but she hoped that Phil wouldn't really care when it came down to that.

329

This little dumpling was something he certainly hadn't counted on, but then neither had Stephie, and she was totally in love with the idea of being a mommy now that she was used to thinking about it. And with Phil gone from her life, she was able to separate her pregnancy from him in her mind, making this baby seem like a second virgin birth and all her own. She glanced through the kitchen door where Gary was making dinner with her mother.

Gary seemed to enjoy spending time with the two Payne women, even if one of them was old enough to . . . well, old enough to be his mother. A smile played at the corners of Stephie's mouth, something that had been happening almost constantly since she boarded that plane in Boston and started the flight across the country. Phil was part of her old life, and if she had her way with the divorce papers and sole custody of the baby, she intended to keep him that way. Dead and gone as far as she was concerned.

"Hey, Steph," Gary called out from the kitchen. "What time am I picking you up tomorrow for the wedding?"

Lisbeth's wedding. Stephie was so excited to be able to go. She didn't think there was any hope of attending when she was living in Boston, but God often has mysterious ways. "We should probably get there a little after one-thirty. The wedding is scheduled to begin at two-thirty, but I want a chance to catch up with my friends."

"I'll pick you up around one then," Gary said. "I hope you're hungry. Your mom is a wicked cook."

Now that she was past the initial days of morning sickness, Stephie was always hungry. That was the problem. She was afraid she was going to swell up into a balloon if she wasn't careful. But tomorrow was Lisbeth's wedding, and she knew there would be all sorts of fun treats. And, knowing Lisbeth, the decorations would be delicious too. Not the kind of delicious that one could eat, but beautiful beyond words, and if she guessed right, the whole place would look, and smell, and feel like they'd stepped right out of Salt Lake and into Hawaii.

Someday, Stephie thought.

"Food's on," her mother called as she and Gary carried plates from the kitchen into the dining area.

"It's looks delicious," Stephie said. "Which one of you made this?" She knew her mom could cook, but this meal was almost gourmet. Beef medallions, sliced cooked carrots in what appeared to be a brown sugar glaze, hot rolls, not to mention the huge bowl of salad that was already waiting on the table.

"Do you even have to ask?" Mrs. Payne shook her head. "In all your days you've never seen me put on a spread like this."

Stephie chuckled. "Well, I didn't want to hurt your feelings."

"No feelings to be hurt here. Stephie, you better hang on to this one 'cause he can cook!"

"Mom!" Stephie blushed with embarrassment.

"You heard your mom," Gary said. "You're eating for two now, and a healthy baby deserves a good cook." He touched his lips to the top of her head, the way her mother used to do when she was a kid.

He kissed me, Stephie thought. *Okay, so it was on the top of my head, but he kissed me!* What on earth was she doing? The divorce papers were barely filed. Was she already thinking about moving into a new relationship? *Not a wise move.*

"A little vain, are we?" she asked, hoping the banter would still her pounding heart.

"Hey, I just call 'em like I see 'em," Gary said as he offered her a pre-served plate.

"It does look delicious," she said.

"And it is," her mom added as she took another bite of the meat.

"There's lots more menus where this one came from," Gary said. "And I'd be happy to make them all for you."

"And we'd be happy to be fed," Stephie said. She couldn't remember how long it had been since she'd felt so happy, and she hoped the mood stuck around.

And Gary, too.

29

"Where's the maid-of-honor?" James called as he poked his head through the front door of Jenny's apartment.

"I'm in my bedroom, getting dressed, and don't you dare come back here," she called.

"Can't I get a sneak peek?" James moved closer to the doorway where her voice was coming from, although he had no intention of actually going anywhere near entering her bedroom. He just thought he'd tease her a little.

A squeal came from her direction. "I said don't you *dare!*"

James laughed at her response. *She sounds like a teenager.* A minute later when she walked into the room, he was struck that she certainly didn't *look* like a teenager though. His heart did a little jump the minute he saw her. She was beautiful, elegant. The bridesmaid dress was stunning in and of itself, but the dress had nothing on the light that shined in Jenny's face. Her upswept hair framed her cheeks and fell softly across her forehead, the rich color deeper with the entire amount of it working together. A low whistle escaped from his lips.

"Do I look okay?" Jenny said, a hint of natural blush coloring her cheeks.

"Gorgeous is more like it," James said. He rocked back on a heel as he gave her a second look. "I'd say this dress is a keeper, and I'll have to take a stick with me to keep the other guys away from you."

"Go on," Jenny said.

"No, seriously. I'm not kidding." James gave a shake of his head, not quite believing how beautiful Jenny looked in her dress for the wedding. *I wonder what she would look like in a bridal gown?*

"I know you're not kidding," Jenny said. "Like I said, go on."

James suddenly realized she was making a joke. Had she ever done that before when she was with him? He didn't think so. It seemed he had learned something new about Jenny and her personality almost every minute of the day since the two of them had been passed over for a promotion and a raise last week, and he didn't mind any of it one bit. A new feeling of caring had developed in his heart, and he wanted to spend as much time as he possibly could with this woman, maybe even all of eternity.

"I think I love you, Jenny Grant." The words had slipped out before he could think to filter them, and he noticed that her first reaction had been to blink, as though she was startled by his admission, but she recovered quickly.

"Well, you're certainly no David Cassidy . . ." She picked up the tiny silk purse that matched the dress. "And as much as I'd love to discuss that possibility, we've got a wedding to go to."

And someday soon, that wedding may be yours, if you'll have me. James knew now that Jenny *was* the reason he'd been inspired to move to Salt Lake. She was the reason he'd gotten hired at Tech Aide. The promotion and raise didn't matter. The only thing that mattered to him was finding the right words that would convince Jenny Grant to become his bride.

The sooner the better, James decided as they were on their way.

***

He said it! He said the LOVE word. Jenny could hardly believe it. No man had ever said he thought he loved her before, and the moment James said it, she knew it was true. But more than that, she knew she loved him too. There was no doubt. But where did they go from here?

Actually she knew where they were headed, Lisbeth and Gary were getting married and Jenny was expected to be there as the maid-of-honor. She was supposed to arrive early to do a walk-through of the reception area with Lisbeth before the guests arrived. Jenny had never gotten around to telling her about the changes she'd made in the flower arrangements, but Jenny knew Lisbeth would be too happy on this day to mind. Flowers were flowers, and as long as the place looked Hawaiian, her best friend would be in heaven.

Lisbeth was getting married, and Jenny began to hope—dream—that she would be getting married too. It was such a different future than she had assigned herself not that many weeks ago, and the possibility really did feel like a dream. If only it was a dream come true.

James stopped the car in the reception hall parking lot, and Jenny got out. Poking her head inside the window, she said, "I'll be back in a few minutes. Oh, and I think I love you too." She was gone before she heard if he had a reply. *Let him wonder if he heard me right*, she thought as she headed inside to meet Lisbeth.

The room was beautiful. The owner of The Rose Shop was bustling around, resetting a seashell here, moving a sprig of flowers there. Jenny gave him a wave, but she didn't want to interrupt him from his work. She walked from table to table, admiring his handiwork, realigning a fork next to a plate, refolding a napkin, or bending to breathe in the luscious aroma of the Hawaiian orchids that were scattered around the various tables. Of course, everything was already perfect, but the actions gave Jenny something to do.

She was startled from her calm when she heard the screech. Turning, she saw Lisbeth, her mother and sister at her side. "What have you done to my wedding?"

Jenny had no idea what Lisbeth was talking about, but she was sure the accusation was directed at her. "Wha . . .?"

"The flowers! Where are my flowers?" Lisbeth's eyes were huge and the redness that came into her face spoke that she was not amused.

Jenny and the owner of The Rose Shop both froze in place. Was Lisbeth upset about the slight change in the

336

flower arrangements? Is that what this was all about? Breaking herself away from the spot where she had stopped, Jenny walked toward her friend, hoping to calm her down. "Your flowers are here, Lisbeth. See? At the head table and at the place where the wedding cake will be, and the petals are everywhere."

"That's *not* what I ordered," Lisbeth whined.

Both her mother and sister stepped in to try to calm her down. The poor guy from The Rose Shop, and the two assistants he had with him looked like they could faint dead away. Jenny knew Lisbeth's anger should be directed at her, not at them, but Lisbeth didn't know that. Lisbeth tried to advance on the three men. Luckily, her mother was able to hold her back.

"No, Lisbeth," Jenny said. "It's my fault, not his. I'm the one who made the change. There was no way they could get enough flowers here, not on time, so I made an executive decision. I forgot to tell you, and I thought everything would be okay. Didn't you want a Hawaiian theme?"

Lisbeth burst into tears. Her mother wrapped her arms around her.

"She's been like this all day," Lisbeth's sister, Kari, said. "Don't worry, Jenny. Everything will be okay."

"I'm so sorry," Jenny said, nearing tears herself. "It's all my fault! I don't know anything about being a maid-of-honor, I was just trying to make things easier for Lisbeth, and now I've messed up everything."

337

Temporary Bridesmaid

Mrs. Conner made a few more shushing sounds above her daughter's head then said, "You've not done anything wrong, Jenny, and the place looks beautiful." She gave a nod toward the three men from The Rose Shop, the owner of which seemed to breathe a sigh of relief. "Brides are like this. They lose a little bit of their sanity on their wedding day. As soon as she sees Gary all of her worries will go away and a year from now she will be telling the story and laughing about the whole thing."

"Are you sure?" Jenny asked, not positive she could believe what Lisbeth's mother was saying. Were brides really this emotional? Is this what she would have to face if she and James *were* ever to get married? She chastised herself for even thinking such a thing. James had only said he *thought* he loved her, and she'd only said the same, yet here she was planning the emotions she was going to feel on her own wedding day. What if she jinxed it and a wedding never became a possibility? After all, she *was* the one who had decided she'd stay single for the rest of her life, and here she was planning a wedding in her head.

"I'm sure," Mrs. Conner said.

"Same sort of thing happened to me," Lisbeth's older sister added. "Of course, my flowers didn't get mixed up, but we should have taste-tested the wedding cake!"

"Yuck!" her mother said. "That thing was naaaaasty!" The two women started to laugh, and Lisbeth raised her head far enough to determine they weren't laughing at her,

338

then shoved her face back into the crook of her mother's shoulder. "You run along now. We'll clean this one up, put her make-up back on, and see you in line, ready for the wedding."

"Okay," Jenny said, although her steps away from the women were reluctant. Once she was outside and had taken a deep breath of the fresh air, Jenny felt a little better, a little more hopeful that Lisbeth's mother was right and that everything would be okay.

"That certainly didn't go well," she said once she was back in the car.

"Something wrong?" James asked, a look of concern shadowing his face.

"Let's just say that reality show *Bridezillas* is more real than fake." Jenny shook her head. "I hope I never act that way, especially on my wedding day."

"You won't," James said as he started the car, ready to drive to the church.

"And how do you know?" Jenny asked, but the thought running through her head was her final words from a minute ago. My *wedding day, my wedding day, my wedding day.* She couldn't believe she had said such a thing to James.

"Because I won't let you," he said.

"Oh? Who says you're going to be there to stop me?"

He gave her a sidelong glance, a wide grin spreading across his face. "Oh, I don't think we need to worry about that. I'll be there."

Jenny suddenly felt all giddy inside, crazy emotions and thoughts flitting through her mind. *James will be there, and I'm going to be his bride!*

***

Stephie couldn't believe how much things had changed in the short time she had been away from Utah. She left a bride, and now she had a baby on the way, but Phil would no longer be a part of her life. She knew she could fall in love again, maybe with someone like Gary. But this time she intended to move slowly. Age didn't matter anymore, but having a good husband who would treat her like a queen, and who would be a wonderful father to her coming baby were the most important things.

Gary had driven Stephie and her mother to the wedding like he'd promised he would. He even stood at her side as she was greeted by the group of friends not involved as a part of the wedding party. Kira and Ben, Isaac and Grace, her tiny new baby nestled in her arms. Even Randy and Tamlyn, who was not that long from having lost her own baby—all of them congratulated Stephie on the pregnancy, waited for her to explain that she and Phil were no longer together, and welcomed Gary as though he were one of their long-lost friends.

The prelude music started, and each of them took a seat. Lisbeth had chosen Pachelbel's Canon instead of the traditional wedding march for her walk down the aisle. Everyone stood and faced the bride as she entered the room.

Stephie didn't expect her to notice that she was there, or who she was with, or not with. The look on Jenny's face though as she walked in front of Lisbeth proved that she'd not only spied Stephie, but that the question *Where is Phil?* had gone through her mind. There would be enough time to explain it to her after the wedding. Of course, Jenny might have known and been part of her decision had she been home to answer the phone that night, but she wasn't and things seemed to be working out great, even without the advice of her friend.

The thought struck her that once her divorce was final, she too would be single again, just like Jenny. Gary slipped his arm across her shoulder as Jenny passed them. But being single might not last so long for Stephie after all, and that would leave Jenny the last woman standing alone in the aisle. She sent out nothing but the best of wishes for her friend then caught Jenny looking at someone sitting a few rows ahead of them. A man, someone she didn't recognize. Maybe things really had changed in the time she was gone. Maybe Jenny would not be alone after all.

Maybe none of them would have to be alone. Stephie leaned a little closer to Gary, enjoying the warmth of his arm around her as the wedding carried on, refusing to think about moving too fast today, Lisbeth's wedding day.

341

30

The final strains of music accompanied the bride and groom on their return trip down the aisle, people hurried to their cars and followed Lisbeth and Gary to the reception hall, and the party was under full swing. Jenny hated the fact that she had to stand in line and greet the guests, while poor James was all alone over at the side. Every once in a while he would get up and shake hands with someone, or perhaps they approached him, their curiosity piqued at why he had accompanied Jenny to the wedding.

She'd only had a moment to catch up with Stephie, but she couldn't remember the last time her friend had been so happy. Maybe it was a good thing Phil would be forever gone from her life, and Gary had stepped back onto Cherry Lane. They would make a good couple, Jenny decided, and went back to the guests until at last the line started to die.

James had seen his chance it seemed. He was standing close to her and tucked his hand under her arm. "Come with me. I need to tell you something."

"Right now?" Jenny asked, glancing toward the line where she was supposed to be standing.

"Yeah, it's important." They moved to a more secluded spot, away from the bustle and noise of the crowded reception floor.

342

"Okay, what's so important that you pulled me away from my responsibilities as the head maid?"

"Maid-of-honor."

"Whatever." Jenny raised her eyebrows, as though to say *Well, get on with it.*

"I've changed my mind."

"Changed your mind?" Jenny felt a sense of panic growing in her heart. Was having him at the wedding too much for James? Did it make him think about the things he had said to her in the past few hours and realize he'd made a mistake?

"Yes, I've changed my mind. I no longer *think* I love you, I *know* it." James wrapped her into his arms, and snuggled his nose against hers for only a minute, but it was enough to send shockwaves through to her spine. "Will you marry me, Jenny Grant?"

Jenny thought her heart would sing louder than her voice could speak, but she couldn't resist a little teasing. "Well, I'm not sure that's such a good idea. An employee really shouldn't marry her supervisor, you know."

"That position was only temporary. I don't think after Tiara's promotion that I am your supervisor anymore."

"You know Tiara will want to take credit," Jenny said.

"Let her. She deserves it. What does this make us—couple twenty-nine?"

"I think so."

When James kissed her, there was no doubt in Jenny's

343

mind. His lips were tender as he placed them upon hers, but there was no doubt this was a lover's kiss. She closed her eyes and enjoyed every moment as his arms pulled her closer, knowing this was the sort of kiss that would keep them together forever. She knew he loved her as much as she loved him, and she decided spending eternity with him made all those years she had spent alone worth the wait.

***

The next few days at work passed quickly, and Jenny had been right. Tiara had gone around bragging that she was responsible for couple number twenty-nine. Jenny didn't mind, and from the looks of things, neither did James. He even sent Tiara a bouquet of flowers, thanking her for taking him and his love life under wing from the very start. The woman strutted around like a beauty queen, showing off her crown of glory. It had been a great couple of weeks for Tiara, first a promotion and a raise, then yet another matchmaking success by getting together James and Jenny.

And things were also moving along nicely on that front for the two of them.

For the next two months, Jenny and James spent a lot of time together, getting to know each other the way a couple should. One night after dinner at her apartment, James stood in front of the calendar, staring at a date. "December 17th—what's happening then?" he asked. His index finger tapped against the entwined hearts Jenny had made on the wall calendar.

344

"Oh, I thought maybe that's the day we'd get married." She picked up the shower invitation she'd gotten in May from Lisbeth, and ran her finger along the organza ribbon that trailed from the bow. *I wonder if she will make the invitations for my shower?*

"So, have you got this wedding all planned?" He stepped away from the calendar, holding out his arms in invitation. She took the hint and stood, ready to be pulled into his embrace. "Do you know how much I love you, Jenny Grant?"

"I'm sure you'd love to remind me."

His kiss was sweet, but the promise of the future they would have together seemed even sweeter as Jenny let her mind wander for only a second. *Now, who will I ask to be my bridesmaid and the maid-of-honor?*

Acknowledgments

On December 17, 1994, I married my best friend, Mike Staheli. Mike and I met in May of 1992 when he came to work at Payson Jr. High School as a substitute teacher—a temp. On the day I met him, I knew we would marry. It took him a little while longer to figure it out, but I am so glad and so blessed that he did. I was 40 and he was 35 the day of our wedding. He has stood by me in all my endeavors, through thick and thin, in sickness and in health. Together we have had twenty exciting and fulfilling years so far. We adopted five sons, have experienced changes in careers, and have grown to love each other more than we thought possible. Love is like that, always changing in form, going up and down the roller coaster, but emerging higher at the top each time. Without Mike, this romance novel wouldn't have been possible. It's not exactly our story, but those who know us well will recognize elements throughout that ring true.

As always, I thank my critique group—Heather (H.B.) Moore, Annette Lyon, Michele Paige Holmes, Sarah M. Eden, Jeff (J. Scott) Savage, and Robison Wells—who put up with many pages of absolute drivel and impossibility before this story became what it is today, a novel that I hope is much better.

Also, a special thank you to Lisa Harrison, Bobette

Bridenbaugh, Jenni Broomhead, and Annalisa Thaler, who read the novel in its entirety and gave me excellent feedback, as well as recognizing me in my own story. If only my mother were still with us so she could see the role she played in making Jenny Grant's life more complete, and of course, more interesting.

And finally, thank you to you, my readers, who have given me this first chance at writing in a new genre and audience—I hope Temporary Bridesmaid does not disappoint.

About the Author

Lu Ann Brobst Staheli got her start as a celebrity paparazzi-stalker-chick, which led to her award-winning career as a ghostwriter for celebrity memoirs. A masochist at heart, she taught junior high school English for 33 years, moved to the school library beginning year 34, and once spent two weeks summer vacation backpacking through Europe with fifteen of her students. She has won three Best of State Medals—two for writing and one for teaching—but refuses to wear them all at the same time because she'd hate to be known as a show-off. Her other published works include *The Explorers: Tides Across the Sea*; *Leona & Me, Helen Marie*; *A Note With Taking*; *When Hearts Conjoin*, the story of the conjoined Herrin twins; *Psychic Madman* about mentalist Jim Karol; *One Day at a Time: Teaching Secondary Language Arts*; and *Books, Books, and More Books: A Parent and Teacher's Guide to Adolescent Literature*. Lu Ann says, "But 2013 will be the year of the eBook for me. A long list of titles are in the finalization stage, and I'm excited to make them available to my readers."

Lu Ann's articles have appeared in Grit, Byline, Scouting, Library Media Connections, and The Writer magazines, and she is featured in the upcoming book release, *Best of The Writer*. She has published invitational essays in *Teaching Secondary Language Arts K-12: It Really Works* (Christopher-Gordon Publishers) and *Famous Family Nights* (Cedar Fort International).

As a Senior Editor with Precision Editing Group, Lu Ann has had a hand in a number of releases from Deseret Book, Shadow Mountain, Covenant Communications, and other regional publishers, including several winners and finalists for the Whitney Award and New York Times bestsellers. A former Associate Producer of Alan Osmond's Stadium of Fire, Lu Ann resides in Spanish Fork, Utah, with her husband, and tries to keep track of their five sons.

349

Praise for Lu Ann's Work

A Note Worth Taking

"This story should be a must-read for every middle grade/junior high girl. The hurt that Laura, the main character, suffers at the hand of Vickie, her supposed best friend, is one that so many girls this age will relate to. How Laura handles the school situation and her pain, along with the growth she experiences throughout the story, are what make this book stand out. Good lessons and good times. Adults reading the story will enjoy the nostalgia of days gone by—as well as being grateful those days are past. We all survived junior high! Laura does too, and you'll cheer for her triumphs over mean girls and her blossoming maturity and self-worth."

—Michele Paige Homes, Whitney Award-winning author

Leona & Me, Helen Marie

"A delightful middle grade novel from award-winning author, Lu Ann Staheli. Readers will fall in love with Helen Marie, a precocious seven-year-old, who looks up to her older sister, Leona Mae, the two of them getting into trouble more often or not (think Laura Ingalls . . .). I laughed out loud at Helen Marie's antics and loved her relationship with her mother and father. Set in 1922 southern Indiana, the family faces financial hardships, like so many around them.

350

But they are blessed with a humble life, rich with country living, and take pride in hard work."

—H. B. Moore, Utah Best of State and Whitney Award-winning author

Tides Across the Sea

"A good read for the 12–16 age range and is a beautiful coming of age and young love story. The author obviously did an extensive amount of research and it shows in the scenery, language and tone of the book. There is plenty of action, following not only the main couple, but also a young slave girl in the palace of Montezuma. Both sides continue to build until the truth of Cortez's expedition comes to a head . . . *Tides Across the Sea* sends young readers deep into history and gives them a story they will find difficult to put down!"

—Stephenia McGee, *InD'Tale Magazine*